Toronto Reprint Library of Canadian Prose and Poetry

Douglas Lochhead, General Editor

This series is intended to provide for
libraries a varied selection of titles of
Canadian prose and poetry which
have been long out-of-print. Each
work is a reprint of a reliable edition,
is in a contemporary library binding,
and is appropriate for public circula-
tion. The Toronto Reprint Library
makes available lesser known works
of popular writers and, in some cases,
the only works of little known poets
and prose writers. All form part of
Canada's literary history; all help to
provide a better knowledge of our
cultural and social past.

T0334449

The Toronto Reprint Library is produced in short-run editions made
possible by special techniques, some
of which have been developed for
the series by the University of Toronto
Press.

This series should not be confused
with Literature of Canada: Poetry
and Prose in Reprint, also under the
general editorship of Douglas Lochhead.

UNIVERSITY OF TORONTO PRESS

Toronto Reprint Library of Canadian Prose and Poetry
© University of Toronto Press 1973
Toronto and Buffalo
Reprinted in paperback 2015
ISBN 978-0-8020-7517-8 (cloth)
ISBN 978-1-4426-3981-2 (paper)

No other edition located.

THE

LADY OF THE ICE.

A NOVEL.

BY
JAMES DE MILLE,
AUTHOR OF
"THE DODGE CLUB ABROAD," "CORD AND CREESE," ETC.

NEW YORK:
D. APPLETON AND COMPANY,
90, 92 & 94 GRAND STREET.
1870.

CONTENTS.

1

THE LADY OF THE ICE.

CHAPTER I.

CONSISTING MERELY OF INTRODUCTORY MAT-
TER.

THIS is a story of Quebec. Quebec is a wonderful city.

I am given to understand that the ridge on which the city is built is Laurentian; and the river that flows past it is the same. On this (not the river, you know) are strata of schist, shale, old red sand-stone, trap, granite, clay, and mud. The upper stratum is ligneous, and is found to be very convenient for pavements.

It must not be supposed from this introduction that I am a geologist. I am not. I am a lieutenant in her Majesty's 129th Bobtails. We Bobtails are a gay and gallant set, and I have reason to know that we are well remembered in every place we have been quartered.

Into the vortex of Quebeccian society I threw myself with all the generous ardor of youth, and was keenly alive to those charms which the Canadian ladies possess and use so fatally. It is a singular fact, for which I will not attempt to account, that in Quebeccian society one comes in contact with ladies only. Where the male element is I never could imagine. I never saw a civilian. There are no young men in Quebec; if there are any, we officers are not aware of it. I've often been anxious to see one, but never could make it out. Now, of these Canadian ladies I cannot trust myself to speak with calmness. An allusion to them will of itself be eloquent to every brother officer. I will simply remark that, at a time when the tendencies of the Canadians generally are a subject of interest both in England and America, and when it is a matter of doubt whether they lean to annexation or British connection, their fair young daughters show an unmistakable tendency not to one, but to both, and make two apparently incompatible principles really inseparable.

You must understand that this is my roundabout way of hinting that the unmarried British officer who goes to Canada generally finds his destiny tenderly folding itself around a Canadian bride. It is the common lot. Some of these take their wives with them around the world, but many more retire from the service, buy farms, and practise love in a cottage. Thus the fair and loyal Canadiennes are responsible for the loss of many and many a gallant officer to her Majesty's service. Throughout these colonial stations there has been, and there will be, a fearful depletion among the numbers of these brave but too impressible men. I make this statement solemnly, as a mournful fact. I have nothing to say against it; and it is not for one who has had an experience like mine to hint at a remedy. But to my story:

Every one who was in Quebec during the winter of 18—, if he went into society at all, must have been struck by the appearance of a young Bobtail officer, who was a joyous and a welcome guest at every house where it was desirable to be. Tall, straight as an arrow, and singularly well-proportioned, the picturesque costume of the 129th Bobtails could add but little to the effect already produced by so martial a figure. His face was whiskerless; his eyes gray; his cheek-bones a little higher than the average; his hair auburn; his nose not Grecian—or Roman—but still impressive: his air one of quiet dignity, mingled with youthful joyance and mirthfulness. Try— O reader!—to bring before you such a figure. Well—that's me.

Such was my exterior; what was my character? A few words will suffice to explain:—bold, yet cautious; brave, yet tender; constant, yet highly impressible; tenacious of affection, yet quick to kindle into admiration at every new form of beauty; many times smitten, yet surviving the wound; vanquished, yet rescued by that very impressibility of temper—such was the man over whose singular adventures you will shortly be called to smile or to weep.

Here is my card:

Lieut. Alexander Macrorie,

129th Bobtails.

And now, my friend, having introduced you to myself, having shown you my pho-tograph, having explained my character, and handed you my card, allow me to lead you to

CHAPTER II.

MY QUARTERS, WHERE YOU WILL BECOME ACQUAINTED WITH OLD JACK RANDOLPH, MY MOST INTIMATE FRIEND, AND ONE WHO DIVIDES WITH ME THE HONOR OF BEING THE HERO OF MY STORY.

I'LL never forget the time. It was a day in April.

But an April day in Canada is a very different thing from an April day in England. In England all Nature is robed in vivid green, the air is balmy; and all those beauties abound which usually set poets rhapsodizing, and young men sentimentalizing, and young girls tantalizing. Now, in Canada there is nothing of the kind. No Canadian poet, for instance, would ever affirm that in the spring a livelier iris blooms upon the burnished dove; in the spring a young man's fancy lightly turns to thoughts of love. No. For that sort of thing—the thoughts of love I mean— winter is the time of day in Canada. The fact is, the Canadians haven't any spring. The months which Englishmen include under that pleasant name are here partly taken up with prolonging the winter, and partly with the formation of a new and nondescript season. In that period Nature, instead of being darkly, deeply, beautifully green, has rather the shade of a dingy, dirty, melancholy gray. Snow covers the ground—not by any means the glistening white robe of Winter—but a rugged substitute, damp, and discolored. It is snow, but snow far gone into decay and decrepitude—snow that seems ashamed of itself for lingering so long after wearing out its welcome, and presenting itself in so revolting a dress—snow, in fact, which is like a man sinking into irremediable ruin, and changing its former glorious state for that condition which is expressed by the unpleasant word "slush." There is not an object, not a circumstance, in visible Nature which does not heighten the contrast. In England there is the luxuriant foliage, the fragrant blossom, the gay flower; in Canada, black twigs—bare, scraggy, and altogether wretched—thrust their repulsive forms forth into the bleak air— there, the soft rain-shower falls; here, the fierce snow-squall, or maddening sleet!— there, the field is traversed by the cheerful plough; here, it is covered with ice-heaps or thawing snow; there, the rivers run babbling onward under the green trees; here, they groan and chafe under heaps of dingy and slowly-disintegrating ice-hummocks; there, one's only weapon against the rigor of the season is the peaceful umbrella; here, one must defend one's self with caps and coats of fur and india-rubber, with clumsy leggings, ponderous boots, steel-creepers, gauntlets of skin, iron-pointed alpenstocks, and forty or fifty other articles which the exigencies of space and time will not permit me to mention. On one of the darkest and most dismal of these April days, I was trying to kill time in my quarters, when Jack Randolph burst in upon my meditations. Jack Randolph was one of Ours—an intimate friend of mine, and of everybody else who had the pleasure of his acquaintance. Jack was in every respect a remarkable man—physically, intellectually, and morally. Present company excepted, he was certainly by all odds the finest-looking fellow in a regiment notoriously filled with handsome men; and to this rare advantage he added all the accomplishments of life, and the

most genial nature in the world. It was difficult to say whether he was a greater favorite with men or with women. He was noisy, rattling, reckless, good-hearted, generous, mirthful, witty, jovial, daring, open-handed, irrepressible, enthusiastic, and confoundedly clever. He was good at every thing, from tracking a moose or caribou, on through all the gamut of rinking, skating, ice-boating, and tobogganing, up to the lightest accomplishments of the drawing-room. He was one of those lucky dogs who are able to break horses or hearts with equal buoyancy of soul. And it was this twofold capacity which made him equally dear to either sex.

A lucky dog? Yea, verily, that is what he was. He was welcomed at every mess, and he had the *entrée* of every house in Quebec. He could drink harder than any man in the regiment, and dance down a whole regiment of drawing-room knights. He could sing better than any amateur I ever heard; and was the best judge of a meerschaum-pipe I ever saw. Lucky? Yes, he was—and especially so, and more than all else—on account of the joyousness of his soul. There was a contagious and a godlike hilarity in his broad, open brow, his frank, laughing eyes, and his mobile lips. He seemed to carry about with him a bracing moral atmosphere. The sight of him had the same effect on the dull man of ordinary life that the Himalayan air has on an Indian invalid; and yet Jack was head-over-heels in debt. Not a tradesman would trust him. Shoals of little bills were sent him every day. Duns without number plagued him from morning to night. The Quebec attorneys were sharpening their bills, and preparing, like birds of prey, to swoop down upon him. In fact, taking it altogether, Jack had full before him the sure and certain prospect of some dismal explosion.

On this occasion, Jack—for the first time in our acquaintance—seemed to have not a vestige of his ordinary flow of spirits. He entered without a word, took up a pipe, crammed some tobacco into the bowl, flung himself into an easy-chair, and began—with fixed eyes and set lips—to pour forth enormous volumes of smoke.

My own pipe was very well under way, and I sat opposite, watching him in wonder. I studied his face, and marked there what I had never before seen upon it—a preoccupied and troubled expression. Now, Jack's features, by long indulgence in the gayer emotions, had immovably moulded themselves into an expression of joyousness and hilarity. Unnatural was it for the merry twinkle to be extinguished in his eyes; for the corners of the mouth, which usually curled upward, to settle downward; for the general shape of feature, out-line of muscle, set of lips, to undertake to become the exponents of feelings to which they were totally unaccustomed. On this occasion, therefore, Jack's face did not appear so much mournful as dismal; and, where another face might have elicited sympathy, Jack's face had such a grewsomeness, such an utter incongruity between feature and expression, that it seemed only droll.

I bore this inexplicable conduct as long as I could, but at length I could stand it no longer.

"My dear Jack," said I, "would it be too much to ask, in the mildest manner in the world, and with all possible regard for your feelings, what, in the name of the Old Boy, happens to be up just now?"

Jack took the pipe from his mouth, sent a long cloud of smoke forward in a straight line, then looked at me, then heaved a deep sigh, and then—replaced the pipe, and began smoking once more.

Under such circumstances I did not know what to do next, so I took up again the study of his face.

"Heard no bad news, I hope," I said at length, making another venture between the puffs of my pipe.

A shake of the head.

Silence again.

"Duns?"

Another shake.

Silence.

"Writs?"

Another shake.

Silence.

"Liver?"

Another shake, together with a contemptuous smile.

"Then I give it up," said I, and betook myself once more to my pipe.

After a time, Jack gave a long sigh, and regarded me fixedly for some minutes, with a very doleful face. Then he slowly ejaculated:

"Macrorie!"

"Well?"

"It's a woman!"

"A woman? Well. What's that? Why need that make any particular difference to you, my boy?"

He sighed again, more dolefully than before.

"I'm in for it, old chap," said he.

"How's that?"

"It's all over."

"What do you mean?"

"Done up, sir—dead and gone!"

"I'll be hanged if I understand you."

"*Hic jacet* Johannes Randolph."

"You're taking to Latin by way of making yourself more intelligible, I suppose."

"Macrorie, my boy—"

"Well?"

"Will you be going anywhere near Anderson's to-day—the stone-cutter, I mean?"

"Why?"

"If you should, let me ask you to do a particular favor for me. Will you?"

"Why, of course. What is it?"

"Well—it's only to order a tombstone for me—plain, neat—four feet by sixteen inches—with nothing on it but my name and date. The sale of my effects will bring enough to pay for it. Don't you fellows go and put up a tablet about me. I tell you plainly, I don't want it, and, what's more, I won't stand it."

"By Jove!" I cried; "my dear fellow, one would think you were raving. Are you thinking of shuffling off the mortal coil? Are you going to blow your precious brains out for a woman? Is it because some fair one is cruel that you are thinking of your latter end? Will you, wasting with despair, die because a woman's fair?"

"No, old chap. I'm going to do something worse."

"Something worse than suicide! What's that? A clean breast, my boy."

"A species of moral suicide."

"What's that? Your style of expression to-day is a kind of secret cipher. I haven't the key. Please explain."

Jack resumed his pipe, and bent down his head; then he rubbed his broad brow with his unoccupied hand; then he raised himself up, and looked at me for a few moments in solemn silence; then he said, in a low voice, speaking each word separately and with thrilling emphasis:

CHAPTER III.

"MACRORIE—OLD CHAP—I'M—GOING—TO—BE—MARRIED ! ! !"

AT that astounding piece of intelligence, I sat dumb and stared fixedly at Jack for the space of half an hour. He regarded me with a mournful smile. At last my feelings found expression in a long, solemn, thoughtful, anxious, troubled, and perplexed whistle.

I could think of only one thing. It was a circumstance which Jack had confided to me as his bosom-friend. Although he had confided the same thing to at least a hundred other bosom-friends, and I knew it, yet, at the same time, the knowledge of this did not make the secret any the less a confidential one; and I had accordingly guarded it like my heart's blood, and all that sort of thing, you know. Nor would I even now divulge that secret, were it not for the fact that the cause for secrecy is removed. The circumstance was this: About a year before, we had been stationed at Fredericton, in the Province of New Brunswick. Jack had met there a young lady from St. Andrews, named Miss Phillips, to whom he had devoted himself with his usual ardor. During a sentimental sleigh-ride he had confessed his love, and had engaged himself to her; and, since his arrival at Quebec, he had corresponded with her very faithfully. He considered himself as destined by Fate to become the husband of Miss Phillips at some time in the dim future, and the only marriage before him that I could think of was this. Still I could not understand why it had come upon him so suddenly, or why, if it did come, he should so collapse under the pressure of his doom.

"Well," said I, after I had rallied somewhat, "I didn't think it was to come off so soon. Some luck has turned up, I suppose."

"Luck!" repeated Jack, with an indescribable accent.

"I assure you, though I've never had the pleasure of seeing Miss Phillips, yet, from your description, I admire her quite fervently, and congratulate you from the bottom of my heart."

"Miss Phillips!" repeated Jack, with a groan.

"What's the matter, old chap?"

"It isn't—*her!*" faltered Jack.

"What!"

"She'll have to wear the willow."

"You haven't broken with her—have you?" I asked.

"She'll have to forgive and forget, and all that sort of thing. If it was Miss Phillips, I wouldn't be so confoundedly cut up about it."

"Why—what is it? who is it? and what do you mean?"

Jack looked at me. Then he looked down, and frowned. Then he looked at me again; and then he said, slowly, and with a powerful effort:

CHAPTER IV.

" IT'S—THE—THE WIDOW! IT'S MRS.—FINNI-MORE!!!"

HAD a bombshell burst—but I forbear. That comparison is, I believe, somewhat hackneyed. The reader will therefore be good enough to appropriate the point of it, and understand that the shock of this intelligence was so overpowering, that I was again rendered speechless.

"You see," said Jack, after a long and painful silence, "it all originated out of an infernal mistake. Not that I ought to be sorry for it, though. Mrs. Finnimore, of course, is a deuced fine woman. I've been round there ever so long, and seen ever so much of her; and all that sort of thing, you know. Oh, yes," he added, dismally; "I ought to be glad, and, of course, I'm a deuced lucky fellow, and all that; but—"

He paused, and an expressive silence followed that "but."

"Well, how about the mistake?" I asked.

"Why, I'll tell you. It was that confounded party at Doane's. You know what a favorite of mine little Louie Berton is —the best little thing that ever breathed, the prettiest, the—full of fun, too. Well, we're awfully thick, you know; and she chaffed me all the evening about my engagement with Miss Phillips. She had heard all about it, and is crazy to find out whether it's going on yet or not. We had great fun—she chaffing and questioning, and I trying to fight her off. Well; the dancing was going on, and I'd been separated from her for some time, and was trying to find her again, and I saw some one standing in a recess of one of the windows, with a dress that was exactly like Louie's. Her back was turned to me, and the curtains half concealed her. I felt sure that it was Louie. So I sauntered up, and stood for a moment or two behind her. She was looking out of the window; one hand was on the ledge, and the other was by her side, half behind her. I don't know what got into me; but I seized her hand, and gave it a gentle squeeze.

"Well, you know, I expected that it would be snatched away at once. I felt immediately an awful horror at my indiscretion, and would have given the world not to have done it. I expected to see Louie's flashing eyes hurling indignant fire at me, and all that. But the hand didn't move from mine at all!"

Jack uttered this last sentence with the doleful accents of a deeply-injured man— such an accent as one would employ in telling of a shameful trick practised upon his innocence.

"It lay in mine," he continued. "There

it was; I had seized it; I had it; I held it; I had squeezed it; and—good Lord!—Macrorie, what was I to do? I'll tell you what I did—I squeezed it again. I thought that now it would go; but it wouldn't. Well, I tried it again. No go. Once more—and once again. On my soul, Macrorie, it still lay in mine. I cannot tell you what thoughts I had. It seemed like indelicacy. It was a bitter thing to associate indelicacy with one like little Louie; but—hang it!—there was the awful fact. Suddenly, the thought struck me that the hand was larger than Louie's. At that thought, a ghastly sensation came over me; and, just at that moment, the lady herself turned her face, blushing, arch, with a mischievous smile. To my consternation, and to my—well, yes —to my horror, I saw Mrs. Finnimore!"

"Good Lord!" I exclaimed.

"A stronger expression would fail to do justice to the occasion," said Jack, helping himself to a glass of beer. "For my part, the thrill of unspeakable horror that was imparted by that shock is still strong within me. There, my boy, you have my story. I leave the rest to your imagination."

"The rest? Why, do you mean to say that this is all?"

"All!" cried Jack, with a wild laugh. "All? My dear boy, it is only the faint beginning; but it implies all the rest."

"What did she say?" I asked, meekly.

"Say—say? What! After—well, never mind. Hang it! Don't drive me into particulars. Don't you see? Why, there I was. I had made an assault, broken through the enemy's lines, thought I was carrying every thing before me, when suddenly I found myself confronted, not by an inferior force, but by an overwhelming superiority of numbers—horse, foot, and artillery, marines, and masked batteries— yes, and baggage-wagons—all assaulting me in front, in flank, and in the rear. Pooh!"

"Don't talk shop, Jack."

"Shop? Will you be kind enough to suggest some ordinary figure of speech that will give an idea of my situation? Plain language is quite useless. At least, I find it so."

"But, at any rate, what did she say?"

"Why," answered Jack, in a more dismal voice than ever, "she said, 'Ah, Jack!'—she called me Jack!—'Ah, Jack! I saw you looking for me. I knew you would come after me.'"

"Good Heavens!" I cried; "and what did you say?"

"Say? Heavens and earth, man! what could I say? Wasn't I a gentleman? Wasn't she a lady? Hadn't I forced her to commit herself? Didn't I have to assume the responsibility and pocket the consequences? Say! Oh, Macrorie! what *is* the use of imagination, if a man *will* not exercise it?"

"And so you're in for it?" said I, after a pause.

"To the depth of several miles," said Jack, relighting his pipe, which in the energy of his narrative had gone out.

"And you don't think of trying to back out?"

"I don't see my way. Then, again, you must know that I've been trying to see if it wouldn't be the wisest thing for me to make the best of my situation."

"Certainly it would, if you cannot possibly get out of it."

"But, you see, for a fellow like me it may be best not to get out of it. You see, after all, I like her very well. She's an awfully fine woman—splendid action. I've been round there ever so much; we've always been deuced thick; and she's got a kind of way with her that a fellow like me can't resist. And, then, it's time for me to begin to think of settling down. I'm getting awfully old. I'll be twenty-three next August. And then, you know, I'm so deuced hard up. I've got to the end of my rope, and you are aware that the sheriff is beginning to be familiar with my name. Yes, I think for the credit of the regiment I'd better take the widow. She's got thirty thousand pounds, at least."

"And a very nice face and figure along with it," said I, encouragingly.

"That's a fact, or else I could never have mistaken her for poor little Louie, and this wouldn't have happened. But, if it *had* only been little Louie—well, well; I suppose it must be, and perhaps it's the best thing."

"If it had been Louie," said I, with new efforts at encouragement, "it wouldn't have been any better for you."

"No; that's a fact. You see, I was never so much bothered in my life. I don't mind an ordinary scrape; but I can't exactly see my way out of this."

"You'll have to break the news to Miss Phillips."

"And that's not the worst," said Jack, with a sigh that was like a groan.

"Not the worst? What can be worse than that?"

"My dear boy, you have not begun to see even the outside of the peculiarly complicated nature of my present situation. There are other circumstances to which all these may be playfully represented as a joke."

"Well, that is certainly a strong way of putting it."

"Couldn't draw it mild—such a situation can only be painted in strong colors. I'll tell you in general terms what it is. I can't go into particulars. You know all

about my engagement to Miss Phillips. I'm awfully fond of her—give my right hand to win hers, and all that sort of thing, you know. Well, this is going to be hard on her, of course, poor thing! especially as my last letters have been more tender than common. But, old chap, that's all nothing. There's another lady in the case!"

"What!" I cried, more astonished than ever.

Jack looked at me earnestly, and said, slowly and solemnly:

CHAPTER V.

"FACT, MY BOY—IT IS AS I SAY.—THERE'S ANOTHER LADY IN THE CASE, AND THIS LAST IS THE WORST SCRAPE OF ALL!"

"ANOTHER lady?" I faltered.

"Another lady!" said Jack.

"Oh!" said I.

"Yes," said he.

"An engagement, too!"

"An engagement? I should think so —and a double-barrelled one, too. An engagement—why, my dear fellow, an engagement's nothing at all compared with this. This is something infinitely worse than the affair with Louie, or Miss Phillips, or even the widow. It's a bad case—yes —an infernally bad case—and I don't see but that I'll have to throw up the widow after all."

"It must be a bad case, if it's infinitely worse than an engagement, as you say it is. Why, man, it must be nothing less than actual marriage. Is that what you're driving at? It must be. So you're a married man, are you?"

"No, not just that, not quite—as yet— but the very next thing to it?"

"Well, Jack, I'm sorry for you, and all

that I can say is, that it is a pity that this isn't Utah. Being Canada, however, and a civilized country, I can't see for the life of me how you'll ever manage to pull through."

Jack sighed dolefully.

"To tell the truth," said he, "it's this last one that gives me my only trouble. I'd marry the widow, settle up some way with Miss Phillips, smother my shame, and pass the remainder of my life in peaceful obscurity, if it were not for *her*."

"You mean by *her*, the lady whose name you don't mention."

"Whose name I don't mention, nor intend to," said Jack, gravely. "Her case is so peculiar that it cannot be classed with the others. I never breathed a word about it to anybody, though it's been going on for six or eight months."

Jack spoke with such earnestness, that I perceived the subject to be too grave a one in his estimation to be trifled with. A frown came over his face, and he once more eased his mind by sending forth heavy clouds of smoke, as though he would thus throw off the clouds of melancholy that had gathered deep and dark over his soul.

"I'll make a clean breast of it, old chap," said he, at length, with a very heavy sigh. "It's a bad business from beginning to end."

"You see," said he, after a long pause, in which he seemed to be collecting his thoughts—"it began last year—the time I went to New York, you know. She went on at the same time. She had nobody with her but a deaf old party, and got into some row at the station about her luggage. I helped her out of it, and sat by her side all the way. At New York I kept up the acquaintance. I came back with them, that is to say, with her, and the deaf old party, you know, and by the time we reached Quebec again we understood one another.

"I couldn't help it—I'll be hanged if I could! You see, Macrorie, it wasn't an ordinary case. She was the loveliest little girl I ever saw, and I found myself awfully fond of her in no time. I soon saw that she was fond of me too. All my other affairs were a joke to this. I wanted to marry her in New York, but the thought of my debts frightened me out of that, and so I put it off. I half wish now I hadn't been so confoundedly prudent. Perhaps it is best, though. Still I don't know. Better be the wife of a poor devil, than have one's heart broken by a mean devil. Heigho!"

H E I G H O are the letters which are usually employed to represent a sigh. I use them in accordance with the customs of the literary world.

"Well," resumed Jack, "after my return I called on her, and repeated my call several times. She was all that could be desired, but her father was different. I found him rather chilly, and not at all inclined to receive me with that joyous hospitality which my various merits deserved. The young lady herself seemed sad. I found out, at last, that the old gentleman amused himself with badgering her about me; and finally she told me, with tears, that her father requested me to visit that house no more. Well, at that I was somewhat taken aback; but, nevertheless, I determined to wait till the old gentleman himself should speak. You know my peculiar coolness, old chap, that which you and the rest call my happy audacity; and you may believe that it was all needed under such circumstances as these. I went to the house twice after that. Each time my little girl was half laughing with joy, half cry ing with fear at seeing me; and each time she urged me to keep away. She said we could write to one another. But letter-writing wasn't in my line. So after trying in vain to obey her, I went once more in desperation to explain matters.

"Instead of seeing her, I found the old fellow himself. He was simply white, hot with rage—not at all noisy, or declamatory, or vulgar—but cool, cutting, and altogether terrific. He alluded to my gentlemanly conduct in forcing myself where I had been ordered off; and informed me that if I came again he would be under the unpleasant necessity of using a horsewhip. That, of course, made me savage. I pitched into him pretty well, and gave it to him hot and heavy, but, hang it! I'm no match for fellows of that sort; he kept so cool, you know, while I was furious—and the long and the short of it is, that I had to retire in disorder, vowing on him some mysterious vengeance or other, which I have never been able to carry out.

"The next day I got a letter from her. It was awfully sad, blotted with tears, and all that. She implored me to write her, told me she couldn't see me, spoke about her father's cruelty and persecution—and ever so many other things not necessary to mention. Well, I wrote back, and she answered my letter, and so we got into the way of a correspondence which we kept up at a perfectly furious rate. It came hard on me, of course, for I'm not much at a pen; my letters were short, as you may suppose, but then they were full of point, and what matters quantity so long as you have quality, you know? Her letters, however, poor little darling, were long and eloquent, and full of a kind of mixture of love, hope, and despair. At first I thought that I should grow reconciled to my situation in the course of time, but, instead of

that, it grew worse every day. I tried to forget all about her, but without success. The fact is, I chafed under the restraint that was on me, and perhaps it was that which was the worst of all. I dare say now if I'd only been in some other place—in Montreal, for instance—I wouldn't have had such a tough time of it, and might gradually have forgotten about her; but the mischief of it was, I was here—in Quebec—close by her, you may say, and yet I was forbidden the house. I had been insulted and threatened. This, of course, only made matters worse, and the end of it was, I thought of nothing else. My very efforts to get rid of the bother only made it a dozen times worse. I flung myself into ladies' society with my usual ardor, only worse; committed myself right and left, and seemed to be a model of a gay Lothario. Little did they suspect that under a smiling face I concealed a heart of ashes—yes, old boy—ashes! as I'm a living sinner. You see, all the time, I was maddened at that miserable old scoundrel who wouldn't let me visit his daughter—me, Jack Randolph, an officer, and a gentleman, and, what is more, a Bobtail! Why, my very uniform should have been a guarantee for my honorable conduct. Then, again, in addition to this, I hankered after her, you know, most awfully. At last I couldn't stand it any longer, so I wrote her a letter. It was only yesterday. And now, old chap, what do you think I wrote?"

"I don't know, I'm sure," said I, mistily; "a declaration of love, perhaps—"

"A declaration of love? pooh!" said Jack; "as if I had ever written any thing else than that. Why, all my letters were nothing else. No, my boy—this letter was very different. In the first place, I told her that I was desperate—then I assured her that I couldn't live this way any longer, and I concluded with a proposal as desperate as my situation. And what do you think my proposal was?"

"Proposal? Why, marriage, of course; there is only one kind of proposal possible under such circumstances. But still that's not much more than an engagement, dear boy, for an engagement means only the same thing, namely, marriage."

"Oh, but this was far stronger—it was different, I can tell you, from any mere proposal of marriage. What do you think it was? Guess."

"Can't. Haven't an idea."

"Well," said Jack—

CHAPTER VI.

"I IMPLORED HER TO RUN AWAY WITH ME, AND HAVE A PRIVATE MARRIAGE, LEAVING THE REST TO FATE. AND I SOLEMNLY ASSURED HER THAT, IF SHE REFUSED, I WOULD BLOW MY BRAINS OUT ON HER DOOR-STEPS. —THERE, NOW! WHAT DO YOU THINK OF THAT?"

SAYING the above words, Jack leaned back, and surveyed me with the stern complacency of despair. After staring at me for some time, and evidently taking some sort of grim comfort out of the speechlessness to which he had reduced me by his unparalleled narrative, he continued his confessions:

"Last night, I made that infernal blunder with the widow—confound her!—that is, I mean of course, bless her! It's all the same, you know. To-day you behold the miserable state to which I am reduced. To-morrow I will get a reply from *her*. Of course, she will consent to fly. I know very well how it will be. She will hint at some feasible mode, and some con-

venient time. She will, of course, expect me to settle it all up, from her timid little hints; and I must settle it up, and not break my faith with her. And now, Macrorie, I ask you, not merely as an officer and a gentleman, but as a man, a fellow-Christian, and a sympathizing friend, what under Heaven am I to do?"

He stopped, leaned back in his chair, lighted once more his extinguished pipe, and I could see through the dense volumes of smoke which he blew forth, his eyes fixed earnestly upon me, gleaming like two stars from behind gloomy storm-clouds.

I sat in silence, and thought long and painfully over the situation. I could come to no conclusion, but I had to say something, and I said it.

"Put it off," said I at last, in a general state of daze.

"Put what off?"

"What? Why, the widow—no, the—the elopement, of course. Yes," I continued, firmly, "put off the elopement."

"Put off the elopement!" ejaculated Jack. "What! after proposing it so desperately—after threatening to blow my brains out in front of her door?"

"That certainly is a consideration," said I, thoughtfully; "but can't you have—well, brain-fever—yes, that's it, and can't you get some friend to send word to her?"

"That's all very well; but, you see, I'd have to keep my room. If I went out, she'd hear of it. She's got a wonderful way of hearing about my movements. She'll find out about the widow before the week's over. Oh, no! that's not to be done."

"Well, then," said I, desperately, "let her find it out. The blow would then fall a little more gently."

"You seem to me," said Jack, rather huffily, "to propose that I should quietly proceed to break her heart. No! Hang it, man, if it comes to that I'll do it openly, and make a clean breast of it, without shamming or keeping her in suspense."

"Well, then," I responded, "why not break off with the widow?"

"Break off with the widow!" cried Jack, with the wondering accent of a man who has heard some impossible proposal.

"Certainly; why not?"

"Will you be kind enough to inform me what thing short of death could ever deliver me out of her hands?" asked Jack, mildly.

"Elope, as you proposed."

"That's the very thing I thought of; but the trouble is, in that case she would devote the rest of her life to vengeance. 'Hell hath no fury like a woman wronged,' you know. She'd move heaven and earth, and never end, till I was drummed out of the regiment. No, my boy. To do that would be to walk with open eyes to disgrace, and shame, and infamy, with a whole community, a whole regiment, and the Horse-Guards at the back of them, all banded together to crush me. Such a fate as this would hardly be the proper thing to give to a wife that a fellow loves."

"Can't you manage to make the widow disgusted with you?"

"No, I can't," said Jack, peevishly. "What do you mean?"

"Why, make it appear as though you only wanted to marry her for her money."

"Oh, hang it, man! how could I do that? I can't play a part, under any circumstances, and that particular part would be so infernally mean, that it would be impossible. I'm such an ass that, if she were even to hint at that, I'd resent it furiously."

"Can't you make her afraid about your numerous gallantries?"

"Afraid? why she glories in them. So many feathers in her cap, and all that, you know."

"Can't you frighten her about your debts and general extravagance—hint that you're a gambler, and so on?"

"And then she'd inform me, very affectionately, that she intends to be my guardian angel, and save me from evil for all the rest of my life."

"Can't you tell her all about your solemn engagement to Miss Phillips?"

"My engagement to Miss Phillips? Why, man alive, she knows that as well as you do."

"Knows it! How did she find it out?"

"How? Why I told her myself."

"The deuce you did!"

Jack was silent.

"Well, then," said I, after some further thought, "why not tell her every thing?"

"Tell her every thing?"

"Yes—exactly what you've been telling me. Make a clean breast of it."

Jack looked at me for some time with a curious expression.

"My dear boy," said he, at length, "do you mean to say that you are really in earnest in making that proposition?"

"Most solemnly in earnest," said I.

"Well," said Jack, "it shows how mistaken I was in leaving any thing to your imagination. You do not seem to understand," he continued, dolefully, "or you will not understand that, when a fellow has committed himself to a lady as I did, and squeezed her hand with such peculiar ardor, in his efforts to save himself and do what's right, he often overdoes it. You don't seem to suspect that I might have overdone it with the widow. Now, unfortunately, that is the very thing that I did. I did happen to overdo it most confoundedly. And so the melancholy fact remains that, if I were to repeat to her, verbatim, all that I've been telling you, she would find an extraordinary discrepancy between such statements and those abominably tender confessions in which I indulged on that other occasion. Nothing would ever convince her that I was not sincere at that time; and how can I go to her now and confess that I am a humbug and an idiot? I don't see it. Come, now, old fellow, what do you think of that? Don't you call it rather a tough situation? Do you think a man can see his way out of it? Own up, now. Don't you think it's about the worst scrape you ever heard of? Come, now, no humbug."

The fellow seemed actually to begin to feel a dismal kind of pride in the very hopelessness of his situation, and looked at me with a gloomy enjoyment of my discomfiture.

For my part, I said nothing, and for the best of reasons: I had nothing to say. So I took refuge in shaking my head.

"You see," Jack persisted, "there's no help for it. Nobody can do any thing. There's only one thing, and that you haven't suggested."

"What's that?" I asked, feebly.

Jack put the tip of his forefinger to his forehead, and snapped his thumb against his third.

"I haven't much brains to speak of," said he, "but if I did happen to blow out what little I may have, it would be the easiest settlement of the difficulty. It would be cutting the knot, instead of attempting the impossible task of untying it. Nobody would blame me. Everybody would mourn for me, and, above all, four tender female hearts would feel a pang of sorrow for my untimely fate. By all four I should be not cursed, but canonized. Only one class would suffer, and those would be wel-

come to their agonies. I allude, of course, to my friends the Duns."

To this eccentric proposal, I made no reply whatever.

"Well," said Jack, thoughtfully, "it isn't a bad idea. Not a bad idea," he repeated, rising from his chair and putting down his pipe, which had again gone out owing to his persistent loquacity. "I'll think it over," he continued, seriously. "You bear in mind my little directions about the head-stone, Macrorie, four feet by eighteen inches, old fellow, very plain, and, mark me, only the name and date. Not a word about the virtues of the deceased, etc. I can stand a great deal, but that I will *not* stand. And now, old chap, I must be off; you can't do me any good, I see."

"At any rate, you'll wait till to-morrow," said I, carelessly.

"Oh, there's no hurry," said he. "Of course, I must wait till then. I'll let you know if any thing new turns up."

And saying this, he took his departure.

CHAPTER VII.

CROSSING THE ST. LAWRENCE.—THE STORM AND THE BREAK-UP.—A WONDERFUL ADVENTURE.—A STRUGGLE FOR LIFE.—WHO IS SHE?—THE ICE-RIDGE.—FLY FOR YOUR LIFE!

ON the following day I found myself compelled to go on some routine duty cross the river to Point Levy. The weather was the most abominable of that abominable season. It was winter, and yet not Winter's self. The old gentleman had lost all that bright and hilarious nature; all that sparkling and exciting stimulus which he owns and holds here so joyously in January, February, and even March. He was decrepit, yet spiteful; a hoary, old, tottering, palsied villain, hurling curses at all who ventured into his evil presence. One look outside showed me the full nature of all that was before me, and revealed the old tyrant in the full power of his malignancy. The air was raw and chill. There blew a fierce, blighting wind, which brought with it showers of stinging sleet. The wooden pavements were overspread with a thin layer of ice, so glassy that walking could only be attempted at extreme hazard; the houses were incrusted with the same cheerful coating; and, of all the beastly weather that I had ever seen, there had never been any equal to this. However, there was no escape from it; and so, wrapping myself up as well as I could, I took a stout stick with a sharp iron ferrule, and plunged forth into the storm.

On reaching the river, the view was any thing but satisfactory. The wind here was tremendous, and the sleet blew down in long, horizontal lines, every separate particle giving its separate sting, while the accumulated stings amounted to perfect torment. I paused for a while to get a little shelter, and take breath before venturing across.

There were other reasons for pausing. The season was well advanced, and the ice was not considered particularly safe. Many things conspired to give indications of a break-up. The ice on the surface was soft, honey-combed, and crumbling. Near the shore was a channel of open water. Farther out, where the current ran strongest, the ice was heaped up in hillocks and mounds, while in different directions appeared crevices of greater or less width. Looking over that broad surface as well as I could through the driving storm, where not long before I had seen crowds passing and repassing, not a soul was now visible.

This might have been owing to the insecurity of the ice; but it might also have been owing to the severity of the weather. Black enough, at any rate, the scene appeared; and I looked forth upon it from my temporary shelter with the certainty that this river before me was a particularly hard road to travel.

"Ye'll no be gangin' ower the day, sewerly?" said a voice near me.

I turned and saw a brawny figure in a reefing-jacket and "sou'-wester." He might have been a sailor, or a scowman, or a hibernating raftsman.

"Why?" said I.

He said nothing, but shook his head with solemn emphasis.

I looked for a few moments longer, and hesitated. Yet there was no remedy for it, bad as it looked. After being ordered forward, I did not like to turn back with an excuse about the weather. Besides, the ice thus far had lasted well. Only the day before, sleds had crossed. There was no reason why I should not cross now. Why should I in particular be doomed to a catastrophe more than any other man? And, finally, was not McGoggin there? Was he not always ready with his warmest welcome? On a stormy day, did he not always keep his water up to the boiling-point, and did not the very best whiskey in Quebec diffuse about his chamber its aromatic odor?

I moved forward. The die was cast.

The channel near the shore was from six to twelve feet in width, filled with floating fragments. Over this I scrambled in safety. As I advanced, I could see that in one day a great change had taken place. The surface-ice was soft and disintegrated, crushing readily under the feet. All around me extended wide pools of water. From beneath these arose occasional groaning sounds—dull, heavy crunches, which seemed to indicate a speedy break-up. The progress of the season, with its thaws and rains, had been gradually weakening the ice; along the shore its hold had in some places at least been relaxed; and the gale of wind that was now blowing was precisely of that description which most frequently sweeps away resistlessly the icy fetters of the river, and sets all the imprisoned waters free. At every step new signs of this approaching break-up became visible. From time to time I encountered gaps in the ice, of a foot or two in width, which did not of themselves amount to much, but which nevertheless served to show plainly the state of things.

My progress was excessively difficult. The walking was laborious on account of the ice itself and the pools through which I had to wade. Then there were frequent gaps, which sometimes could only be traversed by a long detour. Above all, there was the furious sleet, which drove down the river, borne on by the tempest, with a fury and unrelaxing pertinacity that I never saw equalled. However, I managed to toil onward, and at length reached the centre of the river. Here I found a new and more serious obstacle. At this point the ice had divided; and in the channel thus formed there was a vast accumulation of ice-cakes, heaped up one above the other in a long ridge, which extended as far as the eye could reach. There were great gaps in it, however, and to cross it needed so much caution, and so much effort, that I paused for a while, and, setting my back to the wind, looked around to examine the situation.

Wild enough that scene appeared. On one side was my destination, but dimly visible through the storm; on the other rose the dark cliff of Cape Diamond, frowning gloomily over the river, crowned with the citadel, where the flag of Old England was streaming straight out at the impulse of the blast, with a stiffness that made it seem as though it had been frozen in the air rigid in that situation. Up the river all was black and gloomy; and the storm which burst from that quarter obscured the view; down the river the prospect was as gloomy, but one thing was plainly visible—a wide, black surface, terminating the gray of the ice, and showing that there at least the break-up had begun, and the river had resumed its sway.

A brief survey showed me all this, and for a moment created a strong desire to go back. Another moment, however, showed that to go forward was quite as wise and as safe. I did not care to traverse again what I had gone over, and the natural reluctance to turn back from the half-way house, joined to the hope of better things for the rest of the way, decided me to go forward.

After some examination, I found a place on which to cross the central channel. It was a point where the heaps of ice seemed at once more easy to the foot, and more secure. At extreme risk, and by violent efforts, I succeeded in crossing, and, on reaching the other side, I found the ice more promising. Then, hoping that the chief danger had been successfully encountered, I gathered up my energies, and stepped out briskly toward the opposite shore.

It was not without the greatest difficulty and the utmost discomfort that I had come thus far. My clothes were coated with frozen sleet; my hair was a mass of ice; and my boots were filled with water. Wretched as all this was, there was no remedy for it, so I footed it as best I could, trying to console myself by thinking over the peaceful pleasures which were awaiting me at the end of my journey in the chambers of the hospitable McGoggin.

Suddenly, as I walked along, peering with half-closed eyes through the stormy sleet before me, I saw at some distance a dark object approaching. After a time, the object drew nearer, and resolved itself into a sleigh. It came onward toward the centre of the river, which it reached at about a hundred yards below the point where I had crossed. There were two occupants in the sleigh, one crouching low and muffled in wraps; the other the driver, who looked like one of the common *habitans*. Knowing the nature of the river there, and wondering what might bring a sleigh out at such a time, I stopped, and watched them with a vague idea of shouting to them to go back. Their progress thus far from the opposite shore, so far at least as I could judge, made me conclude that the ice on this side must be comparatively good, while my own journey had proved that on the Quebec side it was utterly impossible for a horse to go.

As they reached the channel where the crumbled ice-blocks lay floating, heaped up as I have described, the sleigh stopped, and the driver looked anxiously around. At that very instant there came one of those low, dull, grinding sounds I have already mentioned, but very much louder than any that I had hitherto heard. Deep, augry thuds followed, and crunching sounds, while beneath all there arose a solemn murmur like the "voice of many waters." I felt the ice heave under my feet, and sway in long, slow undulations, and one thought, quick as lightning, flashed horribly into my mind. Instinctively I leaped forward toward my destination, while the ice rolled and heaved beneath me, and the dread sounds grew louder at every step.

Scarcely had I gone a dozen paces when a piercing scream arrested me. I stopped and looked back. For a few moments only had I turned away, yet in that short interval a fearful change had taken place. The long ridge of ice which had been heaped up in the mid-channel had increased to thrice its former height, and the crunching and grinding of the vast masses arose above the roaring of the storm. Far up the river there came a deeper and fuller sound of the same kind, which, brought down by the wind, burst with increasing terrors upon the ear. The ridge of ice was in constant motion, being pressed and heaped up in ever-increasing masses, and, as it heaped itself up, toppling over and falling with a noise like thunder. There could be but one cause for all this, and the fear which had already flashed through my brain was now confirmed to my sight. The ice on which I stood was breaking up!

As all this burst upon my sight, I saw the sleigh. The horse had stopped in front of the ridge of ice in the mid-channel, and was rearing and plunging violently. The driver was lashing furiously and trying to turn the animal, which, frenzied by terror, and maddened by the stinging sleet, refused to obey, and would only rear and kick. Suddenly the ice under the sleigh sank down, and a flood of water rolled over it, followed by an avalanche of ice-blocks which had tumbled from the ridge. With a wild snort of terror, the horse turned, whirling round the sleigh, and with the speed of the wind dashed back toward the shore. As the sleigh came near, I saw the driver upright and trying to regain his command of the horse, and at that instant the other passenger started erect. The cloak fell back. I saw a face pale, overhung with dishevelled hair, and filled with an anguish of fear. But the pallor and the fear could not conceal the exquisite loveliness of that woman-face, which was thus so suddenly revealed in the midst of the storm and in the presence of death; and which now, beautiful beyond all that I had ever dreamed of, arose before my astonished eyes. It was from her that the cry had come but a few moments before. As she passed she saw me, and another cry escaped her. In another moment she was far ahead.

And now I forgot all about the dangers around me, and the lessening chances of an interview with McGoggin. I hurried on, less to secure my own safety than to assist the lady. And thus as I rushed onward I became aware of a new danger which arose darkly between me and the shore. It was a long, black channel, gradually opening itself up, and showing in its gloomy surface a dividing line between me and life. To go back seemed now impossible—to go forward was to meet these black waters.

Toward this gulf the frightened horse ran at headlong speed. Soon he reached the margin of the ice. The water was before him and headed him off. Terrified again at this, he swerved aside, and bounded up the river. The driver pulled frantically at the reins. The lady, who had fallen back again in her seat, was motionless. On went the horse, and, at every successive leap in his mad career, the sleigh swung wildly first to one side and then to the other. At last there occurred a curve in the line of ice, and reaching this the horse turned once more to avoid it. In doing so, the sleigh was swung toward the water. The shafts broke. The harness was torn asunder. The off-runner of the sleigh slid from the ice—it tilted over; the driver jerked at the reins and made a wild leap. In vain. His feet were entangled in the fur robes which dragged him back. A shriek, louder, wilder, and far more fearful than before, rang

out through the storm; and the next instant down went the sleigh with its occupants into the water, the driver falling out, while the horse, though free from the sleigh, was yet jerked aside by the reins, and before he could recover himself fell with the rest into the icy stream.

All this seemed to have taken place in an instant. I hurried on, with all my thoughts on this lady who was thus doomed to so sudden and so terrible a fate. I could see the sleigh floating for a time, and the head of the horse, that was swimming. I sprang to a place which seemed to give a chance of assisting them, and looked eagerly to see what had become of the lady. The sleigh drifted steadily along. It was one of that box-shaped kind called *pungs*, which are sometimes made so tight that they can resist the action of water, and float either in crossing a swollen stream, or in case of breaking through the ice. Such boat-like sleighs are not uncommon; and this one was quite buoyant. I could see nothing of the driver. He had probably sunk at once, or had been drawn under the ice. The horse, entangled in the shafts, had regained the ice, and had raised one foreleg to its surface, with which he was making furious struggles to emerge from the water, while snorts of terror escaped him. But where was the lady? I hurried farther up, and, as I approached, I could see something crouched in a heap at the bottom of the floating sleigh. Was it she—or was it only the heap of buffalo-robes? I could not tell.

The sleigh drifted on, and soon I came near enough to see that the bundle had life. I came close to where it floated. It was not more that six yards off, and was drifting steadily nearer. I walked on by the edge of the ice, and shouted. There was no answer. At length I saw a white hand clutching the side of the sleigh. A thrill of exultant hope passed through me. I shouted again and again, but my voice was lost in the roar of the crashing ice and the howling gale. Yet, though my voice had not been heard, I was free from suspense, for I saw that the lady thus far was safe, and I could wait a little longer for the chance of affording her assistance. I walked on, then, in silence, watching the sleigh which continued to float. We travelled thus a long distance—I, and the woman who had thus been so strangely wrecked in so strange a bark. Looking back, I could no longer see any signs of the horse. All this time the sleigh was gradually drifted nearer the edge of the ice on which I walked, until at last it came so near that I reached out my stick, and, catching it with the crooked handle, drew it toward me. The shock, as the sleigh struck against the ice, roused its occupant. She started up, stood upright, stared for a moment at me, and then, at the scene around. Then she sprang out, and, clasping her hands, fell upon her knees, and seemed to mutter words of prayer. Then she rose to her feet, and looked around with a face of horror. There was such an anguish of fear in her face, that I tried to comfort her. But my efforts were useless.

"Oh! there is no hope! The river is breaking up!" she moaned. "They told me it would. How mad I was to try to cross!"

Finding that I could do nothing to quell her fears, I began to think what was best to be done. First of all, I determined to secure the sleigh. It might be the means of saving us, or, if not, it would at any rate do for a place of rest. It was better than the wet ice for the lady. So I proceeded to pull it on the ice. The lady tried to help me, and, after a desperate effort, the heavy pung was dragged from the water upon the frozen surface. I then made her sit in it, and wrapped the furs around her as well as I could.

She submitted without a word. Her white face was turned toward mine; and once or twice she threw upon me, from her dark, expressive eyes, a look of speechless gratitude. I tried to promise safety, and encouraged her as well as I could, and she seemed to make an effort to regain her self-control.

In spite of my efforts at consolation, her despair affected me. I looked all around to see what the chances of escape might be. As I took that survey, I perceived that those chances were indeed small. The first thing that struck me was, that Cape Diamond was far behind the point where I at present stood. While the sleigh had drifted, and I had walked beside it, our progress had been down the river; and since then the ice, which itself had all this time been drifting, had borne us on without ceasing. We were still drifting at the very moment that I looked around. We had also moved farther away from the shore which I wished to reach, and nearer to the Quebec side. When the sleigh had first gone over, there had not been more than twenty yards between the ice and the shore; but now that shore was full two hundred yards away. All this time the fury of the wind, and the torment of the blinding, stinging sleet, had not in the least abated; the grinding and roaring of the ice had increased; the long ridge had heaped itself up to a greater height, and opposite us it towered up in formidable masses.

I thought at one time of intrusting myself with my companion to the sleigh, in the hope of using it as a boat to gain the shore. But I could not believe that it would float with both of us, and, if it would, there were no means of moving or guiding it. Better to remain on the ice than to attempt that. Such a refuge would only do as a last resort. After giving up this idea, I watched to see if there was any chance of drifting back to the shore, but soon saw that there was none. Every moment drew us farther off. Then I thought of a score of desperate undertakings, but all of them were given up almost as soon as they suggested themselves.

All this time the lady had sat in silence—deathly pale, looking around with that same anguish of fear which I had noticed from the first, like one who awaits an inevitable doom. The storm beat about her pitilessly; occasional shudders passed through her; and the dread scene around affected me far less than those eyes of agony, that pallid face, and those tremulous white lips that seemed to murmur prayers. She saw, as well as I, the widening sheet of water between us and the shore on the one side, and on the other the ever-increasing masses of crumbling ice.

At last I suddenly offered to go to Quebec, and bring back help for her. So wild a proposal was in the highest degree impracticable; but I thought that it might lead her to suggest something. As soon as she heard it, she evinced fresh terror.

"Oh, sir!" she moaned, "if you have a human heart, do not leave me! For God's sake, stay a little longer."

"Leave you!" I cried; "never while I have breath. I will stay with you to the last."

But this, instead of reassuring her, merely had the effect of changing her feelings. She grew calmer.

"No," said she, "you must not. I was mad with fear. No—go. You at least can save yourself. Go—fly—leave me!"

"Never!" I repeated. "I only made that proposal—not thinking to save you, but merely supposing that you would feel better at the simple suggestion of something."

"I implore you," she reiterated. "Go—there is yet time. You only risk your life by delay. Don't waste your time on me."

"I could not go if I would," I said, "and I swear I would not go if I could," I cried, impetuously. "I hope you do not take me for any thing else than a gentleman."

"Oh, sir, pardon me. Can you think that?—But you have already risked your life once by waiting to save mine—and, oh, do not risk it by waiting again."

"Madame," said I, "you must not only not say such a thing, but you must not even think it. I am here with you, and, being a gentleman, I am here by your side either for life or death. But come—rouse yourself. Don't give up. I'll save you, or die with you. At the same time, let me assure you that I haven't the remotest idea of dying."

She threw at me, from her eloquent eyes, a look of unutterable gratitude, and said not a word.

I looked at my watch. It was three o'clock. There was no time to lose. The day was passing swiftly, and at this rate evening would come on before one might be aware. The thought of standing idle any longer, while the precious hours were passing, was intolerable. Once more I made a hasty survey, and now, pressed and stimulated by the dire exigencies of the hour, I determined to make an effort toward the Quebec side. On that side, it seemed as though the ice which drifted from the other shore was being packed in an unbroken mass. If so, a way over it might be found to a resolute spirit.

I hastily told my companion my plan. She listened with a faint smile.

"I will do all that I can," said she, and I saw with delight that the mere prospect of doing something had aroused her.

My first act was to push the sleigh with its occupant toward the ice-ridge in the centre of the river. The lady strongly objected, and insisted on getting out and helping me. This I positively forbade. I assured her that my strength was quite sufficient for the undertaking, but that hers was not; and if she would save herself, and me, too, she must husband all her resources and obey implicitly. She submitted under protest, and, as I pushed her along, she murmured the most touching expressions of sympathy and of gratitude. But pushing a sleigh over the smooth ice is no very difficult work, and the load that it contained did not increase the labor in my estimation. Thus we soon approached that long ice-ridge which I have so frequently mentioned. Here I stopped, and began to seek a place which might afford a chance for crossing to the ice-field on the opposite side.

The huge ice-blocks gathered here, where the fields on either side were forced against one another, grinding and breaking up. Each piece was forced up, and, as the grinding process continued, the heap rose higher. At times, the loftiest parts of the ridge toppled over with a tremendous crash, while many other piles seemed about to do the same. To attempt to pass that ridge would be to encounter the greatest peril. In the first place, it would be to invite an avalanche; and then, again, wherever the piles fell, the force of that fall broke the field-ice below, and the water rushed up, making a passage through it quite as hazardous as the former. For a long time I examined without seeing any place which was at all practicable. There was no time, however, to be discouraged; an effort had to be made, and that without delay; so I determined to try for myself, and test one or more places. One place appeared less dangerous than others—a place where a pile of uncommon size had recently fallen. The blocks were of unusual size, and were raised up but a little above the level of the ice on which I stood. These blocks, though swaying slowly up and down, seemed yet to be strong enough for my purpose. I sprang toward the place, and found it practicable. Then I returned to the lady. She was eager to go. Here we had to give up the sleigh, since to transport that also was not to be thought of.

"Now," said I, "is the time for you to exert all your strength."

"I am ready," said she.

"Hurry, then."

At that moment there burst a thunder-shock. A huge pile farther down had fallen, and bore down the surface-ice. The water rushed boiling and seething upward, and spread far over. There was not a moment to lose. It was now or never; so, snatching her hand, I rushed forward. The water was up to my knees, and sweeping past and whirling back with a furious impetuosity. Through that flood I dragged her, and she followed bravely and quickly. I pulled her up to the first block, then onward to another. Leaping over a third, I had to relinquish her hand for a moment, and then, extending mine once more, I caught hers, and she sprang after me. All these blocks were firm, and our weight did not move their massive forms. One huge piece formed the last stage in our hazardous path. It overlapped the ice on the opposite side. I sprang down, and the next instant the lady was by my side. Thank Heaven! we were over.

Onward then we hurried for our lives, seeking to get as far as possible from that dangerous channel of ice-avalanches and seething waters; and it was not till a safe distance intervened, that I dared to slacken my pace so as to allow my companion to take breath. All this time she had not spoken a word, and had shown a calmness and an energy which contrasted strongly with her previous lethargy and terror.

I saw that the ice in this place was rougher than it had been on the other side. Lumps were upheaved in many places. This was a good sign, for it indicated a close packing in this direction, and less danger of open water, which was the only thing now to be feared. The hope of reaching the shore was now strong within me. That shore, I could perceive, must be some distance below Quebec; but how far I could not tell. I could see the dark outline of the land, but Quebec was now no longer perceptible through the thick storm of sleet.

For a long time, my companion held out nobly, and sustained the rapid progress which I was trying to keep up; but, at length, she began to show evident signs of exhaustion. I saw this with pain, for I was fearful every moment of some new circumstance which might call for fresh exertion from both of us. I would have given any thing to have had the sleigh which we were forced to relinquish. I feared that her strength would fail at the trying moment. The distance before us was yet so great that we seemed to have traversed but little. I insisted on her taking my arm and leaning on me for support, and tried to cheer her by making her look back and see how far we had gone. She tried to smile; but the smile was a failure. In her weakness, she began to feel more sensibly the storm from which she had been shel-tered to some extent before she left the sleigh. She cowered under the fierce pelt of the pitiless sleet, and clung to me, trembling and shivering with cold.

On and on we walked. The distance seemed interminable. The lady kept up well, considering her increasing exhaustion, saying nothing whatever; but her quick, short breathing was audible, as she panted with fatigue. I felt every shudder that ran through her delicate frame. And yet I did not dare to stop and give her rest; for, aside from the imminent danger of losing our hope of reaching land, a delay, even to take breath, would only expose her the more surely to the effect of the cold. At last, I stopped for a moment, and drew off my overcoat. This, in spite of her protestations, I forced her to put on. She threatened, at one time, to sit down on the ice and die, rather than do it.

"Very well, madame," said I. "Then, out of a punctilio, you will destroy, not only yourself, but me. Do I deserve this?"

At this, tears started to her eyes. She submitted.

"Oh, sir," she murmured, "what can I say? It's for your sake that I refuse. I will submit. God bless you—who sent you to my help! God forever bless you!"

I said nothing.

On and on!

Then her steps grew feebler—then her weight rested on me more heavily.

On and on!

She staggered, and low moans succeeded to her heavy panting. At last, with a cry of despair, she fell forward.

I caught her in my arms, and held her up.

"Leave me!" she said, in a faint voice. "I cannot walk any farther."

"No; I will wait for a while."

"Oh, leave me! Save yourself! Or go ashore, and bring help!"

"No; I will go ashore with you, or not at all."

She sighed, and clung to me.

After a time, she revived a little, and insisted on going onward. This time she walked for some distance. She did this with a stolid, heavy step, and mechanically, like an automaton moved by machinery. Then she stopped again.

"I am dizzy," said she, faintly.

I made her sit down on the ice, and put myself between her and the wind. That rest did much for her. But I was afraid to let her sit more than five minutes. Her feet were saturated, and, in spite of my overcoat, she was still shivering.

"Come," said I; "if we stay any longer, you will die."

She staggered up. She clung to me, and I dragged her on. Then, again, she stopped.

I now tried a last resort, and gave her some brandy from my flask. I had thought of it often, but did not wish to give this until other things were exhausted; for, though the stimulus is an immediate remedy for weakness, yet on the ice and in the snow the reaction is dangerous to the last degree. The draught revived her wonderfully.

Starting once more, with new life, she was able to traverse a very great distance; and at length, to my delight, the shore began to appear very near. But now the reaction from the stimulant appeared. She sank down without a word; and another draught, and yet another, was needed to infuse some false strength into her. At length, the shore seemed close by us. Here she gave out utterly.

"I can go no farther," she moaned, as she fell straight down heavily and suddenly on the ice.

"Only one more effort," I said, imploringly. "Take some more brandy."

"It is of no use. Leave me! Get help!"

"See—the shore is near. It is not more than a few rods away."

"I cannot."

I supported her in my arms, for she was leaning on her hand, and slowly sinking downward. Once more I pressed the brandy upon her lips, as her head lay on my shoulder. Her eyes were closed. Down on her marble face the wild storm beat savagely; her lips were bloodless, and her teeth were fixed convulsively. It was only by an effort that I could force the brandy into her mouth. Once more, and for the last time, the fiery liquid gave her a momentary strength. She roused herself from the stupor into which she was sinking, and, springing to her feet with a wild, spasmodic effort, she ran with outstretched hands toward the shore. For about twenty or thirty paces she ran, and, before I could overtake her, she fell once more.

I raised her up, and again supported her. She could move no farther. I sat by her side for a little while, and looked toward the shore. It was close by us now; but, as I looked, I saw a sight which made any further delay impossible.

Directly in front, and only a few feet away, was a dark chasm lying between us and that shore for which we had been striving so earnestly. It was a fathom wide; and there flowed the dark waters of the river, gloomily, warningly, menacingly! To me, that chasm was nothing; but how could she cross it? Besides, there was no doubt that it was widening every moment.

I started up.

"Wait here for a moment," said I, hurriedly.

I left her half reclining on the ice, and ran hastily up and down the chasm. I could see that my fears were true. The whole body of ice was beginning to break away, and drift from this shore also, as it had done from the other. I saw a place not more than five feet wide. Back I rushed to my companion. I seized her, and, lifting her in my arms, without a word, I carried her to that place where the channel was narrowest; and then, without stopping to consider, but impelled by the one fierce desire for safety, I leaped forward, and my feet touched the opposite side.

With a horrible crash, the ice broke beneath me, and I went down. That sound, and the awful sensation of sinking, I shall never forget. But the cake of ice which had given way beneath my feet, though it went down under me, still prevented my sinking rapidly. I flung myself forward, and held up my almost senseless burden as I best could with one arm, while with the other I dug my sharp-pointed stick into the ice and held on for a moment. Then, summoning up my strength, I passed my left arm under my companion, and raised her out of the water upon the ice. My feet seemed sucked by the water underneath the shelf of ice against which I rested; but the iron-pointed stick never slipped, and I succeeded. Then, with a spring, I raised myself up from the water, and clambered out.

My companion had struggled up to her knees, and grasped me feebly, as though to assist me. Then she started to her feet. The horror of sudden death had done this, and had given her a convulsive energy of recoil from a hideous fate. Thus she sprang forward, and ran for some distance. I hastened after her, and, seizing her arm, drew it in mine. But at that moment her short-lived strength failed her, and she sank

once more. I looked all around—the shore was only a few yards off. A short distance away was a high, cone-shaped mass of ice, whose white sheen was distinct amid the gloom. I recognized it at once.

"Courage, courage!" I cried. "We are at Montmorency. There is a house not far away. Only one more effort."

She raised her head feebly.

"Do you see it? Montmorency! the ice-cone of the Falls!" I cried, eagerly.

Her head sank back again.

"Look! look! We are saved! we are near houses!"

The only answer was a moan. She sank down lower. I grasped her so as to sustain her, and she lay senseless in my arms.

There was now no more hope of any further exertion from her. Strength and sense had deserted her. There was only one thing to be done.

I took her in my arms, and carried her toward the shore. How I clambered up that steep bank, I do not remember. At any rate, I succeeded in reaching the top, and sank exhausted there, holding my burden under the dark, sighing evergreens.

Rising once more, I raised her up, and made my way to a house. The inmates were kind, and full of sympathy. I committed the lady to their care, and fell exhausted on a settee in front of the huge fireplace.

CHAPTER VIII.

I FLY BACK, AND SEND THE DOCTOR TO THE RESCUE.—RETURN TO THE SPOT.—FLIGHT OF THE BIRD.—PERPLEXITY, ASTONISHMENT, WONDER, AND DESPAIR.—"PAS UN MOT, MONSIEUR!"

A LONG time passed, and I waited in great anxiety. Meanwhile, I had changed my clothes, and sat by the fire robed in the picturesque costume of a French *habitant*, while my own saturated garments were drying elsewhere. I tried to find out if there was a doctor anywhere in the neighborhood, but learned that there was none nearer than Quebec. The people were such dolts, that I determined to set out myself for the city, and either send a doctor or fetch one. After immense trouble, I succeeded in getting a horse; and, just before starting, I was encouraged by hearing that the lady had recovered from her swoon, and was much better, though somewhat feverish.

It was a wild journey.

The storm was still raging; the road was abominable, and was all one glare of frozen sleet, which had covered it with a slippery surface, except where there arose disintegrated ice-hummocks and heaps of slush—the *débris* of giant drifts. Moreover, it was as dark as Egypt. My progress, therefore, was slow. A boy went with me as far as the main road, and, after seeing me under way, he left me to my own devices. The horse was very aged, and, I fear, a little rheumatic. Besides, I have reason to believe that he was blind. That did not make any particular difference, though; for the darkness was so intense, that eyes were as useless as they would be to the eyeless fishes of the Mammoth Cave. I don't intend to prolong my description of this midnight ride. Suffice it to say that the horse walked all the way, and, although it was midnight when I started, it was near morning when I reached my quarters.

I hurried at once to the doctor, and, to his intense disgust, roused him and implored his services. I made it a personal matter, and put it in such an affecting light, that he consented to go: but he assured me that it was the greatest sacrifice to friendship that he had ever made in his life. I gave him the most explicit directions, and did not leave him till I saw him on horseback, and trotting, half asleep, down the street.

Then I went to my room, completely used up after such unparalleled exertions. I got a roaring fire made, established myself on my sofa immediately in front of it, and sought to restore my exhausted frame by hot potations. My intention was to rest for a while, till I felt thoroughly warmed, and then start for Montmorency to see about the lady. With this in my mind, and a pipe in my mouth, and a tumbler of toddy at my elbow, I reclined on my deep, soft, old-fashioned, and luxurious sofa; and, thus situated, I fell off before I knew it into an exceedingly profound sleep.

When I awoke, it was broad day. I started up, looked at my watch, and, to my horror, found that it was half-past twelve. In a short time, I had flung off my *habitant* clothes, dressed myself, got my own horse, and galloped off as fast as possible.

I was deeply vexed at myself for sleeping so long; but I found comfort in the thought that the doctor had gone on before. The storm had gone down, and the sky was clear. The sun was shining brightly. The roads were abominable, but not so bad as they had been, and my progress was rapid. So I went on at a rattling pace, not sparing my horse, and occupying my mind with thoughts of the lady whom I had saved, when suddenly, about three miles from Quebec, I saw a familiar figure advancing toward me.

It was the doctor!

He moved along slowly, and, as I drew nearer, I saw that he looked very much worn out, very peevish, and very discontented.

"Well, old man," said I, "how did you find her?"

"Find her?" growled the doctor—"I didn't find her at all. If this is a hoax," he continued, "all I can say, Macrorie, is this, that it's a devilish stupid one."

"A hoax? What—didn't find her?" I gasped.

"Find her? Of course not. There's no such a person. Why, I could not even find the house."

"What—do you mean? I—I don't understand—" I faltered.

"Why," said the doctor, who saw my deep distress and disappointment, "I mean simply this: I've been riding about this infernal country all day, been to Montmorency, called at fifty houses, and couldn't find anybody that knew any thing at all about any lady whatever."

At this, my consternation was so great that I couldn't say one single word. This news almost took my breath away. The doctor looked sternly at me for some time, and then was about to move on.

This roused me.

"What!" I cried; "you're not thinking of going back?"

"Back? Of course, I am. That's the very thing I'm going to do."

"For God's sake, doctor," I cried, earnestly, "don't go just yet! I tell you, the lady is there, and her condition is a most perilous one. I told you before how I saved her. I left there at midnight, last night, in spite of my fatigue, and travelled all night to get you. I promised her that you would be there early this morning. It's now nearly two in the afternoon. Good Heavens! doctor, you won't leave a fellow in such a fix?"

"Macrorie," said the doctor, "I'm half dead with fatigue. I did it for your sake, and I wouldn't have done it for another soul—no, not even for Jack Randolph. So be considerate, my boy."

"Doctor," I cried, earnestly, "it's a case of life and death!"

A long altercation now followed; but the end of it was that the doctor yielded, and, in spite of his fatigue, turned back, grumbling and growling.

So we rode back together—the doctor, groaning and making peevish remarks; I, oblivious of all this, and careless of my friend's discomfort. My mind was full of visions of the lady—the fair unknown. I was exceedingly anxious and troubled at the thought that all this time she had been alone, without any medical assistance. I pictured her to myself as sinking rapidly into fever and delirium. Stimulated by all these thoughts, I hurried on, while the doctor with difficulty followed. At length, we arrived within half a mile of the Falls; but I could not see any signs of the house which I wished to find, or of the road that led to it. I looked into all the roads that led to the river; but none seemed like that one which I had traversed.

The doctor grew every moment more vexed.

"Look here now, Macrorie," said he, at last—"I'll go no farther—no, not a step. I'm used up. I'll go into the nearest house, and wait."

Saying this, he turned abruptly, and went to a house that was close by.

I then dismounted, went to the upper bank of the Montmorency, where it joins the St. Lawrence below the Falls, and looked down.

The ice was all out. The place which yesterday had been the scene of my struggle for life was now one vast sheet of dark-blue water. As I looked at it, an involuntary shudder passed through me; for now I saw the full peril of my situation.

Looking along the river, I saw the place where I must have landed, and on the top of the steep bank I saw a house which seemed to be the one where I had found refuge. Upon this, I went back, and, getting the doctor, we went across the fields to this house. I knocked eagerly at the door. It was opened, and in the person of the *habitant* before me I recognized my host of the evening before.

"How is madame?" I asked, hurriedly and anxiously.

"Madame?"

"Yes, madame—the lady, you know."

"Madame? She is not here."

"Not here!" I cried.

"Non, monsieur."

"Not here? What! Not here?" I cried again. "But she must be here. Didn't I bring her here last night?"

"Certainly, monsieur; but she's gone home."

At this, there burst from the doctor a peal of laughter—so loud, so long, so savage, and so brutal, that I forgot in a moment all that he had been doing for my sake, and felt an almost irresistible inclination to punch his head. Only I didn't; and, perhaps, it was just as well. The sudden inclination passed, and there remained nothing but an overwhelming sense of disappointment, by which I was crushed for a few minutes, while still the doctor's mocking laughter sounded in my ears.

"How was it?" I asked, at length— "how did she get off? When I left, she was in a fever, and wanted a doctor."

"After you left, monsieur, she slept, and awoke, toward morning, very much better. She dressed, and then wanted us to get a conveyance to take her to Quebec. We told her that you had gone for a doctor, and that she had better wait. But this, she said, was impossible. She would not

think of it. She had to go to Quebec as soon as possible, and entreated us to find some conveyance. So we found a wagon at a neighbor's, threw some straw in it and some skins over it, and she went away."

"She went!" I repeated, in an imbecile way.

"Oui, monsieur."

"And didn't she leave any word?"

"Monsieur?"

"Didn't she leave any message for—for me?"

"Non, monsieur."

"Not a word?" I asked, mournfully and despairingly.

The reply of the *habitant* was a crushing one:

"*Pas un mot, monsieur!*"

The doctor burst into a shriek of sardonic laughter.

CHAPTER IX.

BY ONE'S OWN FIRESIDE.—THE COMFORTS OF A BACHELOR.—CHEWING THE CUD OF SWEET AND BITTER FANCY.—A DISCOVERY FULL OF MORTIFICATION AND EMBARRASSMENT.—JACK RANDOLPH AGAIN.—NEWS FROM THE SEAT OF WAR.

By six o'clock in the evening I was back in my room again. The doctor had chaffed me so villanously all the way back that my disappointment and mortification had vanished, and had given place to a feeling of resentment. I felt that I had been ill-treated. After saving a girl's life, to be dropped so quietly and so completely, was more than flesh and blood could stand. And then there was that confounded doctor. He fairly revelled in my situation, and forgot all about his fatigue. However, before I left him, I extorted from him a promise to say nothing about it, swearing if he didn't I'd sell out and quit the ser-vice. This promise he gave, with the re-mark that he would reserve the subject for his own special use.

Once within my own room, I made my-self comfortable in my own quiet way, viz.:

1. A roaring, red-hot fire.
2. Curtains close drawn.
3. Sofa pulled up beside said fire.
4. Table beside sofa.
5. Hot water.
6. Whiskey.
7. Tobacco.
8. Pipes.
9. Fragrant aromatic steam.
10. Sugar.
11. Tumblers.
12. Various other things not necessary to mention, all of which contributed to throw over my perturbed spirit a certain divine calm.

Under such circumstances, while every moment brought forward some new sense of rest and tranquillity, my mind wandered back in a kind of lazy reverie over the events of the past two days.

Once more I wandered over the crum-bling ice; once more I floundered through the deep pools of water; once more I halted in front of that perilous ice-ridge, with my back to the driving storm and my eyes searching anxiously for a way of progress. The frowning cliff, with its flag floating out stiff in the tempest, the dim shore opposite, the dark horizon, the low moan of the river as it struggled against its icy burden, all these came back again. Then, through all this, I rushed forward, scrambling over the ice-ridge, reaching the opposite plain to hurry forward to the shore. Then came the rushing sleigh, the recoiling horse, the swift retreat, the mad race along the brink of the icy edge, the terrible plunge into the deep, dark water. Then came the wild, half-human shriek of the drowning horse, and the sleigh with its despairing freight drifting down toward me. Through all this there broke forth amid the clouds of that reverie, the vision of that pale, agonized face, with its white lips and imploring eyes—the face of her whom I had saved.

So I had saved her, had I? Yes, there was no doubt of that. Never would I lose the memory of that unparalleled journey to Montmorency Fall, as I toiled on, dragging with me that frail, fainting, despairing companion. I had sustained her; I had cheered her; I had stimulated her; and, finally, at that supreme moment, when she fell down in sight of the goal, I had put forth the last vestige of my own strength in bearing her to a place of safety.

And so she had left me.

Left me—without a word—without a hint—without the remotest sign of any thing like recognition, not to speak of grati-tude!

Pas un mot!

Should I ever see her again?

This question, which was very natural under the circumstances, caused me to make an effort to recall the features of my late companion. Strange to say, my effort was not particularly successful. A white, agonized face was all that I remem-bered, and afterward a white, senseless face, belonging to a prostrate figure, which I was trying to raise. This was all. What that face might look like in repose, I found it impossible to conjecture.

And now here was a ridiculous and mor-tifying fact. I found myself haunted by this white face and these despairing eyes, yet for the life of me I could not reduce that face to a natural expression so as to learn what it might look like in common life. Should I know her again if I met her? I could not say. Would she know me? I could not answer that. Should I ever be able to find her? How could I tell?

Baffled and utterly at a loss what to do toward getting the identity of the subject of my thoughts, I wandered off into various moods. First I became cynical, but, as I was altogether too comfortable to be morose, my cynicism was of a good-natured character. Then I made merry over my own mishaps and misadventures. Then I reflected, in a lofty, philosophic frame of mind, upon the faithlessness of woman, and, passing from this into metaphysics, I soon boozed off into a gentle, a peaceful, and a very consoling doze. When I awoke, it was morning, and I concluded to go to bed.

On the morrow, at no matter what o'clock, I had just finished breakfast, when I heard a well-known footstep, and Jack Randolph burst in upon me in his usual style.

"Well, old chap," he cried, "where the mischief have you been for the last two days, and what have you been doing with yourself? I heard that you got back from Point Levi—though how the deuce you did it I can't imagine—and that you'd gone off on horseback nobody knew where. I've been here fifty times since I saw you last. Tell you what, Macrorie, it wasn't fair to me to give me the slip this way, when you knew my delicate position, and all that. I can't spare you for a single day. I need your advice. Look here, old fellow, I've got a letter."

And saying this, Jack drew a letter from his pocket, with a grave face, and opened it.

So taken up was Jack with his own affairs, that he did not think of inquiring into the reasons of my prolonged absence. For my part, I listened to him in a dreamy way, and, when he drew out the letter, it was only with a strong effort that I was able to conjecture what it might be. So much had passed since I had seen him, that our last conversation had become very dim and indistinct in my memory.

"Oh," said I, at last, as I began to recall the past, "the letter—h'm—ah—the—the widow. Oh, yes, I understand."

Jack looked at me in surprise.

"The widow?" said he. "Pooh, man! what are you talking about? Are you crazy? This is from *her*—from Miss —— that is—from the other one, you know."

"Oh, yes," said I, confusedly. "True—I remember. Oh, yes—Miss Phillips."

"Miss Phillips!" cried Jack. "Hang it, man, what's the matter with you to-day? Haven't I told you all about it? Didn't I tell you what I wouldn't breathe to another soul—that is, excepting two or three?—and now, when I come to you at the crisis of my fate, you forget all about it."

"Nonsense!" said I. "The fact is, I went to bed very late, and am scarcely awake yet. Go on, old boy, I'm all right. Well, what does she say?"

"I'll be hanged if you know what you're talking about," said Jack, pettishly.

"Nonsense! I'm all right now; go on."

"You don't know who this letter is from."

"Yes, I do."

"Who is it?" said Jack, watching me with jealous scrutiny.

"Why," said I, "it's that other one—the —hang it! I don't know her name, so I'll call her Number Three, or Number Four, whichever you like."

"You're a cool hand, any way," said Jack, sulkily. "Is this the way you take a matter of life and death?"

"Life and death?" I repeated.

"Life and death!" said Jack. "Yes,

life and death. Why, see here, Macrorie, I'll be hanged if I don't believe that you've forgotten every word I told you about my scrape. If that's the case, all I can say is, that I'm not the man to force my confidences where they are so very unimportant."

And Jack made a move toward the door.

"Stop, Jack," said I. "The fact is, I've been queer for a couple of days. I had a beastly time on the river. Talk about life and death! Why, man, it was the narrowest scratch with me you ever saw. I didn't go to Point Levi at all."

"The deuce you didn't!"

"No; I pulled up at Montmorency."

"The deuce you did! How's that?"

"Oh, never mind; I'll tell you some other time. At any rate, if I seem dazed or confused, don't notice it. I'm coming round. I'll only say this, that I've lost a little of my memory, and am glad I didn't lose my life. But go on. I'm up to it now, Jack. You wrote to Number Three, proposing to elope, and were staking your existence on her answer. You wished me to order a head-stone for you at Anderson's, four feet by eighteen inches, with nothing on it but the name and date, and not a word about the virtues, et cetera. There, you see, my memory is all right at last. And now, old boy, what does she say? When did you get it?"

"I got it this morning," said Jack. "It was a long delay. She is always prompt. Something must have happened to delay her. I was getting quite wild, and would have put an end to myself if it hadn't been for Louie. And then, you know, the widow's getting to be a bit of a bore. Look here—what do you think of my selling out, buying a farm in Minnesota, and taking little Louie there?"

"What!" I cried. "Look here, Jack, whatever you do, don't, for Heaven's sake, get poor little Louie entangled in your affairs."

"Oh, don't you fret," said Jack, dolefully. "No fear about her. She's all right, so far.—But, see here, there's the letter."

And saying this, he tossed over to me the letter from "Number Three," and, filling a pipe, began smoking vigorously.

The letter was a singular one. It was highly romantic, and full of devotion. The writer, however, declined to accept of Jack's proposition. She pleaded her father; she couldn't leave him. She implored Jack to wait, and finally subscribed herself his till death. But the name which she signed was "Stella," and nothing more; and this being evidently a pet name or a *nom de plume*, threw no light whatever upon her real personality.

"Well," said Jack, after I had read it over about nine times, "what do you think of that?"

"It gives you some reprieve, at any rate," said I.

"Reprieve?" said Jack. "I don't think it's the sort of letter that a girl should write to a man who told her that he was going to blow his brains out on her doorstep. It doesn't seem to be altogether the right sort of thing under the circumstances."

"Why, confound it, man, isn't this the very letter that you wanted to get? You didn't really want to run away with her? You said so yourself."

"Oh, that's all right; but a fellow likes to be appreciated."

"So, after all, you wanted her to elope with you?"

"Well, not that, exactly. At the same time, I didn't want a point-blank refusal."

"You ought to be glad she showed so much sense. It's all the better for you.

3

It is an additional help to you in your difficulties."

"I don't see how it helps me," said Jack, in a kind of growl. "I don't see why she refused to run off with a fellow."

Now such was the perversity of Jack that he actually felt ill-natured about this letter, although it was the very thing that he knew was best for him. He was certainly relieved from one of his many difficulties, but at the same time he was vexed and mortified at this rejection of his proposal. And he dwelt upon his disappointment until at length he brought himself to believe that "Number Three's." letter was something like a personal slight, if not an insult.

He dropped in again toward evening.

"Macrorie," said he, "there's one place where I always find sympathy. What do you say, old fellow, to going this evening to—

CHAPTER X.

"BERTON'S ?—BEST PLACE IN THE TOWN.—GIRLS ALWAYS GLAD TO SEE A FELLOW.—PLENTY OF CHAT, AND LOTS OF FUN.—NO END OF LARKS, YOU KNOW, AND ALL THAT SORT OF THING."

IN order to get rid of my vexation, mortification, humiliation, and general aggravation, I allowed Jack to persuade me to go that evening to Colonel Berton's. Not that it needed much persuasion. On the contrary, it was a favorite resort of mine. Both of us were greatly addicted to dropping in upon that hospitable and fascinating household. The girls were among the most lively and genial good fellows that girls could ever be. Old Berton had retired from the army with enough fortune of his own to live in good style, and his girls had it all their own way. They were essentially

of the military order. They had all been brought up, so to speak, in the army, and their world did not extend beyond it. There were three of them—Laura, the eldest, beautiful, intelligent, and accomplished, with a strong leaning toward Ritualism; Nina, innocent, childish, and kitten-like; and Louie, the universal favorite, absurd, whimsical, fantastic, a desperate tease, and as pretty and graceful as it is possible for any girl to be. An aunt did the maternal for them, kept house, chaperoned, duennaed, and generally overlooked them. The colonel himself was a fine specimen of the *vieux militaire*. He loved to talk of the life which he had left behind, and fight his battles over again, and all his thoughts were in the army. But the girls were, of course, the one attraction in his hospitable house. The best of it was, they were all so accustomed to homage, that even the most desperate attentions left them heart-whole, in maiden meditation, fancy free. No danger of overflown sentiment with them. No danger of blighted affections or broken hearts. No nonsense there, my boy. All fair, and pleasant, and open, and above-board, you know. Clear, honest eyes, that looked frankly into yours; fresh, youthful faces; lithe, elastic figures; merry laughs; sweet smiles; soft, kindly voices, and all that sort of thing. In short, three as kind, gentle, honest, sound, pure, and healthy hearts as ever beat.

The very atmosphere of this delightful house was soothing, and the presence of these congenial spirits brought a balm to each of us, which healed our wounded hearts. In five minutes Jack was far away out of sight of all his troubles—and in five minutes more I had forgotten all about my late adventure, and the sorrows that had resulted from it.

After a time, Jack gravitated toward

Louie, leaving me with Laura, talking me-diævalism. Louie was evidently taking Jack to task, and very energetically too. Fragments of their conversation reached my ears from time to time. She had heard something about Mrs. Finnimore, but what it was, and whether she believed it or not, could not be perceived from what she said. Jack fought her off skilfully, and, at last, she made an attack from another quarter.

"Oh, Captain Randolph," said she, "what a delightful addition we're going to have to our Quebec society!"

"Ah!" said Jack, "what is that?"

"How very innocent! Just as if you are not the one who is most concerned."

"I?"

"Of course. You. Next to me."

"I don't understand."

"Come, now, Captain Randolph, how very ridiculous to pretend to be so igno-rant!"

"Ignorant?" said Jack; "ignorant is not the word. I am in Egyptian darkness, I assure you."

"Egyptian darkness — Egyptian non-sense! Will it help you any if I tell you her name?"

"Her name! Whose name? What 'her?'"

Louie laughed long and merrily.

"Well," said she, at length, "for pure, perfect, utter, childlike innocence, commend me to Captain Randolph! And now, sir," she resumed, "will you answer me one question?"

"Certainly—or one hundred thousand."

"Well, what do you think of Miss Phil-lips?"

"I think she is a very delightful per-son," said Jack, fluently—"the most de-lightful I have ever met with, present com-pany excepted."

"That is to be understood, of course;

but what do you think of her coming to live here?"

"Coming to live here!"

"Yes, coming to live here," repeated Louie, playfully imitating the tone of evi-dent consternation with which Jack spoke.

"What! Miss Phillips?"

"Yes, Miss Phillips."

"Here?"

"Certainly."

"Not here in Quebec?"

"Yes, here in Quebec—but I *must* say that you have missed your calling in life. Why do you not go to New York and make your fortune as an actor? You must take part in our private theatricals the next time we have any."

"I assure you," said Jack, "I never was so astonished in my life."

"How well you counterfeit!" said Louie; "never mind. Allow me to congratulate you. We'll overlook the little piece of act-ing, and regard rather the delightful fact. Joined once more—ne'er to part—hand to hand—heart to heart—memories sweet—ne'er to fade—all my own—fairest maid! And then your delicious remembrances of Sissiboo."

"Sissiboo?" gasped Jack.

"Sissiboo," repeated Louie, with admir-able gravity. "*Her* birth-place, and hence a sacred spot. She used to be called 'the maid of Sissiboo.' But, in choosing a place to live in, let me warn you against Sissiboo. Take some other place. You've been all over New Brunswick and Nova Scotia. Take Petitcodiac, or Washe Aemoak, or Shubenacadie, or Memramcook, or Reche-bucto, or Chiputneeticook, or the Kenne-becasis Valley. At the same time, I have my preferences for Piserinco, or Quaco."

At all this, Jack seemed for a time com-pletely overwhelmed, and sat listening to Louie with a sort of imbecile smile. Her allusion to Miss Phillips evidently troubled him, and, as to her coming to Quebec, he did not know what to say. Louie twitted him for some time longer, but at length he got her away into a corner, where he began a conversation in a low but very earnest tone, which, however, was sufficiently audible to make his remarks understood by all in the room.

And what was he saying?

He was disclaiming all intentions with regard to Miss Phillips.

And Louie was listening quietly!

Perhaps believing him!!

The scamp!!!

And now I noticed that Jack's unhappy tendency to—well, to *conciliate* ladies—was in full swing.

Didn't I see him, then and there, slyly try to take poor little Louie's hand, utterly forgetful of the disastrous result of a former attempt on what he believed to be that same hand? Didn't I see Louie civilly draw it away, and move her chair farther off from his? Didn't I see him flush up and begin to utter apologies? Didn't I hear Louie begin to talk of operas, and things in general; and soon after, didn't I see her rise and come over to Laura, and Nina, and me, as we were playing dummy? Methinks I did. Oh, Louie! Oh, Jack! Is she destined to be Number Four! or, good Heavens! Number Forty? Why, the man's mad! He engages himself to every girl he sees!

Home again.

Jack was full of Louie.

"Such fun! such life! Did you ever see any thing like her?"

"But the widow, Jack?"

"Hang the widow!"

"Miss Phillips?"

"Bother Miss Phillips!"

"And Number Three?"

Jack's face grew sombre, and he was silent for a time. At length a sudden thought seized him.

"By Jove!" he exclaimed, "I got a letter to-day, which I haven't opened. Excuse me a moment, old chap."

So saying, he pulled a letter from his pocket, opened it, and read it.

He told me the contents.

It was from Miss Phillips, and she told her dearest Jack that her father was about moving to Quebec to live.

CHAPTER XI.

"MACRORIE, MY BOY, HAVE YOU BEEN TO ANDERSON'S YET?" — "NO." — "WELL, THEN, I WANT YOU TO ATTEND TO THAT BUSINESS OF THE STONE TO-MORROW. DON'T FORGET THE SIZE—FOUR FEET BY EIGHTEEN INCHES; AND NOTHING BUT THE NAME AND DATE. THE TIME'S COME AT LAST. THERE'S NO PLACE FOR ME BUT THE COLD GRAVE, WHERE THE PENSIVE PASSER-BY MAY DROP A TEAR OVER THE MOURNFUL FATE OF JACK RANDOLPH. AMEN. R. I. P."

SUCH was the remarkable manner in which Jack Randolph accosted me, as he entered my room on the following day at about midnight. His face was more rueful than ever, and, what was more striking, his clothes and hair seemed *neglected*. This convinced me more than any thing that he had received some new blow, and that it had struck home.

"You seem hard hit, old man," said I. "Where is it? Who is it?"

Jack groaned.

"Has Miss Phillips come?"

"No."

"Is it the widow?"

"No."

"Number Three?"

Jack shook his head.

"Not duns ? "

"No."

"Then I give up."

"It's Louie," said Jack, with an expression of face that was as near an approximation to what is called sheepishness as any thing I ever saw.

"Louie ? " I repeated.

"Yes—"

"What of her ? What has she been doing ? How is it possible ? Good Heavens ! you haven't—" I stopped at the fearful suspicion that came to me.

"Yes, I have !" said Jack, sulkily. "I know what you mean. I've proposed to her."

I started up from the sofa on which I was lounging—my pipe dropped to the ground—a tumbler followed. I struck my clinched fist on the table.

"Randolph !" said I, "this is too much. Confound it, man ! are you mad, or are you a villain ? What the devil do you mean by trifling with the affections of that little girl ? By Heavens ! Jack Randolph, if you carry on this game with her, there's not a man in the regiment that won't join to crush you."

"Pitch in," said Jack quietly, looking at me at the same time with something like approval. "That's the right sort of thing. That's just what I've been saying to myself. I've been swearing like a trooper at myself all the way here. If there's any one on earth that every fellow ought to stand up for, it's little Louie. And now you see the reason why I want you to attend to that little affair of the gravestone."

At Jack's quiet tone, my excitement subsided. I picked up my pipe again, and thought it over.

"The fact is, Jack," said I, after about ten minutes of profound smoking, "I think you'll have to carry out that little plan of yours. Sell out as soon as you can, and take Louie with you to a farm in Minnesota."

"Easier said than done," said Jack, sententiously.

"Done ? why, man, it's easy enough. You can drop the other three, and retire from the scene. That'll save Louie from coming to grief."

"Yes ; but it won't make her come to Minnesota."

"Why not ? She's just the girl to go anywhere with a fellow."

"But not with Jack Randolph."

"What humbug are you up to now ? I don't understand you."

"So I see," said Jack, dryly. "You take it for granted that because I proposed, Louie accepted. Whereas, that didn't happen to be the case. I proposed, but Louie disposed of me pretty effectually."

"Mittened ? " cried I.

"Mittened !" said Jack, solemnly. "Hence the gravestone."

"But how, in the name of wonder, did that happen ?"

"Easily enough. Louie happens to have brains. That's the shortest way to account for her refusal of my very valuable devotions. But I'll tell you all about it, and, after that, we'll decide about the headstone.

"You see, I went up there this evening, and the other girls were off somewhere, and so Louie and I were alone. The aunt was in the room, but she soon dozed off. Well, we had great larks, no end of fun— she chaffing and twitting me about no end of things, and especially the widow ; so, do you know, I told her I had a great mind to tell her how it happened ; and excited her curiosity by saying it all originated in a mistake. This, of course, made her wild to know all about it, and so I at last told her the whole thing—the mistake, you know, about the hand, and all that—and my horror. Well, hang me, if I didn't think she'd go into fits. I never saw her laugh so much before. As soon as she could speak, she began to remind me of the approaching advent of Miss Phillips, and asked me what I was going to do. She didn't appear to be at all struck by the fact that lay at the bottom of my disclosures; that it was her own hand that had caused the mischief, but went on at a wild rate about my approaching 'sentimental see-saw,' as she called it, when my whole time would have to be divided between my two *fiancées.* She remarked that the old proverb called man a pendulum between a smile and a tear, but that I was the first true case of a human pendulum which she had ever seen.

"Now the little scamp was so perfectly fascinating while she was teasing me, that I felt myself overcome with a desperate fondness for her; so, seeing that the old aunt was sound asleep, I blurted out all my feelings. I swore that she was the only—"

"Oh, omit all that. I know—but what bosh to say to a sensible girl!"

"Well, you know, Louie held her handkerchief to her face, while I was speaking, and I—ass, dolt, and idiot that I was—felt convinced that she was crying. Her frame shook with convulsive shivers, that I took for repressed sobs. I saw the little hand that held the little white handkerchief to her face—the same slender little hand that was the cause of my scrape with Mrs. Finnimore—and, still continuing the confession of my love, I thought I would soothe her grief. I couldn't help it. I was fairly carried away. I reached forward my hand, and tried to take hers, all the time saying no end of spooney things.

"But the moment I touched her hand, she rolled her chair back, and snatched it away—

"And then she threw back her head—

"And then there came such a peal of musical laughter, that I swear it's ringing in my ears yet.

"What made it worse was, not merely what she considered the fun of my proposal, but the additional thought that suddenly flashed upon her, that I had just now so absurdly mistaken her emotion. For, confound it all! as I reached out my hand, I said a lot of rubbish, and, among other things, implored her to let me wipe her tears. This was altogether too much. Wipe her tears! And, Heavens and earth, she was shaking to pieces all the time with nothing but laughter. Wipe her tears! Oh, Macrorie! Did you *ever* hear of such an ass?

"Well, you know she couldn't get over it for ever so long, but laughed no end, while I sat utterly amazed at the extent to which I had made an ass of myself. However, she got over it at last.

"'Well,' said I, 'I hope you feel better.'

"'Thanks, yes; but don't get into a temper. Will you promise to answer me one question?'

"'Certainly; most happy. If you think it worth while to do any thing else but laugh at me, I ought to feel flattered.'

"'Now, that's what I call temper, and you must be above such a thing. After all, I'm only a simple little girl, and you—that is, *it* was so awfully absurd.'

"And here she seemed about to burst forth afresh. But she didn't.

"'What I was going to ask,' she began, in a very grave way, 'what I was going to ask is this, If it is a fair question, how many of these little entanglements do you happen to have just now?'

"'Oh, Louie!' I began, in mournful and reproachful tones.

"'Oh don't, don't,' she cried, covering her face, 'don't begin; I can't stand it. If you only knew how absurd you look when you are sentimental. You are always so funny, you know; and, when you try to be solemn, it looks so awfully ridiculous! Now, don't—I really cannot stand it. Please—ple-e-e-e-ease don't, like a good Captain Randolph.'

"At this she clasped her hands and looked at me with such a grotesque expression of mock entreaty, that I knocked under, and burst out laughing.

"She at once settled herself comfortably in her easy-chair.

"'Now that's what I call,' said she, placidly, 'a nice, good, sensible, old-fashioned Captain Randolph, that everybody loves, and in whose affairs all his innumerable friends take a deep interest. And now let me ask my question again: How many?'

"'How many what?' said I.

"'Oh, you know very well.'

"'How can I know, when you won't say what you mean?'

"'How many entanglements?'

"'Entanglements?'

"'Yes. Engagements, if you wish me to be so very explicit.'

"'What nonsense! Why you know all about it, and the cause—'

"'Ah, now, that is not frank; it isn't friendly or honest,' said the little witch. 'Come, now. Are there as many as—as—fifty?'

"'Nonsense!'

"'Twenty, then?'

"'How absurd!'

"'Ten?'

"'Of course not.'

"'Five?'

"'No.'

"'Four?'

"'Why, haven't I told you all?'

"'Four,' she persisted.

"'No—'

"'Three, then—'

"'It isn't fair,' said I, 'to press a fellow this way.'

"'Three?' she repeated.

"I was silent. I'm not very quick, and was trying, in a dazed way, to turn it off.

"'Three!' she cried. 'Three! I knew it. Oh, tell me all about it. Oh, do tell me! Oh, do—please tell me all. Oh, do, ple-e-e-e-ease tell me.'

"And then she began, and she teased and she coaxed, and coaxed and teased, until at last—"

Jack hesitated.

"Well," said I.

"Well," said he.

"You didn't really tell her," said I.

"Yes, but I did," said he.

"You didn't—you couldn't."

"I'll be hanged if I didn't!"

"Not about Number Three?"

"Yes, Number Three," said Jack, looking at me with a fixed and slightly stony stare.

Words were useless, and I sought expression for my feelings in the more emphatic whistle, which now was largely protracted.

"And how did she take it?" I asked, at length, as soon as I found voice to speak.

"As usual. Teased me, no end. Alluded to my recent proposal. Asked me if I had intended her to be Number Four, and declared her belief that I had thirty rather than three. Finally, the aunt waked up, and wanted to know what we were laughing at. Whereupon Louie said that she was laughing at a ridiculous story of mine, about an

Indian juggler who could keep three oranges in the air at the same time.

"'Captain Randolph,' said she 'you know all about Frederick the Great, of course?'

"'Of course,' I said, 'and Alexander the Great also, and Julius Cæsar, and Nebuchadnezzar, as the poet says.'

"'Perhaps you remember,' said Louie, in a grave tone, for her aunt was wide awake now, 'that the peculiar excellence of the genius of that great monarch consisted in his successful efforts to encounter the coalition raised against him. Though subject to the attacks of the three united powers of France, Austria, and Russia, he was still able to repel them, and finally rescued himself from destruction. Three assailants could not overpower him, and surely others may take courage from his example.'

"And after that little speech I came away, and here I am."

For some time we sat in silence. Jack did not seem to expect any remarks from me, but appeared to be rapt in his own thoughts. For my part, I had nothing whatever to say, and soon became equally rapt in my meditations.

And what were they about?

What? Why, the usual subject which had filled my mind for the past few days —my adventure on the river, and my mysterious companion. Mysterious though she was, she was evidently a lady, and, though I could not be sure about her face, I yet could feel sure that she was beautiful. So very romantic an adventure had an unusual charm, and this charm was heightened to a wonderful degree by the mystery of her sudden and utter disappearance.

And now, since Jack had been so very confidential with me, I determined to return that confidence, and impart my secret to him. Perhaps he could help me. At any rate, he was the only person to whom I could think of telling it.

So you see—

CHAPTER XII.

MY ADVENTURES REHEARSED TO JACK RANDOLPH.—"MY DEAR FELLOW, YOU DON'T SAY SO!"—"'PON MY LIFE, YES."—"BY JOVE! OLD CHAP, HOW CLOSE YOU'VE BEEN! YOU MUST HAVE NO END OF SECRETS. AND WHAT'S BECOME OF THE LADY? WHO IS SHE?"

WHO is she? Ay. Who, indeed? Hadn't I been torturing my brain for seventy-nine hours, sleeping as well as waking, with that one unanswered and apparently unanswerable question?

"Who is she?" repeated Jack.

"Well," said I, "that's the very thing that I wish to find out, and I want you to help me in it. I told you that she didn't leave any message—"

"But, didn't you find out her name?"

"No."

"By Jove! You're a queer lot. Why, I'd have found out her name the first thing."

"But I didn't—and now I want your help to find out not only her name, but herself."

At this Jack rose, loaded his pipe solemnly, and, with the air of one who is making preparations for a work of no common kind, lighted it, flung himself back in the easy-chair, and sent forth vast volumes of smoke, which might have been considered as admirably symbolical of the state of our minds.

"Well, Macrorie," said he, at last, "I'll tell you what I'd do. I'd go round to all the hotels, and examine the lists."

"Pooh!"

"Well, then, take the directory and hunt up all the names."

"Nonsense!"

"Why 'nonsense?'"

"Because I don't know her name. Didn't I impress that upon your mind?"

"By Jove!" cried Jack Randolph, after which he again relapsed into silence.

"See here, Macrorie," said he, at length.

"I have it."

"What?"

"Go round next Sunday to all the churches."

"What's the use of that?"

"Go round to the churches," repeated Jack, "scan every bonnet—and then, if you don't see her, why then, why—go to the photographic saloons. You'll be sure to find her picture there. By Jove! Why, Macrorie, the game's all in your own hands. These photographic saloons are better than a whole force of detective police. There's your chance, old man. You'll find her. Do that, and you're all right. Oh, yes— you'll find her, as sure as my name's Jack Randolph."

"No go, Jack," said I. "You see I couldn't recognize her even if I were to see her."

"Couldn't what?"

"Couldn't recognize her."

"You surely would know her if you saw her."

"I don't think I should."

"Well, of all the confounded fixes that ever I met with, this is the greatest!"

"That's the peculiarity of my present situation."

Jack relapsed into smoky silence.

"The fact is," said Jack, after a brief pause, "we've got to go to work systematically. Now, first of all, I want to know what she looks like."

"Well, that's the very thing I don't know."

"Nonsense! You must know something about it. Is she a blonde or a brunette? You can answer that, at least."

"I'm not sure that I can."

"What! don't you know even the color of her complexion?"

"When I saw her, she was as white as a sheet. Even her lips were bloodless. You see, she was frightened out of her wits."

"Well, then, her hair—her hair, man! Was that dark or light?"

"I didn't see it."

"Didn't see it?"

"No. You see it was covered by her hood. Think of that driving sleet. She had to cover herself up as much as she could from the terrible pelting of the storm."

"Well, then, I'll ask only one question more," said Jack, dryly. "I hope you'll be able to answer it. A great deal depends upon it. In fact, upon a true answer to this question the whole thing rests. Gather up all your faculties now, old chap, and try to answer me correctly. No shirking now—no humbug, for I won't stand it. On your life, Macrorie, and, by all your future hopes, answer me this—was your friend—a woman or a man?"

At the beginning of this solemn question, I had roused myself and sat upright, but at its close I flung myself down in disgust.

"Well," said Jack, "why don't you answer?"

"Jack," said I, severely, "I'm not in the humor for chaff."

"Chaff! my dear fellow, I only want to get a basis of action—a base of operations. Are you sure your friend was a woman? I'm in earnest—really."

"That's all rubbish—of course she was a woman—a lady—young—beautiful—but the anguish which she felt made her face seem like that of Niobe, or—or—well like some marble statue representing woe or despair, and all that sort of thing. What's the use of humbugging a fellow? Why not talk sense, or at least hold your tongue?"

"Don't row, old boy. You were so utterly in the dark about your friend that I wanted to see how far your knowledge extended. I consider now that a great point is settled, and we have something to start from. Very well. She was really a woman!"

"A lady," said I.

"And a lady," repeated Jack.

"Young?"

"Young."

"And beautiful as an angel," I interposed, enthusiastically.

"And beautiful as an angel," chimed in Jack. "By-the-by, Macrorie, do you think you would know her by her voice?"

"Well, n—no, I don't think I would. You see, she didn't say much, and what she did say was wrung out of her by terror or despair. The tones of that voice might be very different if she were talking about—well, the weather, for instance. The voice of a woman in a storm, and in the face of death, is not exactly the same in tone or modulation as it is when she is quietly speaking the commonplaces of the drawing-room."

"There's an immense amount of truth in that," said Jack, "and I begin to understand and appreciate your position."

"Never, while I live," said I, earnestly, "will I forget the face of that woman as I held her fainting form in my arms, and cheered her, and dragged her back to life; never will I forget the thrilling tones of her voice, as she implored me to leave her and save myself; but yet, as I live, I don't think that I could recognize her face or her

voice if I were to encounter her now, under ordinary circumstances, in any drawing-room. Do you understand?"

"Dimly," said Jack; "yes, in fact, I may say thoroughly. You have an uncommonly forcible way of putting it too. I say, Macrorie, you talk just like our chaplain."

"Oh, bother the chaplain!"

"That's the very thing I intend to do before long."

"Well, it'll be the best thing for you. Married and done for, you know."

"Nonsense! I don't mean that. It's something else—the opposite of matrimony."

"What is it?"

"Oh, never mind, I'll let you know when the time comes. It's a little idea of my own to countermine the widow. But come —don't let's wander off. Your business is the thing to be considered now—not mine. Now listen to me."

"Well."

"Let's put your case in a plain, simple, matter-of-fact way. You want to find a person whose name you don't know, whose face you can't recognize, and whose voice even is equally unknown. You can't give any clew to her at all. You don't know whether she lives in Quebec or in New York. You only know she is a woman?"

"A lady," said I.

"Oh, of course—a lady."

"And an English lady," I added. "I could tell that by the tone of her voice."

"She may have been Canadian."

"Yes. Many of the Canadian ladies have the English tone."

"Well, that may be all very true," said Jack, after some moments' thought; "but at the same time it isn't any guide at all. Macrorie, my boy, it's evident that in this instance all the ordinary modes of investigation are no good. Streets, churches, drawing-rooms, photographic saloons, hotel registers, directories, and all that sort of thing are utterly useless. We must try some other plan."

"That's a fact," said I, "but what other plan can be thought of?"

Jack said nothing for some time.

He sat blowing and puffing, and puffing and blowing, apparently bringing all the resources of his intellect to bear upon this great problem. At last he seemed to hit upon an idea.

"I have it!" he exclaimed. "I have it. It's the only thing left."

"What's that?"

"Macrorie, my boy," said Jack, with an indescribable solemnity, "I'll tell you what we must do. Let's try—

CHAPTER XIII.

"ADVERTISING!!!"

"ADVERTISING?" said I, dubiously.

"Yes, advertising," repeated Jack. "Try it. Put a notice in all the papers. Begin with the Quebec papers, and then send to Montreal, Ottawa, Toronto, Hamilton, Kingston, London, and all the other towns. After that, send notices to the leading papers of New York, Philadelphia, Baltimore, Richmond, St. Louis, New Orleans, Cincinnati, Portland, Chicago, Boston, and all the other towns of the United States."

"And while I'm about it," I added, "I may as well insert them in the English, Irish, Scotch, French, German, Spanish, Italian, Turkish, and Indian journals."

"Oh, bosh!" said Jack, "I'm in earnest. What's the use of nonsense? Really, my dear fellow, why not advertise in the Quebec papers? She'll be sure to see it."

"Well," said I, after some thought, "on the whole it isn't a bad idea. It can't do any harm at any rate."

"Harm? Why, my dear boy, it's your only chance."

"All right, then; let's try advertising."

And saying this, I brought out my entire writing-apparatus and displayed it on the table.

"Will you try your fist at it, Jack?" I asked.

"I? nonsense! I'm no good at writing. It's as much as I can do to write an 'I. O. U.,' though I've had no end of practice. And then, as to my letters—you ought to see them! No, go ahead, old boy. You write, and I'll be critic. That's about the style of thing, I fancy."

At this I sat down and commenced the laborious task of composing an advertisement. In a short time I had written out the following:

"*A gentleman who accompanied a lady across the ice on the 3d of April, was separated from her, and since then has been anxious to find out what became of her. Any information will console a distracted breast. The gentleman implores the lady to communicate with him. Address Box 3,333.*"

I wrote this out, and was so very well satisfied with it, that I read it to Jack. To my surprise and disgust, he burst out into roars of laughter.

"Why, man alive!" he cried, "that will never do. You must never put out that sort of thing, you know. You'll have the whole city in a state of frantic excitement. It's too rubbishy sentimental. No go. Try again, old man, but don't write any more of that sort of thing."

I said nothing. I felt wounded; but I had a dim idea that Jack's criticism was just. It *was* rather sentimental. So I tried again, and this time I wrote out something very different.

With the following result:

"*If the party who crossed the ice on the 3d of April with A. Z. will give her address, she will confer an unspeakable favor. Write to Box No. 3,333.*"

"Oh, that'll never do at all!" cried Jack, as I read it to him. "In the first place, your 'A. Z.' is too mysterious; and, in the second place, you are still too sentimental with your 'unspeakable favor.' Try again."

I tried again, and wrote the following:

"*A gentleman is anxious to learn the address of a party who accompanied him over the ice on the 3d of April. Address Box No. 3,333.*"

"Oh, that'll never do!" said Jack.

"Why not?"

"Why, man, it's too cold and formal."

"Hang it all! What *will* suit you? One is too warm; another is too cold."

Saying this, I tried once more, and wrote the following:

"*A. B. has been trying in vain to find the address of the party who accompanied him over the ice on the 3d of April. Will she have the kindness to communicate with him to Box No. 3,333?*"

"No go," said Jack.

"Why not?"

"Well, you see, you call her a 'party,' and then announce that this 'party' is a woman. It won't do. I wouldn't like to call any lady a 'party.' You'll have to drop that word, old boy."

At this I flung down the pen in despair.

"Well, hang it!" said I. What *will* do? You try it, Jack."

"Nonsense!" said he. "I can't write; I can only criticise. Both faculties are very good in their way. You'll have to start from another direction. I'll tell you what to do —try a roundabout way."

"A roundabout way?" I repeated, doubtfully.

"Yes."

"What's that?"

"Why, advertise for—let me see—oh, yes—advertise for the French driver. He was drowned—wasn't he?"

"Yes."

"Well, if you advertise for him, she will respond, and thus you will come into contact with her without making a fool of yourself."

"By Jove, Jack," said I, "that's not a bad idea! I think I get your meaning. Of course, if she has any soul, she'll sympathize with the lost driver. But what name shall I put?"

"Was he a common driver? I gathered this from your story."

"Oh, yes. It was a sleigh from the country—hired, you know, not a private sleigh."

"She couldn't have known his name, then?"

"I suppose not. It looked like a sleigh picked up hap-hazard to take her across."

"Well, risk it, and put in an assumed name. Make up something. Any name will do. The lady, I dare say, hasn't the smallest idea of the driver's name. Trot out something—Napoleon Bonaparte Gris, or any thing else you like."

"How would Lavoisier do?"

"Too long."

"Well, Noir, then."

"I don't altogether like that."

"Rollin."

"Literary associations," objected Jack.

"Well, then, Le Verrier," said I, after a moment's thought.

"Le Verrier—" repeated Jack. "Well, leave out the article, and make it plain Verrier. That'll do. It sounds natural."

"Verrier," said I. "And for the Christian name what?"

"Paul," suggested Jack.

"Paul—very well. Paul Verrier — a very good name for a Canadian. All right. I'll insert an advertisement from his distracted parent."

And I wrote out this:

"Notice.—*Paul Verrier, of Chaudière, left his home on the 3d of April last, to convey a lady to Quebec across the ice. He has not since been heard of. As the river broke up on that day, his friends are anxious to know his fate. Any one who can give any information about those who crossed on that date will confer a great favor on his afflicted father. Address Pierre Verrier, Box 3,333.*"

"That's about the thing," said Jack, after I had read it to him. "That'll fetch her down. Of course, she don't know the name of the *habitant* that drove her; and, of course, she'll think that this is a notice published by the afflicted father. What then? Why, down she comes to the rescue. Afflicted father suddenly reveals himself in the person of the gallant Macrorie. Grand excitement—mutual explanations—tableau—and the curtain falls to the sound of light and joyous music."

"Bravo, Jack! But I don't like to settle my affairs this way, and leave yours in disorder."

"Oh, I'm all right," said Jack. "There's no immediate danger. I'm settling down into a state of stolid despair, you know. If it wasn't for that last business with Louie, I could be quite calm. That's the only thing that bothers me now."

"I should think the widow would bother you more."

"Well, to tell the truth, she's getting to be a bit of a bore. She's too affectionate and *exigeante*, and all that, you know. But, then, I always leave early. I dine with her at seven, and get away before nine. Then I go to Louie's—or, at least, that's the way I intend to do."

"You're going to Louie's again, then?"

"Going to Louie's again? Why, man alive, what do you take me for? Going again? I should think I was. Why, Louie's the only comfort I have left on earth."

"But Number Three?"

Jack sighed.

"Poor little thing!" said he. "She seems to be rather down just now. I think she's regretting that she didn't take my offer. But I wrote her a note to-day, telling her to cheer up, and all that."

"But Miss Phillips? What'll you do when she comes? When will she be here?"

"She's expected daily."

"That will rather complicate matters—won't it?"

"Sufficient for the day," said Jack.

"I tell you what it is, my boy. I feel very much struck by Louie's idea about the three oranges. You'll find it precious hard to keep your three affairs in motion. You must drop one or two."

"Come, now, Macrorie—no croaking. You've got me into a placid state of mind by telling me of your little affair. It gave me something to think of besides my own scrapes. So don't you go to work and destroy the good effect that you've produced. For that matter, I won't let you. I'm off, old chap. It's fifteen minutes to three. You'd better seek your balmy couch. No—don't stop me. You'll croak me into despair again. Good-night, old man!"

CHAPTER XIV.

A CONCERT.—A SINGULAR CHARACTER.—" GOD
SAVE THE QUEEN."—A FENIAN.—A GENE-
RAL ROW.—MACRORIE TO THE RESCUE!—
MACRORIE'S MAIDEN SPEECH, AND ITS SIN-
GULAR EFFECTIVENESS. — O'HALLORAN. — A
STRANGE COMPANION. — INVITED TO PAR-
TAKE OF HOSPITALITY.

ON the following day I sent my notice to
the papers.

On the evening of that day there was to
be a concert. Everybody was going. It
was under the patronage of the military,
and of course everybody had to go. For
you must know that, in a garrison-town like
Quebec, we of the military order have it all
our own way. If we smile on an undertaking, it succeeds. If we don't, it languishes.
If we frown, the only result is ruin. But,
as we are generally a good-natured lot, we
smile approvingly on almost every thing.
It gets to be an awful bore; but what can
we do? Societies wish our countenance
at their public gatherings, and we have to
give it. Benevolent associations ask our
subscriptions; joint-stock companies wish
our names; missionaries and musicians,
lawyers and lecturers, printers and preach-
ers, tailors and teachers, operas and orato-
rios, balls and Bible-meetings, funerals and
festivities, churches and concerts—in short,
every thing that lives and moves and has its
being awaits the military smile. And the
smile is smiled. And so, I tell you what
it is, my dear fellow, it amounts to this,
that the life of an officer isn't by any means
the butterfly existence that you imagine it
to be. What with patronizing Tom, Dick,
and Harry, inspecting militia, spouting at
volunteers, subscribing to charities, buying
at bazaars, assisting at concerts, presiding
at public dinners, and all that sort of thing
no end, it gets to be a pretty difficult matter to keep body and soul together.

The concert under consideration happened to be a popular one. The best of
the regimental bands had been kindly lent
to assist, and there were songs by amateurs
who belonged to the first circles in Quebec,
both civil and military. It was quite a
medley, and the proceeds were intended for
some charitable purpose or other. The
house was crowded, and I could not get a
seat without extreme difficulty.

The concert went on. They sang " An-
nie Laurie," of course. Then followed " La
ci darem;" then "D'un Pescator Igno-
bile;" then "Come gentil;" then "Auld
Lang-syne;" then "Ah, mon Fils!" then
"Roy's Wife of Aldivalloch;" then "The
Last Rose of Summer;" then "Allister
MacAllister;" then "The Harp that once
through Tara's Halls."

As this last song was being sung, I became aware of an old gentleman near me
who seemed to be profoundly affected.
"The Last Rose of Summer" had evidently touched him, but Tara had an overpowering effect on him. It was sung confoundedly well, too. The band came in with a
wild, wailing strain, that was positively
heart-breaking. The party just mentioned
was, as I said, old, and a gentleman, but he
was tall, robust, broad-shouldered, with
eagle-like beak, and keen gray eyes that
were fitting accompaniments to so distinguished a feature. His dress was rather
careless, but his air and the expression of
his face evinced a mixture of eccentricity
and a sense of superiority. At least, it
had evinced this until the singing of Tara.
Then he broke down. First he bowed his
head down, resting his forehead upon his
hands, which were supported by his cane,
and several deep-drawn sighs escaped him.

Then he raised his head again, and looked up at the ceiling with an evident effort to assume a careless expression. Then he again hid his face. But the song went on, and the melancholy wail of the accompaniment continued, and at last the old gentleman ceased to struggle, and gave himself up to the influence of that wonderful music. He sat erect and rigid; his hands in front of him clasped tightly round his stick; and his eyes fixed on vacancy; and as I looked at him I saw big tears slowly coursing down his cheeks.

At length the song ceased, and he impatiently dashed his tears away, and looked furtively and suspiciously around, as though trying to see if any one had detected his weakness. I, of course, looked away, so that he had not the smallest reason for supposing that I had seen him.

After this the concert went on through a varied collection of pieces, and all the time I wondered who the old gentleman with the eagle face and tender sensibilities might be. And in this state of wonder I continued until the close.

At last came the usual concluding piece —"God save the Queen."

Of course, as everybody knows, when the national anthem is sung, it is the fashion all over the British empire for the whole audience to rise, and any one who remains seated is guilty of a deliberate insult to the majesty of that empire. On this occasion, as a matter of course, everybody got up, but I was surprised to see that the old gentleman remained seated, with his hands clinched tightly about his cane.

I was not the only one who had noticed this.

The fact is, I had got into a part of the hall which was not altogether congenial to my taste. I had got my ticket at the door, and found that all the reserved seats were taken up. Consequently I had to take my chance among the general public. Now this general public happened to be an awfully loyal public, and the moment they found that a man was among them who deliberately kept his seat while the national anthem was being sung, they began to get into a furious state of excitement.

Let me say also that there was very sufficient reason for this excitement. All Canada was agog about the Fenians. Blood had been shed. An invasion had taken place. There was no joke about it. The Fenians were not an imaginary danger, but a real one. All the newspapers were full of the subject. By the Fenians every Canadian understood an indefinite number of the disbanded veteran soldiers of the late American war, who, having their hand in, were not willing to go back to the monotony of a peaceful life, but preferred rather a career of excitement. Whether this suspicion were well founded or not doesn't make the slightest difference. The effect on the Canadian mind was the same as if it were true. Now, since the Canadian mind was thus roused up to this pitch of universal excitement, there existed a very general watch for Fenian emissaries, and any of that brotherhood who showed himself too openly in certain quarters ran a very serious risk. It was not at all safe to defy popular opinion. And popular opinion ran strongly toward the sentiment of loyalty. And anybody who defied that sentiment of loyalty did it at his peril. A serious peril, too, mind you. A mob won't stand nonsense. It won't listen to reason. It has a weakness for summary vengeance and broken bones.

Now, some such sort of a mob as this began to gather quickly and menacingly round my elderly friend, who had thus so rashly shocked their common sentiment. In a few moments a wild uproar began.

"Put him out!"

"Knock him down!"

"Hustle him!"

"He's a Fenian!"

"Down with him!"

"Punch his head!"

"Hold him up, and make him stand up!"

"Stand up, you fool!"

"Get up!"

"Up with him! Let's pass him out over our heads!"

"A Fenian!"

"We'll show him he's in bad company!"

"He's a spy!"

"A Fenian spy!"

"Up with him!" "Down with him!" "Pitch into him!" "Out with him!" "Toss him!" "Hustle him!" "Punch his head!" "Throttle him!" "Level him!" "Give it to him!" "Turn him inside out!" "Hold up his boots!" "Walk him off!"

All these, and about fifty thousand more shouts of a similar character, burst forth from the maddened mob around. All mobs are alike. Any one who has ever seen a mob in a row can understand the action of this particular one. They gathered thick and fast around him. They yelled. They howled. The music of the national anthem was drowned in that wild uproar. They pressed close to him, and the savage eyes that glared on him menaced him with something little less than death itself.

And what did he do?

He?

Why he bore himself splendidly.

As the row began, he rose slowly, holding his stick, which I now saw to be a knotted staff of formidable proportions, and at length reared his figure to its full height. It was a tall and majestic figure which he revealed—thin, yet sinewy, and towering over the heads of the roaring mob around him.

He confronted them all with a dark frown on his brow, and blazing eyes.

"Ye beggars!" he cried. "Come on—the whole pack of ye! A Fenian, ye say? That's thrue for you. Ye've got one, an' ye'll find him a tough customer! Come on—the whole thousand of ye!"

And saying this, he swung his big, formidable knotted stick about his head.

Those nearest him started back, but the crowd behind rushed forward. The row increased. The people in the reserved seats in front looked around with anxious eyes, not knowing what was going on.

The crowd yelled and hooted. It surged nearer. A moment more and the tall figure would go down.

Now, I'm a loyal man. None more so. I'm an officer and a gentleman. I'm ready at any moment to lay down my life for the queen and the rest of the royal family. I'm ready to pitch into the Fenians on any proper occasion, and all that.

But somehow this didn't seem to me to be the proper occasion. It was not a Fenian that I saw. It was an elderly gentleman; so sensitive, that but a few minutes before he had been struggling with his tears; so lion-hearted, that now he drew himself up and faced a roaring, howling mob of enemies—calmly, unflinchingly—hurling desperate defiance at them. And was that the sort of thing that I could stand? What! to see one man attacked by hundreds—a man like that, too—an old man, alone, with nothing to sustain him but his own invincible pluck? Pooh! what's the use of talking? I am an officer and a gentleman, and as such it would have been a foul disgrace to me if I had been capable of standing there quietly and looking at the old man at the mercies of the mob.

But, as it happened, I did nothing of the kind.

On the contrary, I sprang forward and stood by the side of the old man.

"Now, look here—you fellows!" I roared—"this is all very fine, and very loyal, but, damn it! don't it strike you that it's an infernally cowardly thing to pitch into an old man in this style? He may be a Fenian, and he may be Old Nick himself, but he's never done you fellows any harm. What the devil do you mean by kicking up such a row as this? You touch him, if you dare, that's all! You see my uniform, and you know what I am. I'm a Bobtail. This man is my friend. He's going out with me, and I'd like to see the fellow that will stop us."

That's the first speech I ever made in my life, and all that I can say is, that it was wonderfully successful. Demosthenes, and Cicero, and the Earl of Chatham, and Burke, and Mirabeau, all rolled into one, couldn't have been more successful. The mob rolled back. They looked ashamed. It was a word of sense spoken in a forcible manner. And that I take it is the essence of true oratory.

The mob rolled back. I gave my new friend my arm. He took it. The door was not far away. We started to go out. The people fell back, and made way for us. After all, they were a good-enough lot, and had only yielded to a kind of panic. All mobs, I suppose, are insane. The very fact of a mob involves a kind of temporary insanity. But these fellows had come to their senses, and so I had no difficulty in making my way through them along with my companion. We got out into the street without any difficulty. My new

friend held my arm, and involuntarily made a turn to the right on leaving the door of the hall. Thus we walked along, and for some time we walked in silence.

At length the silence was broken by my companion.

"Well—well—well!" he ejaculated—"to think of me, walking with a British officer—arrum-in-arrum!"

"Why not?" said I.

"Why not?" said he, "why there's iviry reason in loife. I'm a Fenian."

"Pooh!" said I, "what's the use of bothering about politics? You're a man, and a confoundedly plucky fellow too. Do you think that I could stand there and see those asses pitching into you? Don't bother about politics."

"An' I won't" said he. "But at any reet, I feeced them. An Oirishman niver sirrinders to an inimy. I feeced them, I did—an' I exprissed meself in shootable sintimints."

The rich Leinster accent of my companion showed his nationality more plainly than even his own explicit statement. But this did not at all lessen the interest that I took in him. His sensitiveness which had been so conspicuous, his courage which had shone so brightly, and his impressive features, all combined to create a feeling of mingled regard and respect for my new acquaintance.

"By Jove!" I cried, "I never saw a pluckier fellow in my life. There you were, alone, with a mad mob howling at you."

"It's meself," said he, "that'll nivir be intimidected. Don't I know what a mob is? An' if I didn't, wouldn't I feece thim all the seeme? An' afther all I don't moind tellin' you that it wasn't disrispict. It was only a kind of absthraction, an' I wasn't conscious that it was the national anthim, so I wasn't. I'd have stood up, if I'd

4

knowed it. But whin those divils began reelin' at me, I had to trait thim with scarrun and contimpt. An' for me—I haven't much toime to live, but what I have ye've seeved for me."

"Oh, nonsense, don't talk about that," said I, modestly.

"Sorr," said he, "I'm very well aware that I'm under deep obleegeetions, an' I owe ye a debt of grateechood. Consequintly, I insist on bein' greetful. I hold iviry British officer as me personal inimy; but, in you, sorr, I'm sinsible of a ginirous frind. Ye've seeved me loife, so ye have, an' there's no doubt about it. We'll weeve politics. I won't spake of the Finians. Phaylim O'Halloran isn't the man that'll mintion onsaisonable politics, or dwell upon uncongainal thames, so he isn't."

"Well," said I, "Mr. O'Halloran, since you've introduced yourself, I must give you my humble address. I'm Lieutenant Macrorie."

"Macrorie?" said he.

"Macrorie," said I, "of the Bobtails, and I assure you I'm very happy to make your acquaintance."

We walked along arm-in-arm in the most friendly manner, chatting about things in general. I found my companion to be very intelligent and very well informed. He had travelled much. He expressed himself fluently on every subject, and though his brogue was conspicuous, he was evidently a gentleman, and very well educated too. I gathered from his conversation that he had studied at Trinity College, Dublin, and that he had been leading a desultory sort of life in the United States for twenty years or so. He had been in Canada for something less than a year, and was anxious to get back to a more southern clime.

Chatting thus, and arm-in-arm, we walked along. I had nothing to do, and so I went with my new-found friend, with a vague idea of seeing him safe home. Of course such an idea was preposterous, for he could have got home just as well without me, but I had taken a fancy to my new acquaintance, and found a strange charm in his conversation. He talked incessantly and on many subjects. He discoursed on theology, literature, science, the weather, the army, the navy, music, painting, sculpture, photography, engraving, geology, chemistry, and on a thousand other arts and sciences, in all of which he showed himself deeply versed, and far beyond my depth. He had a brogue, and I had none, but as for intellectual attainments I was only a child in comparison with him.

At length we reached a house where he stopped.

"I'm infeenetely obloiged to ye," said he. "And now, won't ye koindly condiscind to step in and parteek of me hospitalitee? It'll give me shuprame deloight."

After such an invitation what could I say? I had nothing to do. Accordingly, I accepted it in a proper spirit, and, thanking him for his kind invitation, I went in along with him.

O'Halloran led the way in. It was a comfortable house. The parlor which we entered was large, and a huge grate filled with blazing coals diffused a cheerful glow. Magazines and periodicals lay on the table. Pictures illustrative of classical scenes hung round the walls, done in the old-fashioned style of line engraving, and representing such subjects as Mutius Scævola before Porsenna; Belisarius begging for an obolus; Æneas carrying his father from Troy; Leonidas at Thermopylæ; Coriolanus quitting Rome; Hamilcar making the boy Hannibal swear his oath of hate against Rome; and others of a similar character. O'Halloran made me sit in a "sleepy-hollow" easy-chair by the fire. Beside me were two huge book-shelves crammed with books. A glance at them showed me that they were largely of a classical order. Longinus, Æschylus, Demosthenes, Dindorf, Plato, Stallbaum—such were the names that I saw in gilt letters on the backs of the volumes.

About the room there was that air of mingled comfort and refinement that is always suggestive of the presence of ladies. A work-basket stood beside the table. And on a little Chinese table in a corner lay some crochet-work. I took in all these things at a glance and while my host was talking to me. After a time he excused himself and said that he would call the "leedies." He retired, leaving me alone, and striving to picture to myself—

CHAPTER XV.

THE O'HALLORAN LADIES.—THEIR APPEAR-
ANCE.—THEIR AGES.—THEIR DRESS.—THEIR
DEMEANOR.—THEIR CULTURE, POLISH, EDU-
CATION, RANK, STYLE, ATTAINMENTS, AND
ALL ABOUT THEM.

"LEEDIES," said O'Halloran, "allow me to inthrojuice to ye Captain Macrorie, an officer an' a gintlemin, an' when I steet that he seeved me life about a half an hour ago, ye'll see what sintimints of grateechood are his jew."

With these words O'Halloran entered the room, followed by two ladies whom he thus introduced, giving my name to them, but in the abstraction of the moment not mentioning their names to me.

The ladies greeted me with smiles, which at once threw a new charm over this very comfortable room, and seated themselves opposite on the other side of the fire, so that I had the best view of them possible.

And now the very first glance that I obtained of these ladies showed me that I had hit upon a wonderful piece of good luck when I went to that concert and met my new friend O'Halloran. For in beauty of face, grace of figure, refinement of manner; in every thing that affects an impressible man—and what man is not impressible?—these ladies were so far beyond all others in Quebec, that no comparison could be made. The Burton girls were nowhere.

The elder of the two might have been—no matter—not over twenty-three or four at any rate; while the younger was certainly not over eighteen or nineteen. There was a good deal of similarity in their styles; both were brunettes; both had abundance of dark, lustrous hair; both had those dark, hazel eyes which can send such a thrill to the soul of the impressible. For my part I thrilled, I glowed, I exulted, I rejoiced and triumphed in the adventure which had led to such a discovery as this. Were there any other women in Canada, in America, or in the world, equal to them? I did not believe there were. And then their voices—low—sweet—musical—voices which spoke of the exquisite refinement of perfect breeding; those voices would have been enough to make a man do or dare any thing.

Between them, however, there were some differences. The elder had an expression of good-natured content, and there was in her a vein of fun which was manifest, while the younger seemed to have a nature which was more intense and more earnest, and there was around her a certain indefinable reserve and *hauteur*.

Which did I admire most?

I declare it's simply impossible to say. I was overwhelmed. I was crushed with equal admiration. My whole soul became instinct with the immortal sentiment—

"How happy could I be with either;" while the cordiality of my reception, which made me at once a friend of this jewel of a family, caused my situation to assume so delicious an aspect that it was positively bewildering.

O'Halloran hadn't mentioned their names, but the names soon came out. They were evidently his daughters. The name of the eldest I found was Nora, and the name of the younger was Marion. The old gentleman was lively, and gave a highly-dramatic account of the affair at the concert, in which he represented my conduct in the most glowing light. The ladies listened to all this with undisguised agitation, interrupting him frequently with anxious questions, and regarding my humble self as a sort of a hero. All this was in the highest degree encouraging to a susceptible mind; and I soon found myself sliding off into an easy, a frank, an eloquent, and a very delightful conversation. Of the two ladies, the elder Miss O'Halloran took the chief share in that lively yet intellectual intercourse. Marion only put in a word occasionally; and, though very amiable, still did not show so much cordiality as her sister. But Miss O'Halloran! what wit! what sparkle! what mirth! what fun! what repartee! what culture! what refinement! what an acquaintance with the world! what a knowledge of men and things! what a faultless accent! what indescribable grace of manner! what a generous and yet ladylike humor! what a merry, musical laugh! what quickness of apprehension! what acuteness of perception! what—words fail. Imagine every thing that is delightful in a first-rate conversationalist, and every thing that is fascinating in a lady, and even then you will fail to have a correct idea of Miss O'Halloran. To have such an idea it would be necessary to see her.

Marion on the other hand was quiet, as I have said. Perhaps this arose from a reticence of disposition; or perhaps it was merely the result of her position as a younger sister. Her beautiful face, with its calm, self-poised expression, was turned toward us, and she listened to all that was said, and at times a smile like a sunbeam would flash over her lovely features; but it was only at times, when a direct appeal was made to her, that she would speak, and then her words were few, though quite to the point. I had not, therefore, a fair chance of comparing her with Miss O'Halloran.

In their accent there was not the slightest sign of that rich Leinster brogue which was so apparent in their father. This, however, may have arisen from an English mother, or an English education. Suffice it to say that in no respect could they be distinguished from English ladies, except in a certain vivacity of manner, which in the latter is not common. O'Halloran was evidently a gentleman, and his house showed that he was at least in comfortable circumstances. What his business now might be I could not tell. What his past had been was equally uncertain. Was he an exiled Young Irelander? Had he been driven from his home, or had he left it voluntarily? Whatever he was, his surroundings and his belongings showed unmistakable signs of culture and refinement; and as to his daughters, why, hang it! a peer of the realm couldn't have shown more glorious specimens of perfect womanhood than these which smiled on me in that pleasant parlor.

Meanwhile, as I flung myself headlong into a lively conversation with Miss O'Halloran, the old gentleman listened for a time and made occasional remarks, but at length relapsed into himself, and after some minutes of thought he reached out his hand and drew from among the periodicals lying on the table—

CHAPTER XVI.

THE DAILY PAPER.

"By the powers!" suddenly interrupted the deep voice of O'Halloran, breaking in upon our lively and delightful conversation.

At which we all started as though we had been shot.

"By the pipers!" continued O'Halloran, after some hesitation. "To think of anybody thryin' to cross the river on the 3d! Why, that was the dee of the breek-up."

At these words I started in new astonishment, and for a moment didn't know what in the world to make of it all. As for the ladies, they didn't say a word. I didn't notice them, in fact; I had turned and was looking at O'Halloran.

"See here," said he. "Did you ever hear the loikes of this? '*Paul Verrier of Chaudière lift his home on the 3d of Epril last, to convce a leedy to Quebec across the oice ;*'" and he read straight through the very advertisement which I had written and inserted in that very paper.

What my emotions were at that moment it is difficult to describe. At first I felt surprise, then I experienced a sense of triumph at this striking proof of the success which my advertisement had met with, but finally I had occasion to feel emotions which were very different from either of these. I had turned as O'Halloran began to read those familiar words, and after he had finished I mechanically settled myself into my former position, partly because of the comfort of the thing, and partly to see how perfectly impartial hearers like these ladies would listen to this composition of mine. My chief feeling was precisely the same as animates the artist who stands *incognito* beside his picture, to listen to the remarks of spectators; or the author who hunts through papers to read the criticism on his first book. This, it is true, was neither a picture nor a book, nor was I either an artist or an author, yet, after all, this advertisement was a literary effort of mine, and, what is more, it was the first one that had appeared in print. Was it any wonder, then, that for these reasons I felt curious to see the effect of that advertisement?

Now, as I turned, I was in expectation of some sign of feeling on the part of the ladies—call it surprise; call it sympathy; call it what you will—but I certainly was not prepared for that very peculiar and very marked effect which my humble effort at composition produced on them.

For there they sat—Marion erect and rigid, with her eyes fixed on her sister, and her hand raised in an attitude of warning; and Miss O'Halloran, in the same fixed attitude, looked eagerly at Marion, her eyes wide open, her lips parted, and one of her hands also half raised in the involuntary expression of amazement, or the mechanical suggestion of secrecy. Miss O'Halloran's emotion was not so strong as that of Marion, but then her nature was more placid, and the attitude of each was in full accordance with their respective characters.

They sat there in that attitude, altogether unconscious of me and of my gaze, with deep emotion visible on their faces, and unmistakable, yet why that emotion should be caused by that advertisement I could not for the life of me imagine.

"Well," said O'Halloran, "what do ye think of that now? Isn't that a spicimin of thrue Canajin grade? The man threw his loife away for a few pince."

As O'Halloran spoke, the ladies recovered

their presence of mind. They started. Miss O'Halloran saw my eyes fixed on her, flushed up a little, and looked away. As for Marion, she too saw my look, but, instead of turning her eyes away, she fixed them on me for an instant with a strange and most intense gaze, which seemed to spring from her dark, solemn, lustrous eyes, and pierce me through and through. But it was only for an instant. Then her eyes fell, and there remained not a trace of their past excitement in either of them.

I confess I was utterly confounded at this. These two ladies perceived in that advertisement of mine a certain meaning which showed that they must have some idea of the cause of the fate of the imaginary Verrier. And what was this that they knew; and how much did they know? Was it possible that they could know the lady herself? It seemed probable.

The idea filled me with intense excitement, and made me determine here on the spot, and at once, to pursue my search after the unknown lady. But how? One way alone seemed possible, and that was by telling a simple, unvarnished tale of my own actual adventure.

This decision I reached in little more than a minute, and, before either of the ladies had made a reply to O'Halloran's last remark, I answered him in as easy a tone as I could assume.

"Oh," I said, "I can tell you all about that."

"You!" cried O'Halloran.

"You!" cried Miss O'Halloran.

"You!" cried Marion, and she and her sister fixed their eyes upon me with unmistakable excitement, and seemed to anticipate all that I might be going to say.

This, of course, was all the more favorable to my design, and, seeing such immediate success, I went on headlong.

"You see," said I, "I put that notice in myself."

"*You!*" cried {O'Halloran, Miss O'Halloran, Marion,} this time in greater surprise than before.

"Yes," said I. "I did it because I was very anxious to trace some one, and this appeared to be the way that was at once the most certain, and at the same time the least likely to excite suspicion."

"Suspicion?"

"Yes—for the one whom I wished to trace was a lady."

"A lady!" said O'Halloran. "Aha! you rogue, so that's what ye'er up to, is it? An' there isn't a word of truth in this about Verrier?"

"Yes, there is," said I. "He was really drowned, but I don't know his name, and Paul Verrier, and the disconsolate father, Pierre, are altogether imaginary names. But I'll tell you all about it."

"Be dad, an' I'd be glad if ye would, for this exorjium sthrikes me as the most schupindous bit of schamin that I've encounthered for a month of Sundays."

While I was saying this, the ladies did not utter a single syllable. But if they were silent, it was not from want of interest. Their eyes were fixed on mine as though they were bound to me by some powerful spell; their lips parted, and, in their intense eagerness to hear what it was that I had to say, they did not pretend to conceal their feelings. Miss O'Halloran was seated in an arm-chair. Her left arm leaned upon it, and her hand mechanically pressed her forehead as she devoured me with her gaze. Marion was seated on a common chair, and sat with one elbow on the table, her hands clasped tight, her body thrown slightly forward, and her eyes fixed on mine with an intensity of gaze that was really embarrassing.

And now all this convinced me that they must know all about it, and emboldened me to go on. Now was the time, I felt, to press my search—now or never.

So I went on—

"Conticuere omnes, intentique ora tenebant
Inde toro Sandy Macrorie sic orsus ab alto:
Infandum, Regina, jubes renovare dolorem.'

That's about it. Rather a hackneyed quotation, of course, but a fellow like me isn't supposed to know much about Latin, and it is uncommonly appropriate. And, I tell you what it is, since Æneas entertained Dido on that memorable occasion, few fellows have had such an audience as that which gathered round me, as I sat in that hospitable parlor, and told about my adventure on the ice.

Such an audience was enough to stimulate any man. I felt the stimulus. I'm not generally considered fluent, or good at description, and I'm not much of a talker; but all that I ever lacked on ordinary occasions I made amends for on that evening. I began at the beginning, from the time I was ordered off. Then I led my spellbound audience over the crumbling ice, till the sleigh came. Then I indulged in a thrilling description of the runaway horse and the lost driver. Then I portrayed the lady floating in a sleigh, and my rescue of her. Of course, for manifest reasons, which every gentleman will appreciate, I didn't bring myself forward more prominently than I could help. Then followed that journey over the ice, the passage of the ice-ridge, the long, interminable march, the fainting lady, the broad channel near the shore, the white gleam of the ice-cone at Montmorency, my wild leap, and my mad dash up the bank to the Frenchman's house.

Up to this moment my audience sat, as I have before remarked, I think, simply spellbound. O'Halloran was on one side of me, with his chin on his breast, and his eyes glaring at me from beneath his bushy eyebrows. Marion sat rigid and motionless, with her hands clasped, and her eyes fixed on the floor. Miss O'Halloran never took her eyes off my face, but kept them on mine as though they were riveted there. At times she started nervously, and shifted her position, and fidgeted in her chair, but never did she remove her eyes. Once, when I came to the time when I led my companion over the ice-ridge, I saw a shudder pass through her. Once again, when I came to that moment when my companion fainted, Marion gave a kind of gasp, and I saw Miss O'Halloran reach out her hand, and clasp the clinched hands of her sister; but with these exceptions there was no variation in their attitude or manner.

And now I tuned my harp to a lighter strain, which means that I proceeded to give an account of my journey after the doctor, his start, my slumbers, my own start, our meeting, the doctor's wrath, my pursuasions, our journey, our troubles, our arrival at the house, our final crushing disappointment, the doctor's brutal raillery, my own meekness, and our final return home. Then, without mentioning Jack Randolph, I explained the object of the advertisement—

"Sic Sandy Macrorie, intentis omnibus, unus
Fata renarrabat Divûm, cursusque docebat,
Conticuit tandem—"

[Hack Latin, of course, but then, you know, if one does quote Latin, that is the only sort that can be understood by the general reader.]

The conclusion of my story produced a marked effect. O'Halloran roused himself, and sat erect with a smile on his face and a good-natured twinkle in his eyes. Miss O'Halloran lowered her eyes and held down her head, and once, when I reached that point in my story where the bird was flown, she absolutely laughed out. Marion's solemn and beautiful face also underwent a change. A softer expression came over it; she raised her eyes and fixed them with burning intensity on mine, her hands relaxed the rigid clasp with which they had held one another, and she settled herself into an easier position in her chair.

"Well, be jakers!" exclaimed old Halloran when I had concluded, "it bates the wurruld. What a lucky dog ye are! Advintures come tumblin' upon ye dee afther dee. But will ye ivir foind the leedee?"

I shook my head.

"I'm afraid not," said I, disconsolately. "I put out that advertisement with a faint hope that the lady's sympathy with the unfortunate driver might lead her to make herself known."

At this point the ladies rose. It was getting late, and they bade adieu and retired. Marion went out rather abruptly, Miss O'Halloran rather slowly, and not without a final smile of bewitching sweetness. I was going too, but O'Halloran would not think of it. He declared that the evening was just begun. Now that the ladies were gone we would have the field to ourselves. He assured me that I had nothing in particular to do, and might easily wait and join him in "somethin' warrum."

CHAPTER XVII.

"SOMETHIN' WARRUM."

I must say I was grievously disappointed at the departure of the ladies. It was late enough in all conscience for such a move, but the time had passed quickly, and I was not aware how late it was. Besides, I had hoped that something would fall from them which would throw light on the great mystery. But nothing of the kind occurred. They retired without saying any thing more than the commonplaces of social life. What made it worse was, the fact that my story had produced a tremendous effect on both of them. That could not be concealed. They evidently knew something about the lady whom I had rescued; and, if they chose, they could put me in the way of discovery. Then, in Heaven's name, why didn't they? Why did they go off in this style, without a word, leaving me a prey to suspense of the worst kind? It was cruel. It was unkind. It was ungenerous. It was unjust. It was unfair.

One thing alone remained to comfort and encourage me, and that was the recollection of Miss O'Halloran's bewitching smile. The sweetness of that smile lingered in my memory, and seemed to give me hope. I would see her again. I would ask her directly, and she would not have the heart to refuse. Marion's graver face did not inspire that confident hope which was caused by the more genial and sympathetic manner of her sprightly elder sister.

Such were my thoughts after the ladies had taken their departure. But these thoughts were soon interrupted and diverted to another channel. O'Halloran rang for a servant, and ordered up what he called "somethin' warrum." That something soon appeared in the shape of two decanters, a kettle of hot water, a sugar-bowl, tumblers, wine-glasses, spoons, and several other things, the list of which was closed by pipes and tobacco.

O'Halloran was beyond a doubt an Irishman, and a patriotic one at that, but for "somethin' warrum" he evidently preferred Scotch whiskey to that which is produced on the Emerald Sod. Beneath the benign influences of this draught he became more confidential, and I grew more serene. We sat. We quaffed the fragrant draught. We inhaled the cheerful nicotic fumes. We became friendly, communicative, sympathetic.

O'Halloran, however, was more talkative than I, and consequently had more to say. If I'm not a good talker, I'm at least an excellent listener, and that was all that my new friend wanted. And so he went on talking, quite indifferent as to any answers of mine; and, as I always prefer the ease of listening to the drudgery of talking, we were both well satisfied and mutually delighted.

First of all, O'Halloran was simply festive. He talked much about my adventure, criticised it from various points of view, and gayly rallied me about the lost "gyerrul."

From a consideration of my circumstances, he wandered gradually away to his own. He lamented his present position in Quebec, which place he found insufferably dull.

"I'd lave it at wanst," he said, "if I wern't deteened here by the cleems of jewty. But I foind it dull beyond all exprission. Me only occupeetion is to walk about the sthraits and throy to preserve the attichood of a shuparior baying. But I'm getting overwarrun an' toired out, an' I'm longing for the toime whin I can bid ajoo to the counthry with its Injins an' Canajians."

"I don't see what you can find to amuse yourself with," said I, sympathetically.

"Oh," said he, "I have veerious purshoots. I've got me books, an' I foind imploymint an' amusemint with thim."

And now he began to enlarge on the theme of his books, and he went on in this way till he became eloquent, enthusiastic, and glorious. He quaffed the limpid and transparent liquid, and its insinuating influences inspired him every moment to nobler flights of fancy, of rhetoric, and of eloquence. He began to grow learned. He discoursed about the Attic drama; the campaigns of Hannibal; the manners and customs of the Parthians; the doctrines of Zoroaster; the wars of Heraclius and Chosroes; the Ommiades, the Abbasides, and the Fatimites; the Comneni; the Paleologi; the writings of Snorro Sturlesson; the round towers of Ireland; the Phœnician origin of the Irish people proved by illustrations from Plautus, and a hundred other things of a similar character.

"And what are you engaged upon now?" I asked, at length, as I found myself fairly lost amid the multiplicity of subjects which he brought forward.

"Engeeged upon?" he exclaimed, "well—a little of iviry thing, but this dee I've been busy with a rayconsthruction of the scholastic thaories rilitiv' to the jureetion of the diluge of Juceelion. Have ye ivir perused the thraitises of the Chubingen school about the Noachic diluge?"

"No."

"Well, ye'll find it moighty foine an' insthructive raidin'. But in addition to this, I've been investigatin' the subject of may-dyayvil jools."

"Jools?" I repeated, in an imbecile way.

"Yis, jools," said O'Halloran, "the orjil, ye know, the weeger of battle."

"Oh, yes," said I, as a light burst in upon me; "duels—I understand."

"But the chafe subject that I'm engeeged upon is a very different one," he resumed, taking another swallow of the oft-replenished draught. "It's a thraitise of moine by which I ixpict to upsit the thaories of the miserable Saxon schaymers that desthort the pleen facts of antiquetee to shoot their own narrow an' disthortid comprayhinsions. An' I till ye what—whin my thraitise is published, it'll make a chumult among thim that'll convulse the litherary wurruld."

"What is your treatise about?" I asked, dreamily, for I only half comprehended him, or rather, I didn't comprehend him at all.

"Oh," said he, "its a foine subject intoirely. It's a thraitise rilitiv' to the Aydipodayan Ipopaya."

"What's that?" I asked. "The what?—"

"The Aydipodayan Ipopaya," said O'Halloran.

"The Aydipodayan Ipopaya?" I repeated, in a misty, foggy, and utterly woe-begone manner.

"Yis," said he, "an' I'd like to have your opinion about that same," saying which, he once more filled his oft-replenished tumbler.

It was too much. The conversation was getting beyond my depth. I had followed him in a vague and misty way thus far, but this Aydipodayan Ipopaya was an obstacle which I could not in any way surmount. I halted short, full in front of that insurmountable obstacle. So far from surmounting it, I couldn't even pretend to have the smallest idea what it was. I could not get over it, and therefore began to think of a general retreat.

I rose to my feet.

"Ye're not going yit?" he said.

"Yes, but I am," said I.

"Why, sure it's airly enough," said he.

"Yes," said I, "it's early enough, but it's early the wrong way. It's now," said I, taking out my watch, "just twenty minutes of four. I must be off—really."

"Well," said O'Halloran, "I'm sorry ye're going, but you know best what you must do."

"And I'm sorrier," said I, "for I've spent a most delightful evening."

"Sure an' I'm glad to hear ye say that. And ye'll come again, won't ye?"

"Nothing would give me greater pleasure."

"Come to-morrow night thin," said he.

"I shall be only too happy," said I; and with these words I took my departure.

I went home, and went to bed at once. But I lay awake, a prey to many thoughts. Those thoughts did not refer to O'Halloran, or to his Aydipodayan Ipopaya. On the contrary, they referred altogether to the ladies, and to the manner in which they had heard my narrative.

What was the meaning of that?

And my speculations on this passed on even into my dreams, and thus carried me away into

CHAPTER XVIII.

THE FOLLOWING MORNING.—APPEARANCE OF JACK RANDOLPH.—A NEW COMPLICATION.—THE THREE ORANGES.—DESPERATE EFFORTS OF THE JUGGLER.—HOW TO MAKE FULL, AMPLE, COMPLETE, AND MOST SATISFACTORY EXPLANATIONS.—MISS PHILLIPS!—THE WIDOW!!—NUMBER THREE!!!—LOUIE RAPIDLY RISING INTO GREATER PROMINENCE ON THE MENTAL AND SENTIMENTAL HORIZON OF JACK RANDOLPH.

"WELL, old chap," cried Jack, as he burst into my room on the following morning, "what the mischief were you doing with yourself all last night? Come, out with it. No humbug. I was here at twelve, lighted up, and smoked till—yes—I'll be hanged if it wasn't half-past two. And you didn't come. What do you mean, my good fellow, by that sort of thing?"

"Oh," said I, meekly, "I was passing the evening with a friend."

"The evening! The night you mean."

"Well, it was rather late," said I. "The fact is, we got talking, and I was telling him about my adventure on the ice. We had been at the concert first, and then I went with him to his quarters. By-the-way, why weren't you there?"

In this dexterous way I parried Jack's question, for I did not feel inclined just yet to return his confidence. I am by nature, as the reader must by this time have seen, uncommonly reticent and reserved, and I wasn't going to pour out my story and my feelings to Jack, who would probably go and tell it everywhere before the close of the day.

"The concert!" cried Jack, contemptuously—"the concert! My dear boy, are you mad? What's a concert to me or I to a concert? A concert? My dear fellow, what kind of an idea have you formed of me, if you think that I am capable of taking part in any festive scene when my soul is crushed under such an accumulated burden of fuss and bother?"

"What, are you bothered still? Haven't you begun to see your way through the woods?"

"See my way?" cried Jack. "Why, it's getting worse and worse—"

"Worse? I thought you had reached the worst when you were repulsed by Louie. What worse thing can happen than that? Weren't all your thoughts on death intent? Didn't you repeat your order for a gravestone?"

"True, old boy; very correct; but then I was just beginning to rally, you know, and all that, when down comes a new bother, and, if I weren't so uncommonly fruitful in resource, this day would have seen an end of Jack Randolph. I see you're rather inclined to chaff me about the gravestone, but I tell you what it is, Macrorie, if this sort of thing continues you'll be in for it. I've pulled through this day, but whether I can pull through to-morrow or not is a very hard thing to say."

At this Jack struck a match, and solemnly lighted his pipe, which all this time he had been filling.

"'Pon my word, old chap," said I, "you seem bothered again, and cornered, and all that. What's up? Any thing new? Out with it, and pour it into this sympathetic ear."

Jack gave about a dozen solemn puffs. Then he removed his pipe with his left hand. Then with his right hand he stroked his brow. Then he said, slowly and impressively:

"*She's here!*"

"She!" I repeated. "What she? Which? When? How?"

"Miss Phillips!" said Jack.

"Miss Phillips!" I cried. "Miss Phillips! Why, haven't you been expecting her? Didn't she write, and tell you that she was coming, and all that?"

"Yes; but then you know I had half an idea that something or other would turn up to prevent her actual arrival. There's many a slip, you know, 'tween cup and lip. How did I know that she was really coming? It didn't seem at all probable that any thing so abominably embarrassing should be added to all my other embarrassments."

"Probable? Why, my dear fellow, it seems to me the most probable thing in the world. It's always so. Misfortunes never come single. Don't you know that they always come in clusters? But come, tell me all about it. In the first place, you've seen her, of course?"

"Oh, of course. I heard of her arrival

yesterday morn, and went off at once to call on her. Her reception of me was not very flattering. She was, in fact, most confoundedly cool. But you know my way. I felt awfully cut up, and insisted on knowing the reason of all this. Then it all came out."

Jack paused.

"Well, what was it?"

"Why, confound it, it seems that she had been here two days, and had been expecting me to come every moment. Now, I ask you, Macrorie, as a friend, wasn't that rather hard on a fellow when he's trying to do the very best he can, and is over head and ears in all kinds of difficulties? You know," he continued, more earnestly, "the awful bothers I've had the last few days. Why, man alive, I had only just got her letter, and hadn't recovered from the shock of that. And now, while I was still in a state of bewilderment at such unexpected news, here she comes herself! And then she begins to pitch into me for not calling on her before."

"It was rather hard, I must confess," said I, with my never-failing sympathy; "and how did it all end?"

Jack heaved a heavy—a very heavy—sigh.

"Well," said he, "it ended all right—for the time. I declared that I had not expected her until the following week; and, when she referred to certain passages in her letter, I told her that I had misunderstood her altogether, which was the solemn fact, for I swear, Macrorie, I really didn't think, even if she did come, that she'd be here two or three days after her letter came. Two or three days—why, hang it all, she must have arrived here the very day I got her letter. The letter must have come through by land, and she came by the way of Portland. Confound those abominable mails, I say! What business have those wretched postmasters to send their letters through the woods and snow? Well, never mind. I made it up all right."

"All right?"

"Oh, yes. I explained it all, you know. I cleared up every thing in the completest way. In fact, I made a full, ample, intelligible, and perfectly satisfactory explanation of the whole thing. I showed that it was all a mistake, you know—that I was humbugged by the mails, and all that sort of thing, you know. So she relented, and we made it all up, and I took her out driving, and we had a glorious time, though the roads were awful—perfect lakes, slush no end, universal thaw, and all that. But we did the drive, and I promised to go there again to-day."

"And did you call on the widow?"

"Oh, yes; but before I went there I had to write a letter to Number Three."

"Number Three! You must have had your hands full?"

"Hands full? I should think I had, my boy. You know what agony writing a letter is to me. It took me two hours to get through it. You see I had written her before, reproaching her for not running off with me, and she had answered me. I got her answer yesterday morning. She wrote back a repetition of her reason for not going, and pleaded her father, who she said would go mad if she did such a thing. Between you and me, Macrorie, that's all bosh. The man's as mad as a March hare now. But this wasn't all. What do you think? She actually undertook to haul me over the coals about the widow."

"What! has she heard about it?"

"Oh, yes. Didn't I tell you before that she kept the run of me pretty closely? Well, she's evidently heard all about me and the widow, and accordingly, after a brief explanation about her father, she proceeded to walk into me about the widow. Now that was another shock. You see, the fact is, I pitched into her first for this very reason, and thought, if I began the attack, she'd have to take up a strictly defensive attitude. But she was too many guns for me. No go, my boy. Not with Number Three. She dodged my blow, and then sprang at me herself, and I found myself thrown on my defence. So you see I had to write to her at once."

Jack sighed heavily, and quaffed some Bass.

"But how the mischief could you handle such a subject? Two hours! I should think so. For my part, I don't see how you managed it at all."

"Oh, I got through," said Jack. "I explained it all, you know. I cleared up every thing in the completest way. In fact, I made a full, perfect, intelligible, ample, and satisfactory explanation—"

"Oh, that's all downright bosh now, old boy," I interrupted. "How could you explain it? It can't be explained."

"But I did though," said Jack. "I don't remember how. I only know the letter struck me as just the thing, and I dropped it into the post-office when on my way to the widow's."

"The widow's?"

"Yes, as soon as I finished the letter, I hurried off to the widow's."

"By Jove!" I cried, aghast. "So that's the style of thing, is it? Look here, old man, will you allow me to ask you, in the mildest manner in the world, how long you consider yourself able to keep up this sort of thing?"

"Allow you? Certainly not. No questions, old chap. I don't question myself, and I'll be hanged if I'll let anybody else. I'm among the breakers. I'm whirling

down-stream. I have a strong sense of the aptness of Louie's idea about the juggler and the oranges. But the worst of it is, I'm beginning to lose confidence in myself."

And Jack leaned his head back, and sent out a long beam of smoke that flew straight up and hit the ceiling. After which he stared at me in unutterable solemnity.

"Well," said I, "go on. What about the widow?"

"The widow—oh—when I got there I found another row."

"Another?"

"Yes, another—the worst of all. But by this time I had grown used to it, and I was as serene as a mountain-lake."

"But—the row—what was it about?"

"Oh, she had heard about my engagement to Miss Phillips, and her arrival; so she at once began to talk to me like a father. The way she questioned me—why the Grand Inquisitor is nothing to it. But she didn't make any thing by it. You see I took up the Fabian tactics and avoided a direct engagement."

"How's that?"

"Why, I wouldn't answer her."

"How could you avoid it?"

"Pooh!—easy enough—I sat and chaffed her, and laughed at her, and called her jealous, and twitted her, no end. Well, you know, at last she got laughing herself, and we made it all up, and all that sort of thing, you know; still, she's very pertinacious, and even after we made up she teased and teased, till she got an explanation out of me."

"An explanation! What, another?"

"Oh, yes—easy enough—I explained it all, you know. I cleared up every thing perfectly. I made an ample, intelligible, full, frank, and thoroughly satisfactory explanation of the whole thing, and—"

"What, again? Hang it, Jack, don't repeat yourself. This is the third time that you've repeated those words *verbatim.*"

"Is it? Did I? Odd, too. Fact is, I believe I made up that sentence for my letter to Number Three, and I suppose I've got it by heart. At any rate, it's all right. You see I had three explanations to make, and they all had to be full, frank, ample, satisfactory, and all the rest of those words, you know. But it's awfully hard work. It's wearing on the constitution. It destroys the nervous system. I tell you what it is, old chap—I'm serious—if this sort of thing is to go on, hang it, I'll die of exhaustion."

"So that was the end of your troubles for that day?"

"Well—yes—but not the end of my day. I got away from the widow by eight o'clock, and then trotted over to Louie."

"Louie?"

"Yes, Louie. Why, man—why not?"

"What, after the late mitten?"

"Mitten? of course. What do you suppose I care for that? Isn't Louie the best friend I have? Isn't she my only comfort? Doesn't she give magnificent advice to a fellow, and all that? Louie? Why, man alive, it's the only thing I have to look forward to! Of course. Well, you see, Louie was luckily disengaged. The other girls were at whist with their father and the aunt. So I had Louie to myself."

"I hope you didn't do the sentimental again."

"Sentimental? Good Lord! hadn't I been overwhelmed and choked with sentiment all day long? Sentiment? Of all the bosh—but, never mind. Louie at least didn't bother me in that way. Yes, it's a fact, Macrorie, she's got an awful knack of giving comfort to a fellow."

"Comfort?"

"Well, I can't exactly explain it."

"I suppose she was very sad, and sympathetic, and all that. At any rate, she didn't know the real trouble that you'd been having?"

"Didn't she, though?"

"No, of course not; how could she?"

"Why, she began questioning me, you know."

"Questioning you?"

"Yes—about—the three oranges, you know."

"Well, and how did you manage to fight her off?"

"Fight her off?"

"Yes."

"Why, I couldn't."

"Couldn't?"

"No."

"Nonsense! A fellow that could baffle the widow, wouldn't have any trouble in baffling Louie."

"Oh, that's all very well; but you don't know the peculiar way she goes to work. She's such an awful tease. And she keeps at it too, like a good fellow."

"Still you were safe from her by reason of the very fact that your daily adventures were things that you *could* not tell her."

"Couldn't I, though?"

"Of course not."

"I don't see why not."

"Impossible."

"But I *did.*"

"You did?"

"I did."

"To Louie?"

"Yes, to Louie."

Again my thoughts and feelings found expression in a whistle.

"You see," resumed Jack, "she badgered and questioned, and teased and teased, till at last she got it all out of me. And the way she took it! Laughing all the time, the provoking little witch, her eyes dancing with fun, and her soul in a perfect ecstasy over my sorrows. I was quiet at first, but at length got huffy. You see if she cared for a fellow she ought to pity him instead of laughing at him."

"But she doesn't pretend to care for you —and lucky for her too."

"That's true," said Jack, dolefully.

"But what did she say about it?"

"Say? Oh, she teased and teased, and then when she had pumped me dry she burst out into one of her fits—and then I got huffy—and she at once pretended to be very demure, the little sinner, though I saw her eyes twinkling with fun all the time. And at last she burst out:

"'Oh, Captain Randolph! You're so awfully absurd. I can't help it, I must laugh. Now ain't you awfully funny? Confess. Please confess, Captain Randolph. Ple-e-e-ease do, like a good Captain Randolph. Ple-e-e-e-e-e-e-e-e-e-e-e-e-case!'

"So my grim features relaxed, and I looked benignly at her, whereupon she burst out laughing again in my face.

"'Well, I can't help it, I'm sure,' she said. 'You do look so droll. You try to make me laugh, and I laugh, and can't help it, and then you blame me for doing the very thing you make me do, and I think it's a shame—there, now.'

"Whereupon she began to pout, and look hurt, and so, you know, I had to go to work and explain to her."

"What! not another explanation, I hope. A 'full, frank, free, fresh, ample,' and all that sort of thing, I suppose."

"Oh, bother, chaff! I'm in earnest. I merely explained that I didn't take any offence from her laughter, but that I thought that if she cared for a fellow she wouldn't laugh at him.

"'But, I never said I cared for you,' said she.

"'Oh, well—you know what I mean— you're my friend, you know, and my only comfort,' said I.

"At this she went off again.

"'Well, then,' said I, 'what are you?'

"She sat and thought.

"'Well,' said she, 'I won't be your friend, for that's too cold; I won't be your sister, for that's too familiar. Let me see—what ought I to be? I can't be your guardian, for I'm too volatile—what, then, can I be? Oh, I see! I'll tell you, Captain Randolph, what I'll be. I'll pretend that I'm your aunt. There, sir.'

"'Well, then,' said I, 'my own dear aunt.'

"'No. That won't do—you are always absurd when you grow affectionate or sentimental. You may call me aunt—but no sentiment.'

"'Well, Aunt Louie.'

"She demurred a little, but finally, I gained my point. After this she gave me some good advice, and I left and came straight to you, to find your room empty."

"Advice? You said she gave you advice? What was it?"

"Well, she advised me to get immediate leave of absence, and go home for a time. I could then have a breathing-space to decide on my future."

"Capital! Why, what a perfect little trump Louie is! Jack, my boy, that's the very thing you'll have to do."

Jack shook his head.

"Why not?"

He shook his head again.

"Well, what did you say to Louie?"

"Why, I told her that it was impossible. She insisted that it was the very thing I ought to do, and wanted to know why I wouldn't. I refused to tell, whereupon she began to coax and tease, and tease and coax, and so the end of it was, I told her."

"What was it?"

"Why, I told her I couldn't think of going away where I couldn't see her; that I would have blown my brains out by this time if it weren't for her; and that I'd blow my brains out when I went home, if it weren't for the hope of seeing her to-morrow."

"The devil you did!" said I, dryly. "What! after being mittened?"

"Yes," said Jack. "It was on my mind to say it, and I said it."

"And how did Louie take it?"

"Not well. She looked coolly at me, and said:

"'Captain Randolph, I happened to be speaking sensibly. You seemed to be in earnest when you asked for my opinion, and I gave it.'

"'And I was in earnest,' I said.

"'How very absurd!' said she. 'The fable of the shepherd-boy who cried wolf, is nothing to you. It seems to be a fixed habit of yours to go about to all the young ladies of your acquaintance threatening to blow your brains out. Now, in getting up a sentiment for my benefit, you ought at least to have been original, and not give to me the same second-hand one which you had already sent to Number Three.'

"She looked so cold, that I felt frightened.

"'You're—you're—not offended?' said I. 'I'm sure—'

"'Oh, no,' said she, interrupting me; 'I'm not offended. I'm only disappointed in you. Don't apologize, for you'll only make it worse.'

"'Well,' said I, 'I'm very much obliged to you for your advice—but circumstances over which I have no control prevent me from taking it. There—is that satisfactory?'

"'Quite,' said Louie, and her old smile returned.

"'Do you wish me to tell you what the circumstances are?'

"'Oh, no—oh, don't—' she cried, with an absurd affectation of consternation. 'Oh, Captain Randolph—please. Ple-e-e-ase, Captain Randolph—don't.'

"So I didn't."

"Well, Jack," said I, "how in the world did you manage to carry on such conversations when the rest of the family were there? Wouldn't they overhear you?"

"Oh, no. You see they were in one room at their whist, and we were in the other. Besides, we didn't speak loud enough for them to hear—except occasionally."

"So Louie didn't take offence."

"Oh, no, we made it up again at once. She gave me a beaming smile as I left. I'll see her again this evening."

"And the others through the day?"

"Oh, yes," said Jack, with a sigh.

"Miss Phillips?"

"Of course—and then I get a note from Number Three, requiring an immediate answer—and then off I go to the widow, who will have a new grievance; and then, after being used up by all these, I fly to Louie for comfort and consolation."

I shook my head.

"You're in for it, old chap," I said, solemnly, "and all that I can say is this: Take Louie's advice, and flit."

"Not just yet, at any rate," said Jack, rising; and with these words he took his departure.

CHAPTER XIX.

O'HALLORAN'S AGAIN.—A STARTLING REVELA-
TION.—THE LADY OF THE ICE.—FOUND AT
LAST.—CONFUSION, EMBARRASSMENT, RETI-
CENCE, AND SHYNESS, SUCCEEDED BY WIT,
FASCINATION, LAUGHTER, AND WITCHING
SMILES.

AFTER waiting impatiently all day, and
beguiling the time in various ways, the hour
at length came when I could go to O'Halloran's. I confess, my feelings were of rather
a tumultuous description. I would see the
ladies again. I would renew my endeavors
to find out the great mystery of the ice.
Such were my intentions, and I had firmly resolved to make direct questions to
Nora and Marion, and see if I couldn't force
them, or coax them, or argue them, into
an explanation of their strange agitation.
Such an explanation, I felt, would be a discovery of the object of my search.

Full of these thoughts, intentions, and
determinations, I knocked at O'Halloran's
door, and was ushered by the servant into
the comfortable parlor. O'Halloran stood
there in the middle of the room. Nora
was standing not far from him. Marion
was not there; but O'Halloran and Nora
were both looking at me, as I entered,
with strange expressions.

O'Halloran advanced quickly, and caught
me by the hand.

"D'ye know what ye've done?" said he,
abruptly, without greeting or salutation of
any kind. "D'ye know what ye've done?
Ye seeved moy loife at the concert. But
are you aweer what you've done be-
soides?"

He looked at me earnestly, and with so
strange an expression that for a moment I
thought he must be mad.

"Well, really," said I, somewhat confusedly, "Mr. O'Halloran, I must confess
I'm not aware of any thing in particular."

"He doesn't know!" cried O'Halloran.
"He doesn't know. 'Tisn't the sloightest
conception that he has! Will, thin, me
boy," said he—and all this time he held my
hand, and kept wringing it hard—"will,
thin—I've another dibt of gratichood, and,
what's more, one that I nivir can raypay.
D'ye know what ye've done? D'ye know
what ye are? No? Will, thin, I'll tell ye.
Ye're the seevior of me Nora, me darlin',
me proide, me own. She was the one that
ye seeved on the oice, and riscued from de-
sthruction. There she stands. Look at
her. But for you, she'd be now lost forivir
to the poor owld man whose light an' loife
an' trisure she always was. Nora, jewel,
there he is, as sure as a gun, though whoy
he didn't recognoize ye last noight passes
moy faible comprayhinsion, so it does."

Saying this, he let go my hand and looked
toward Nora.

At this astounding announcement I stood
simply paralyzed. I stared at each in succession. To give an idea of my feelings is
simply impossible. I must refer every thing
to the imagination of the reader; and, by
way of comparison to assist his imagination, I beg leave to call his attention to our
old friend, the thunder-bolt. "Had a thun-
der-bolt burst," and all that sort of thing.
Fact, sir. Dumbfounded. By Jove! that
word even does not begin to express the
idea.

Now for about twenty hours, in dreams
as well as in waking moments, I had been
brooding over the identity of the lady of
the ice, and had become convinced that the
O'Halloran ladies knew something about it;
yet so obtuse was I that I had not suspected
that the lady herself might be found in this
house. In fact, such an event was at once

5

so romantic and so improbable that it did not even suggest itself. But now here was the lady herself. Here she stood. Now I could understand the emotion, the agitation, and all that, of the previous evening. This would at once account for it all. And here she stood—the lady herself—and that lady was no other than Miss O'Halloran.

By Jove!

Miss O'Halloran looked very much confused, and very much embarrassed. Her eyes lowered and sought the floor, and in this way she advanced and took my proffered hand. 'Pon my life, I don't think I ever saw any thing more beautiful than she was as this confusion covered her lovely face; and the eyes which thus avoided mine seemed to my imagination still more lovely than they had been before.

And this was the one—I thought, as I took her hand—this was the one—the companion of my perilous trip—the life that I had saved. Yet this discovery filled me with wonder. This one, so gay, so genial, so laughter-loving—this one, so glowing with the bloom of health, and the light of life, and the sparkle of wit—this one! It seemed impossible. There swept before me on that instant the vision of the ice, that quivering form clinging to me, that pallid face, those despairing eyes, that expression of piteous and agonizing entreaty, those wild words of horror and of anguish. There came before me the phantom of that form which I had upraised from the ice when it had sunk down in lifelessness, whose white face rested on my shoulder as I bore it away from the grasp of death; and that vision, with all its solemn, tragic awfulness seemed out of keeping with this. Miss O'Halloran? Impossible! But yet it must be so, since she thus confessed it. My own memory had been at fault. The face on the ice which haunted me was not

the face that I saw before me; but, then, Miss O'Halloran in despair must have a different face from Miss O'Halloran in her happy and peaceful home. All these thoughts passed through me as I took her hand; but they left me with the impression that my vision was a mistake, and that this lady was in very deed the companion of that fearful journey.

I pressed her hand in silence. I could not speak. Under the pressure of thoughts and recollections that came sweeping in upon me, I was dumb; and so I wandered away, and fell into a seat. Yet, in my stupefaction, I could see that Miss O'Halloran showed an emotion equal to mine. She had not spoken a word. She sat down, with her eyes on the floor, and much agitation in her manner.

"Nora, me pet," said O'Halloran, "haven't ye any exprission of gratichood?"

Miss O'Halloran raised her face, and looked at me with earnest eyes.

"Indeed—indeed," she said—"it is not from want of gratitude that I am silent. My gratitude is too strong for words. Lieutenant Macrorie needs no assurance of mine, I know, to convince him how I admire his noble conduct—"

The sound of her voice roused me from my own abstraction.

"Oh, of course," said I, "a fellow knows all that sort of thing, you know; and I feel so glad about the service I was able to render you, that I'm positively grateful to you for being there. Odd, though—wasn't it?—that I didn't recognize you. But then, you see, the fact is, you looked so different then from what you do now. Really, you seem like another person—you do, by Jove!"

At this Miss O'Halloran looked down, and seemed embarrassed.

"But what made you clear out so soon

from the Frenchman's?" said I, suddenly. "You've no idea how it bothered me. By Jove! it didn't seem altogether fair to me, you know. And then you didn't even leave your address."

Miss O'Halloran's confusion seemed to increase. She murmured something about having to hurry home—pressed for time—fear of her friends being anxious—and all that.

Then I asked her anxiously if she had been any the worse for it.

"Oh, no," she said; "no ill consequences had resulted."

By this time I had sense enough to perceive that the subject was an extremely unpleasant one. A moment's further thought showed me that it couldn't be any thing else. Unpleasant! I should think so. Was it not suggestive of sorrow and of despair? Had she not witnessed things which were never to be forgotten? Had she not seen her hapless driver go down beneath the icy waters? Had she not herself stood face to face with an awful doom? Had she not twice—yes, and thrice—tasted of the bitterness of death?

"I beg pardon," said I, as these thoughts came to me—"it's a painful subject. I spoke thoughtlessly; but I won't allude to it again. It was bad enough for me; but it must have been infinitely worse for you. The fact is, my curiosity got the better of my consideration for your feelings."

"That's thrue," said O'Halloran; "it's a peenful subjict."

At this Miss O'Halloran looked immensely relieved. She raised her head, and involuntarily cast upon me a touching look of gratitude. Yes; it must, indeed, have been a painful subject. The consciousness of this made me eager to make amends for my fault, and so I began to rattle on in a lively strain about a thousand things; and Miss

O'Halloran, seizing the opportunity thus held out of casting dull care away, at once rose superior to her embarrassment and confusion, and responded to my advances with the utmost liveliness and gayety. The change was instantaneous and marked. A moment ago she had been constrained and stiff and shy; now she was gay and lively and spirited. This change, which thus took place before my eyes, served in some measure to explain that difference which I saw between the Lady of the Ice and Miss O'Halloran in her own home.

O'Halloran himself joined in. He was gay, and genial, and jocose. At about nine o'clock Marion came in. She seemed dull and distrait. She gave me a cold hand, and then sat down in silence. She did not say any thing whatever. She did not seem even to listen, but sat, with her head leaning on her hand, like one whose thoughts are far away. Yet there was a glory about her sad and melancholy beauty which could not but arrest my gaze, and often and often I found my eyes wandering to that face of loveliness. Twice—yes, three times—as my gaze thus wandered, I found her eyes fixed upon me with a kind of eager scrutiny—a fixed intensity which actually was startling to encounter. And strange, vague, wild, unformed memories arose, and odd ideas, and fantastic suspicions. Her face became thus like one of those which one sees in a crowd hastily, and then loses, only to rack his brain in vain endeavors to discover who the owner of the face might be. So it was with me as I saw the dark face and the lustrous eyes of Marion.

And now, 'pon my life, I cannot say which one of these two excited the most of my admiration. There was Nora, with her good-nature, her wit, her friendliness, her witchery, her grace, the sparkle of her eye, the music of her laugh. But there, too, was Marion, whose eyes seemed to pierce to my soul, as twice or thrice I caught their gaze, and whose face seemed to have some weird influence over me, puzzling and bewildering me by suggestions of another face, which I had seen before. I was fascinated by Nora; I was in love with her; but by Marion I was thrown under a spell.

On the whole, Nora seemed to me more sympathetic. With all her brightness and joyousness, there was also a strange timidity, at times, and shyness, and furtive glances. An occasional flush, also, gave her a sweet confusion of manner, which heightened her charms. All these were signs which I very naturally interpreted in my own favor. What else should I do?

I have been calling her indiscriminately Miss O'Halloran and Nora. But to her face I did not call her by any name. Nora, of course, was not to be thought of. On the other hand, Miss O'Halloran seemed too distant. For the memory of our past experience made me feel very near to her, and intimate. Had we not been together on a journey where hours create the familiarities of years? Was not her life mine? In fact, I felt to her as a man feels when he meets the old flame of his boyhood. She is married, and has passed beyond him. But her new name is too cold, and her old name may not be used. So he calls her nothing. He meets her as a friend, but does not know how to name her.

As we talked, O'Halloran sat there, and sometimes listened, and sometimes chimed in. An uncommonly fine-looking old fellow he was, too. Although about sixty, his form was as erect as that of a young man, and his sinewy limbs gave signs of great strength. He sat in an easy-chair—his iron-gray hair clustering over his broad brow; his eyes keen, penetrating, but full of fun; his nose slightly curved, and his lips quivering into smiles; small whiskers of a vanished fashion on either cheek; and small hands—a right royal, good fellow—witty, intellectual, and awfully eccentric—at once learned and boyish, but for all that perhaps all the better adapted for social enjoyment, and perhaps I may add conviviality. There was a glorious flow of animal spirits in the man, which could not be repressed, but came rolling forth, expressed in his rich Leinster brogue. He was evidently proud of his unparalleled girls; but of these all his tenderness seemed to go forth toward Nora. To her, and apparently to her alone, he listened, with a proud affection in his face and in his eyes; while any little sally of hers was always sure to be received with an outburst of rollicking laughter, which was itself contagious, and served to increase the general hilarity.

But the general hilarity did not extend to Marion. She was like a star, and sat apart, listening to every thing, but saying nothing. I caught sometimes, as I have said, the lustrous gleam of her eyes, as they pierced me with their earnest gaze; and when I was looking at Nora, and talking with her, I was conscious, at times, of Marion's eyes. O'Halloran did not look at her, or speak to her. Was she under a cloud? Was this her usual character? Or was she sad and serious with the pressure of some secret purpose? Such were my thoughts; but then I suddenly decided that by such thoughts I was only making an ass of myself, and concluded that it was nothing more than her way. If so, it was an uncommonly impressive way.

The ladies retired early that evening. Marion, on leaving, gave me a last searching glance; while Nora took leave with her most bewildering smile. The glance and the smile both struck home; but, which affected me most, it is impossible to say.

CHAPTER XX.

"OUR SYMPOSIUM," AS O'HALLORAN CALLED IT.—HIGH AND MIGHTY DISCOURSE.—GENERAL INSPECTION OF ANTIQUITY BY A LEARNED EYE.—A DISCOURSE UPON THE "OIONEESOIZIN" OF THE ENGLISH LANGUAGE.—HOMERIC TRANSLATIONS.—O'HALLORAN AND BURNS.—A NEW EPOCH FOR THE BROGUE.—THE DINNER OF ACHILLES AND THE PALACE OF ANTINOUS.

THE servants brought us the generous preparations for the evening—sugar, spoons, hot water, tumblers, and several other things.

O'Halloran began by expressing his gratitude, and saying that Nora could not speak on the subject. He hoped I would see, by that, why it was that she had not answered my questions. Whereupon I hastened to apologize for asking questions which so harshly reminded her of a terrible tragedy. Our mutual explanations were soon exhausted, and we turned to subjects in general.

As our symposium proceeded, O'Halloran grew more and more eloquent, more discursive, more learned, more enthusiastic. He didn't expect me to take any part in the conversation. He was only anxious that I should "take it hot," and keep my pipe and my tumbler well in hand. He was like Coleridge, and Johnson, and other great men who abhor dialogues, and know nothing but monologues.

On this occasion he monologued on the following subjects: The Darwinian hypothesis, the positive philosophy, Protestant missions, temperance societies, Fichte, Lessing, Hegel, Carlyle, mummies, the Apocalypse, Maimonides, John Scotus Erigena, the steam-engine of Hero, the Serapeium, the Dorian Emigration, and the Trojan War. This at last brought him on the subject of Homer.

He paused for a moment here.

"D'ye want to know," said he, "the thrue business of me loife, an' me sowl occupeetion?"

I bowed and gave a feeble smile. I thought of Fenian agencies and a dozen other things, and fancied that in this hour of confidence he would tell all. I had several times wondered why he lived in a place which he hated so, and had a vague idea that he was some kind of a secret emissary, though there was certainly not a single thing in his character which might warrant such a supposition.

"Me object," said O'Halloran, looking solemnly at me, "and the whole eem of me loife is the Oioneesoizin of the language of the Saxon. He's thrust his language on us, an' my eem is to meek it our own, to illivate it—an' by one schtoopindous illusthreetion to give it a pleece among the lethcrary doialicts of the wurruld."

"Oioneesoizin?" said I, slowly.

"Yis, Oioneesoizin," said O'Halloran. "An' I'm going to do this by mains of a thransleetion of Homer. For considher. Since Chapman no thransleetion has been made. Pope and Cowper are contimptible. Darby is onraydable. Gladstone's attimpt on the fust buk, an' Mat Arnold's on the seem, an' Worsley's Spinsayrians are all feclures. Ye see, they think only of maythers, an' don't considher doialicts. Homer wrote in the Oionic doialict, an' shud be thranslated into the modern ayquivalint of that same."

"Oh, I see," said I, "but is there such an equivalent?"

"Yis," said he, solemnly. "Ye see, the Scotch doialict has been illivatid into a Doric by the janius of a Burruns; and so loikewise shall the Oirish be illivatid into an Oioneean doialict by the janius of O'Halloran.

"For Oirish is the natural an' conjayneal ripriseentitive of the ancient Oioneean. It's vowel-sounds, its diphthongs, its shuperabundince of leginds, all show this most pleenly. So, too, if we apploy this modern Oineean to a thransleetion of Homer, we see it has schtoopindous advantages. The Homeric neems, the ipithets, and the woild alterneetion of dacthyls an' spondees, may all be riprisinted boy a neetive and conjayneal mayther. Take for a spicimin *Barny O'Brallaghan.* ''Twas on a windy night about two o'clock in the mornin.' That is the neetive misure of the Oirish bards, an' is iminintly adapted to rendher the Homeric swinge. It consists of an Oiambic pinthimitir followed by a dacthylic thripody; an' in rhythm projuices the effects of the dacthylic hixamitir. Compeer wid this the ballad mayther, an' the hayroic mayther, and the Spinserian stanzas, of Worsley, an' Gladstone's Saxon throchaics, and Darby's dull blank verse, an' the litheral prose, an' Mat Arnold's attimpts at hixameters, an' Dain somebody's hindicasyllabics. They're one an' all ayqually contimptible. But in this neetive Oirish loine we have not only doialictic advantages, but also an ameezing number of others. It's the doirict riprisinteetive of the Homiric loine, fust, in the number of fate; secindly, in the saysural pause; thirdly, in the capaceetee for a dactylic an' spondaic inding, an' fowerthly, in the shuperabundince of sonorous ipithits and rowling syllabeefeeceetions. An' all this I can prove to ye by spicimins of me oun thransleetion."

With this he went to a Davenport at one end of the room, and brought out a pile of manuscript closely written. Then he seated himself again.

"I'll raid ye passages here an' there,"

said he. "The fust one is the receptiou of the imbassy by Achilles." Saying this, he took the manuscript and began to read the following in a very rich, broad brogue, which made me think that he cultivated this brogue of his purposely, and out of patriotic motives, from a desire to elevate his loved Irish dialect to an equality with the literary standard English :.

"'He spake. Pat Rokles heard, an' didn't dacloine for till do it,
But tuk the mate-thray down, an' into the foyre he threw it :
A shape's choine an' a goat's he throwed on top of the platter,
An' wan from a lovely pig, than which there wor nivir a fatter ;
Thase O'Tommedon tuk, O'Kelly devoided thim nately,
He meed mince-mate av thim all, an' thin he spitted thim swately ;
To sich cntoicin' fud they all extinded their arrums,
Till fud and dhrink loikewise had lost their jaynial charrums ;
Thin Ajax winked at Phaynix, O'Dishes tuke note of it gayly,
An' powerin' oat some woine, he dhrunk till the health ov O'Kelly.'"

After this he read the description of the palace of Antinous in the "Odyssey :"

"'For beuchus hoights ov brass aich wee wos firrumlee buildid,
From the front dure till the back, an' a nate blue corrinis filled it ;
An' there was gowldin dures, that tastee dome securin',
An' silver posts loikewise that slid the breezin' dure in ;
An' lovely gowldin dogs the intherrance wee stud fast in,
Thim same, H. Phaestus meed, which had a turrun for castin'.
Widont that speecious hall there grew a gyardin, be Jakers !
A fince purticts that seeme ov fower (I think it is) acres.'"

I have but an indistinct recollection of the rest of the evening. If I was not sound asleep, I must have been in a semi-doze, retaining just sufficient consciousness to preserve the air of an absorbed listener. I had nothing but an innumerable multitude of visions, which assumed alternately the shape of Nora and of Marion. When at length I rose to go, O'Halloran begged me to stay longer. But, on looking at my watch, I found it was half-past three, and so suggested in a general way that perhaps I'd better be in bed. Whereupon he informed me that he would not be at home on the following evening, but wouldn't I come the evening after. I told him I'd be very happy. But suddenly I recollected an engagement. " Well, will you be at leisure on the next evening ? " said he. I told him I would be, and so I left, with the intention of returning on the third evening from that time.

I got home and went to bed; and in my dreams I renewed the events of that evening. Not the latter part of it, but the former part. There, before me, floated the forms of Nora and of Marion, the one all smiles, the other all gloom—the one all jest and laughter, the other silent and sombre—the one casting at me the glowing light of her soft, innocent, laughing eyes; the other flinging at me from her dark, lustrous orbs glances that pierced my soul. I'm an impressible man. I own it. I can't help it. I was so made. I'm awfully susceptible. And so, 'pon my honor, for the life of me I couldn't tell which I admired most of these two fascinating, bewildering, lovely, bewitching, yet totally different beings. " Oh, Nora ! " I cried—and immediately after, " Oh, Marion ! "

CHAPTER XXI.

JACK ONCE MORE.—THE WOES OF A LOVER.—
NOT WISELY BUT TOO MANY.—WHILE JACK
IS TELLING HIS LITTLE STORY, THE ONES
WHOM HE THUS ENTERTAINS HAVE A SEPA-
RATE MEETING.—THE BURSTING OF THE
STORM.—THE LETTER OF " NUMBER THREE."
—THE WIDOW AND MISS PHILLIPS.—JACK
HAS TO AVAIL HIMSELF OF THE AID OF A
CHAPLAIN OF HER MAJESTY'S FORCES.—
JACK AN INJURED MAN.

IT was late on the following morning when I rose. I expected to see Jack bouncing in, but there were no signs of him. I went about on my usual round, but he didn't turn up. I asked some of the other fellows, but none of them had seen him. I began to be anxious. Duns were abroad. Jack was in peril. The sheriff was near. There was no joke in it. Perhaps he was nabbed, or perhaps he was in hiding. The fact that no one had seen him was a very solemn and a very portentous one. I said nothing about my feelings, but, as the day wore on without bringing any sign of him, I began to be more anxious ; and as the evening came I retired to my den, and there thoughts of Jack intermingled themselves with visions of Nora and Marion.

The hours of that evening passed very slowly. If I could have gone to O'Halloran's, I might have forgotten my anxiety; but, as I couldn't go to O'Halloran's, I could not get rid of my anxiety. What had become of him ? Was he in limbo ? Had he taken Louie's advice and flitted ? Was he now gnashing his splendid set of teeth in drear confinement; or was he making a fool of himself, and an ass, by persisting in indulging in sentiment with Louie ?

In the midst of these cogitations, eleven

o'clock came, and a few moments after in bounced Jack himself.

I met him as the prodigal son was met by his father.

He was gloomy. There was a cloud on his broad, Jovian, hilarious, Olympian brow, with its clustering ambrosial locks.

"Jack, old fellow! You come like sunshine through a fog. I've been bothering about you all day. Have you been nabbed? Are the duns abroad? Has the sheriff invited you to a friendly and very confidential conversation? You haven't been here for two days."

"Yes, I have," said Jack, "I was here last night, and waited till three, and then walked off to sleep on it. You're up to something yourself, old man, but look out. Take warning by me. Don't plunge in too deep. For my part, I haven't the heart to pursue the subject. I've got beyond the head-stone even. The river's the place for me. But, Macrorie, promise me one thing."

"Oh, of course—all right—go ahead."

"Well, if I jump into the river, don't let them drag for me. Let me calmly drift away, and be borne off into the Atlantic Ocean. I want oblivion. Hang head-stones! Let Anderson slide."

Saying this, Jack crammed some tobacco into his pipe, lighted it, flung himself into a chair, and began smoking most vigorously. I watched him for some time in silence. There was a dark cloud on his sunny brow; he looked woe-begone and dismal, and, though such expressions were altogether out of harmony with the style of his face, yet to a friendly eye they were sufficiently visible. I saw that something new had occurred. So I waited for a time, thinking that he would volunteer his confidence; but, as he did not, I thought I would ask for it.

"By Jove!" said I, at last. "Hang it, Jack, do you know, old man, you seem to be awfully cut up about something—hit hard—and all that sort of thing. What's up? Any thing new? Out with it—clean breast, and all that. 'Pon my life, I never saw you so cut up before. What is it?"

Jack took his pipe from his mouth, rubbed his forehead violently, stared at me for a few moments, and then slowly ejaculated

"There's a beastly row—tremendous—no end—that's what there is."

"A row?"

"Yes—no end of a row."

"Who? What? Which of them?"

"All of them. Yesterday, and to-day, and to be continued to-morrow. Such is life. Sic transit, et cetera. Good Lord! Macrorie, what's a fellow to do but drown himself? Yes, my boy—oblivion! that's what I want. And I'll have it. This life isn't the thing for me. I was never made to be badgered. The chief end of man is for other things than getting snubbed by woman. And I'm not going to stand it. Here, close by, is a convenient river. I'll seek an acquaintance with its icy tide, rather than have another day like this."

"But I'm all in the dark. Tell what it is that has happened."

Jack inhaled a few more whiffs of the smoke that cheers but not inebriates, and then found voice to speak:

"You see it began yesterday. I started off at peace with the world, and went most dutifully to call on Miss Phillips. Well, I went in and found her as cool as an icicle. I didn't know what was up, and proceeded to do the injured innocent. Whereupon she turned upon me, and gave it to me then and there, hot and heavy. I didn't think it was in her. I really didn't—by Jove! The way she gave it to me," and Jack paused in wonder.

"What about?" said I.

"The widow!" groaned Jack.

"The widow?" I repeated.

"Yes—the widow."

"But how did she hear about it so soon?"

"Oh, easy enough. It's all over town now, you know. Her friends here heard of it, and some were incredulous, and others were indignant. At any rate, both classes rushed with delightful unanimity to inform her, so you may imagine the state of mind I found her in.

"You can easily imagine what she said. I don't think much of your imagination, Macrorie, but in this case it don't require a very vivid one. The worst of it is, she was quite right to feel indignant. The only thing about it all that gave me the smallest relief, was the fact that she didn't do the pathetic. She didn't shed a tear. She simply questioned me. She was as stiff as a ramrod, and as cold as a stone. There was no mercy in her, and no consideration for a fellow's feelings. She succeeded in making out that I was the most contemptible fellow living."

"And what did you say?"

"Say? What could I say? She forced me to own up about the widow. Hang it, you know I can't lie. So, after trying to dodge her questions, I answered them. She wouldn't let me dodge them. But there was one thing left. I swore to her, by all that was true, that I didn't care a fig for the widow, that my engagement with her arose altogether through a mistake. She pressed me hard on this, and I had to tell this too."

"What? Look here, Jack—you didn't drag in Louie into your confounded scrape?"

"Do you think I'm such a villain as that?" said Jack, indignantly. "No—of course I didn't. Louie—I'd die first. No. I told her some story about my mistaking her for a friend, whose name I didn't mention. I told her that I took the widow's hand by mistake—just in fun, you know—thinking it was my friend, and all that; and before I knew it the widow had nabbed me."

"Well?"

"Well, she didn't condescend to ask the name of my friend. She thought the widow was enough at a time, I suppose, and so she asked me about the state of my feelings toward her. And here I expressed myself frankly. I told her that my only desire was to get out of her clutches—that it was all a mistake, and that I was in an infernal scrape, and didn't know how to get out of it.

"Such strong language as this mollified her a little, and she began to believe me. Yet she did not soften altogether. At last, I pitched into the widow hot and heavy. This restored her to her usual self. She forgave me altogether. She even said that she was sorry for me. She hinted, too, that if she ever saw the widow, she'd have it out with her."

"Heaven forbid!" said I. "Keep them apart, Jack, if you can,"

Jack groaned.

"So it's all right, is it? I congratulate you—as far as it's worth congratulation, you know. So you got out of it, did you? A 'full, fresh, frank, free, formal, ample, exhaustive, and perfectly satisfactory explanation,' hey? That's the style of thing, is it?"

Jack gnashed his teeth.

"Come, now—old boy—no chaff. I'm beyond that. Can't stand it. Fact is, you haven't heard the whole story yet, and I don't feel like telling the rest of it, if you interrupt a fellow with your confounded humbug."

"Go ahead—don't fear, Jack—I won't chaff."

Jack drew a long breath.

"Well, then—I took her out for a drive. We had a very good time, though both of us were a little preoccupied, and I thought she had altered awfully from what she used to be; and then, you know, after leaving her, I went to see the widow."

"You didn't tell her where you were going, of course?"

"No," said Jack, with a sigh. "Well, you see, I went to the widow, and I found that she had heard about my calling on Miss Phillips, and driving out with her for a couple of hours, and I don't know what else. She was calm, and quiet, and cool, and simply wanted to know what it all meant. Well, do you know that sort of coolness is the very thing that I can't stand. If she'd raved at me, or scolded, or been passionate, or gone on in any kind of a way, I could have dealt with her; but with a person like that, who is so calm, and cool, and quiet, I haven't the faintest idea how to act.

"I mumbled something or other about 'old friendship'—'stranger in a strange land'—horrid rot—what an ass she must have thought me!—but that's the way it was. She didn't say any thing. She began to talk about something else in a conventional way — the weather, I think. I couldn't do any thing. I made a vague attempt at friendly remonstrance with her about her coolness; but she didn't notice it. She went on talking about the weather. She was convinced that it would snow. I, for my part, was convinced that there was going to be a storm—a hurricane—a tornado—any thing. But she only smiled at my vehemence, and finally I left, with a general idea that there was thunder in the air.

"Well, you know, I then went off to see Louie. But I didn't get any satisfaction there. The other girls were present, and the aunt. There wasn't any whist, and so I had to do the agreeable to the whole party. I waited until late, in the hope that some chance might turn up of a private chat with Louie, but none came. So at last I came home, feeling a general disgust with the world and the things of the world."

"Rather hard, that," said I, as Jack relapsed into moody silence.

"Hard?" said he; "that was yesterday, but it was nothing to what I met with to-day."

"To-day?—why, what's up worse than that?"

"Every thing. But I'll go on and make a clean breast of it. Only don't laugh at me, Macrorie, or I'll cut."

"Laugh? Do I ever laugh?"

Jack took a few more puffs, and relieved his sorrow-laden breast by several preliminary and preparatory sighs, after which he proceeded:

"To-day," he began, "I got up late. I felt heavy. I anticipated a general row. I dressed. I breakfasted, and, just as I was finishing, the row began. A letter was brought in from the post-office. It was from Number Three."

"Number Three?" I cried.

"Number Three," repeated Jack. "As if it wasn't bad enough already, she must come forward to add herself to those who were already crushing me to the earth, and driving me mad. It seemed hard, by Jove! I tell you what it is, old chap, nobody's so remorseless as a woman. Even my duns have been more merciful to me than these friends whom I love. It's too bad, by Jove, it is!

"Well. Number Three's letter was simply tremendous. She had heard every thing. I've already told you that she keeps the run of me pretty well, though how she manages it I can't imagine—and now it seems she heard, on the same day, of my engagement to the widow, and of the arrival of Miss Phillips, to whom I was also engaged. This news seemed to drive her wild with indignation. She mentioned these facts to me, and ordered me to deny them at once. She declared that it was impossible for any gentleman to act so dishonorably, and said that nothing but the character of her informant could lead her to ask me to deny such foul slanders.

"That's the way she put it. That's the style of thing she flung at me when I was already on my back. That's Number Three for you! And the worst of it is, I don't know what to say in reply. I tell you what it is now, Macrorie, that was a pretty tough beginning for the day. I felt it, and I left my room with a dark presentiment in my mind, and the same general idea of a brooding thunder-storm, which I had experienced the evening before.

"Then I went to see Miss Phillips, and this was my frame of mind. I found her calm, cold, and stiff as an iceberg. Not a single kind word. No consideration for a fellow at all. I implored her to tell me what was the matter. She didn't rail at me; she didn't reproach me; but proceeded in the same cruel, inconsiderate, iceberg fashion, to tell me what the matter was. And I tell you, old boy, the long and the short of it was, there was the very mischief to pay, and the last place in Quebec that I ought to have entered was that particular place. But then, how did I know? Besides, I wanted to see her."

"What was it?" I asked, seeing Jack hesitate.

"What! Why, who do you think had been there? The widow herself! She had come to call on Miss Phillips, and came with a fixed design on me. In a few moments she managed to introduce my name. Trotting me out in that fashion doesn't strike me as being altogether fair, but she did it. Mrs. Llewelopen, who is Miss Phillips's aunt, took her up rather warmly, and informed her that I was engaged to Miss Phillips. The widow smiled, and said I was a sad man, for I had told her, when I engaged myself to her, that my affair with Miss Phillips was all broken off, and had repeated the same thing two evenings before. She also informed them that I visited her every day, and was most devoted. To all this Miss Phillips had to listen, and could not say one word. She had sense enough, however, to decline any altercation with the widow, and reserve her remarks for me. And now, old boy, you see what I caught on entering the presence of Miss Phillips. She did not weep; she did not sigh; she did not reproach; she did not cry—she simply questioned me, standing before me cold and icy, and flinging her bitter questions at me. The widow had said this and that. The widow had repeated such and such words of mine. The widow had also subjected her to bitter shame and mortification. And what had I to say? She was too much of a lady to denounce or to scold, and too high-hearted even to taunt me; too proud, too lofty, to deign to show that she felt the cut; she only questioned me; she only asked me to explain such and such things. Well, I tried to explain, and gave a full and frank account of every thing, and, as far as the widow was concerned, I was perfectly truthful. I declared again that it was all a mistake, and that I'd give any thing to get rid of her. This was all perfectly true, but it wasn't by any means satisfactory to Miss Phillips. She's awfully high-strung, you know. She couldn't overlook the fact that I had given the widow to understand that it was all broken off with us. I had never said so, but I had let the widow think so, and that was enough.

"Well, you know, I got huffy at last, and said she didn't make allowances for a fellow, and all that. I told her that I was awfully careless, and was always getting into confounded scrapes, but that it would all turn out right in the end, and some day she'd understand it all. Finally, I felt so confoundedly mean, and so exactly like some infernal whipped cur, that I then and there asked her to take me, on the spot, as I was, and fulfil her vow to me. I swore that the widow was nothing to me, and wished she was in Jericho. At this she smiled slightly, and said that I didn't know what I was saying, and, in fact, declined my self-sacrificing offer. So there I was—and I'll be hanged, Macrorie, isn't it odd?— there's the third person that's refused to marry me off-hand! I vow I did what I could. I offered to marry her at once, and she declined just as the others did. With that I turned the tables on her, reproached her for her coldness, told her that I had given her the highest possible mark of my regard, and bade her adieu. We shook hands. Hers was very languid, and she looked at me quite indifferently. I told her that she'd feel differently to-morrow, and she said perhaps she might. And so I left her.

"Well, then, I had the widow to visit, but the letter and the affair with Miss Phillips had worn out my resources. In any ordinary case, the widow was too many guns for me, but, in a case like this, she was formidable beyond all description. So I hunted up the chaplain, and made him go with me. He's a good fellow, and is acquainted with her a little, and I knew that she liked him. So we went off there together. Well, do you know, Macrorie, I believe that woman saw through the whole thing, and knew why the chaplain had come as well as I did. She greeted me civilly, but rather shortly; and there was a halfsmile on her mouth, confound it! She's an awfully pretty woman, too! We were there for a couple of hours. She made us dine— that is to say, I expected to dine as a matter of course, and she invited the chaplain. So we stayed, and I think for two hours I did not exchange a dozen words with her. She directed her conversation almost exclusively to the chaplain. I began to feel jealous at last, and tried to get her attention, but it was no go. I'm rather dull, you know —good-natured, and all that, but not clever —while the chaplain is one of the cleverest men going; and the widow's awfully clever, too. They got beyond me in no time. They were talking all sorts of stuff about Gregorian chants, ecclesiastic symbolism, mediæval hymns, the lion of St. Mark, chasuble, alb, and all that sort of thing, you know, no end, and I sat like a log listening, just the same as though they spoke Chinese, while the widow took no more notice of me than if I'd been a Chinaman. And she kept up that till we left. And that was her way of paying me off. And the chaplain thought she was an awfully clever woman, and admired her—no end. And I felt as jealous as Othello.

"Then I hurried off to Louie. But luck was against me. There was a lot of fellows there, and I didn't get a chance. I only got a pleasant greeting and a bright look, that was all. I was longing to get her into a corner, and have a little comfort, and a little good advice. But I couldn't. Misfortunes never come singly. To-day every thing has been blacker than midnight. Number Three, Miss Phillips, and the widow, are all turning against a fellow. I think it's infernally hard. I feel Miss Phillips's treatment worst. She had no business to come here at all when I thought she was safe in New Brunswick. I dare say I could have wriggled through, but she came and precipitated the catastrophe, as the saying is. Then, again, why didn't she take me when I offered myself? And, for that matter, why didn't Number Three take me that other time when I was ready, and asked her to fly with me? I'll be hanged if I don't think I've had an abominably hard time of it! And now I'm fairly cornered, and you must see plainly why I'm thinking of the river. If I take to it, they'll all mourn, and even Louie'll shed a tear over me, I know; whereas, if I don't, they'll all pitch into me, and Louie'll only laugh. Look here, old boy, I'll give up women forever."

"What! And Louie, too?"

"Oh, that's a different thing altogether," said Jack; and he subsided into a deep fit of melancholy musing.

CHAPTER XXII.

I REVEAL MY SECRET.—TREMENDOUS EFFECTS OF THE REVELATION.—MUTUAL EXPLANATIONS, WHICH ARE BY NO MEANS SATISFACTORY.—JACK STANDS UP FOR WHAT HE CALLS HIS RIGHTS.—REMONSTRANCES AND REASONINGS, ENDING IN A GENERAL ROW. —JACK MAKES A DECLARATION OF WAR, AND TAKES HIS DEPARTURE IN A STATE OF UNPARALLELED HUFFINESS.

I COULD hold out no longer. I had preserved my secret jealously for two entire days, and my greater secret had been seething in my brain, and all that, for a day. Jack had given me his entire confidence. Why shouldn't I give him mine? I longed

to tell him all. I had told him of my adventure, and why should I not tell of its happy termination? Jack, too, was fairly and thoroughly in the dumps, and it would be a positive boon to him if I could lead his thoughts away from his own sorrows to my very peculiar adventures.

"Jack," said I, at last, "I've something to tell you."

"Go ahead," cried Jack, from the further end of his pipe.

"It's about the Lady of the Ice," said I.

"Is it?" said Jack, dolefully.

"Yes; would you like to hear about it?"

"Oh, yes, of course," said Jack, in the same tone.

Whereupon I began with the evening of the concert, and told him all about the old man, and my rush to the rescue. I gave a very animated description of the scene, but, finding that Jack did not evince any particular interest, I cut it all short.

"Well," said I, "I won't bore you. I'll merely state the leading facts. I got the old fellow out. He took my arm, and insisted on my going home with him. I went home, and found there the Lady of the Ice."

"Odd, too," said Jack, languidly, puffing out a long stream of smoke; "don't see how you recognized her—thought you didn't remember, and all that. So you've found her at last, have you? Well, my dear fellow, 'low me to congratulate you. Deuced queer, too. By-the-way, what did you say her name was?"

"I didn't mention her name," said I.

"Ah, I see; a secret?"

"Oh, no. I didn't suppose you'd care about knowing."

"Bosh! Course I'd care. What was it, old boy? Tell a fellow. I'll keep dark —you know me."

"Her name," said I, "is Miss O'Hallo-ran."

No sooner had I uttered that name, than an instantaneous and most astonishing change came over the whole face, the whole air, the whole manner, the whole expression, and the whole attitude, of Jack Randolph. He sprang up to his feet, as though he had been shot, and the pipe fell from his hands on the floor, where it lay smashed.

"WHAT!!!" he cried, in a loud voice.

"Look here," said I—"what may be the meaning of all that? What's the row now?"

"What name did you say?" he re-peated.

"Miss O'Halloran," said I.

"O'Halloran?" said he — "are you sure?"

"Of course, I'm sure. How can I be mistaken?"

"And her father—what sort of a man is he?"

"A fine old fellow," said I—"full of fun, well informed, convivial, age about sixty, well preserved, splendid face—"

"Is—is he an Irishman?" asked Jack, with deep emotion.

"Yes."

"Does — does he live in—in Queen Street?" asked Jack, with a gasp.

"The very street," said I.

"Number seven hundred and ninety-nine?"

"The very number. But see here, old chap, how the mischief do you happen to know so exactly all about that house? It strikes me as being deuced odd."

"And you saved her?" said Jack, with-out taking any notice of my question.

"Haven't I just told you so? Oh, both-er! What's the use of all this fuss?"

"Miss O'Halloran?" said Jack.

"Miss O'Halloran," I repeated. "But will you allow me to ask what in the name of common-sense is the matter with you? Is there a bee in your bonnet, man? What's Miss O'Halloran to you, or you to Miss O'Halloran? Haven't you got enough women on your conscience already? Do you mean to drag her in? Don't try it, my boy—for I'm concerned there."

"Miss O'Halloran!" cried Jack. "Look here, Macrorie—you'd better take care."

"Take care?"

"Yes. Don't you go humbugging about there."

"I don't know what you're up to, dear boy. What's your little joke?"

"There's no joke at all about it," said Jack, harshly. "Do you know who Miss O'Halloran is?"

"Well, I know that she's the daughter of Mr. O'Halloran, and that he's a fine old fellow. Any further information, however, I shall be delighted to receive. You talk as though you knew something about her. What is it? But don't slander. Not a word against her. That I won't stand."

"Slander! A word against her!" cried Jack. "Macrorie, you don't know who she is, or what she is to me. Macrorie, this Miss O'Halloran is that lady that we have been calling 'Number Three.'"

It was now my turn to be confounded. I, too, started to my feet, and not only my pipe, but my tumbler also, fell crash-ing on the floor.

"The devil she is!" I cried.

"She is—I swear she is—as true as I'm alive."

At this moment I had more need of a good, long, low whistle than ever I had in my life before. But I didn't whistle. Even a whistle was useless here to express the emotions that I felt at Jack's revelation. I stood and stared at him in silence. But I didn't see him. Other visions came before my mind's eye, Horatio, which shut out Jack from my view. I was again in that delightful parlor; again Nora's form was near— her laughing face, her speaking eyes, her expression—now genial and sympathetic, now confused and embarrassed. There was her round, rosy, smiling face, and near it the sombre face of Marion, with her dark, penetrating eyes. And this winning face, this laughter-loving Venus—this was the one about whom Jack raved as his Number Three. This was the one whom he asked to run off with him. She! *She* run off, and with him! The idea was simple insanity. She had written him a letter—had she?— and it was a scorcher, according to his own confession. She had found him out, and thrown him over. Was not I far more to her than a fellow like Jack—I who had saved her from a hideous death? There could be no question about that. Was not her bright, beaming smile of farewell still lingering in my memory? And Jack had the audacity to think of her yet!

"Number Three," said I—"well, that's odd. At any rate, there's one of your troubles cut off."

"Cut off?"

"Yes."

"What do you mean?"

"I mean this, that Number Three won't bother you again."

Jack stood looking at me for some time in silence, with a dark frown on his brow.

"Look here, Macrorie," said he; "you force me to gather from your words what I am very unwilling to learn."

"What!" said I. "Is it that I admire Miss O'Halloran? Is that it? Come, now; speak plainly, Jack. Don't stand in the sulks. What is it that you want to say? I confess that I'm as much amazed as you are at finding that my Lady of the Ice is the same as your 'Number Three.' But such is the case; and now what are you going to do about it?"

"First of all," said Jack, coldly, "I want to know what you are proposing to do about it."

"I?" said I. "Why, my intention is, if possible, to try to win from Miss O'Halloran a return of that feeling which I entertain toward her."

"So that's your little game—is it?" said Jack, savagely.

"Yes," said I, quietly; "that's exactly my little game. And may I ask what objection you have to it, or on what possible right you can ground any conceivable objection?"

"Right?" said Jack—"every right that a man of honor should respect."

"Right?" cried I. "Right?"

"Yes, right. You know very well that she's mine."

"Yours! Yours!" I cried. "Yours! You call her 'Number Three.' That very name of itself is enough to shut your mouth forever. What! Do you come seriously to claim any rights over a girl, when by your own confession there are no less than two others to whom you have offered yourself? Do you mean to look me in the face, after what you yourself have told me, and say that you consider that you have any claims on Miss O'Halloran?"

"Yes, I do!" cried Jack. "I do, by Jove! Look here, Macrorie. I've given you my confidence. I've told you all about my affair with her. You know that only a day or two ago I was expecting her to elope with me—"

"Yes, and hoping that she wouldn't," I interrupted.

"I was not. I was angry when she refused, and I've felt hard about it ever since.

But she's mine all the same, and you know it."

"Yours? And so is Miss Phillips yours," I cried, "and so is Mrs. Finnimore; and I swear I believe that, if I were to be sweet on Louie, you'd consider yourself injured. Hang it, man! What are you up to? What do you mean? At this rate, you'll claim every woman in Quebec. Where do you intend to draw the line? Would you be content if I were sweet on Miss Phillips? Wouldn't you be jealous if I were to visit the widow? And what would you say if I were seized with a consuming passion for Louie? Come, Jack—don't row; don't be quite insane. Sit down again, and take another pipe, and let's drop the subject."

"I won't drop the subject," growled Jack. "You needn't try to argue yourself out of it. You know very well that I got her first."

"Why, man, at this rate, you might get every woman in America. You seem to think that this is Utah."

"Come, no humbug, Macrorie. You know very well what I am to that girl."

"You! you!" I cried. "Why, you have told me already that she has found you out. Hang it, man! if it comes to that, what are you in her eyes compared with me? You've been steadily humbugging her ever since you first knew her, and she's found it out. But I come to her as the companion of the darkest hour of her life, as the one who saved her from death. You—good Lord! —do you pretend to put yourself in comparison with me? You, with your other affairs, and your conscious falsity to her, with me! Why, but for me, she would by this time be drifting down the river, and lying stark and dead on the beach of Anticosti. That is what I have done for her. And what have you done? I might have laughed over the joke of it before I knew her; but now, since I know her, and love her, when you force me to say what you have done, I declare to you that you have wronged her, and cheated her, and humbugged her, and she knows it, and you know it, and I know it. These things may be all very well for a lark; but, when you pretend to make a serious matter of them, they look ugly. Confound it! have you lost your senses?"

"You'll see whether I've lost my senses or not," said Jack, fiercely.

"You've got trouble enough on your shoulders, Jack," said I. "Don't get into any more. You actually have the face to claim no less than three women. Yes, four. I must count Louie, also. If this question were about Louie, wouldn't you be just as fierce?"

Jack did not answer.

"Wouldn't you? Wouldn't you say that I had violated your confidence? Wouldn't you declare that it was a wrong to yourself, and a bitter injury? If I had saved Louie's life, and then suddenly fallen in love with her, wouldn't you have warned me off in the same way? You know you would. But will you listen to reason? You can't have them all. You must choose one of them. Take Miss Phillips, and be true to your first vow. Take the widow, and be rich. Take Louie, and be happy. There you have it. There are three for you. As for Miss O'Halloran, she has passed away from you forever. I have snatched her from death, and she is mine forever."

"She shall never be yours!" cried Jack, furiously.

"She shall be mine!" cried I, in wrathful tones.

"Never! never!" cried Jack. "She's mine, and she shall be mine."

"Damn it, man! are you crazy? How many wives do you propose to have?"

"She shall be mine!" cried Jack. "She, and no other. I give up all others. They may all go and be hanged. She, and she alone, shall be mine."

Saying this, he strode toward the door, opened it, passed through, and banged it behind him. I heard his heavy footsteps as he went off, and I stood glaring after him, all my soul on fire with indignation.

CHAPTER XXIII.

A FRIEND BECOMES AN ENEMY.—MEDITATIONS ON THE ANCIENT AND VENERABLE FABLE OF THE DOG IN THE MANGER.—THE CORRUPTION OF THE HUMAN HEART.—CONSIDERATION OF THE WHOLE SITUATION.—ATTEMPTS TO COUNTERMINE JACK, AND FINAL RESOLVE.

So Jack left, and so I stood staring after him in furious indignation.

"By Jove!" I exclaimed, addressing my own honorable self, "are you going to stand that sort of thing, Macrorie? And at your time of life, my boy! You, twenty-two years of age, six feet high, and with your knowledge of the world! You're not altogether an ass, are you? I think I can depend on you, my boy. You'll stand up for your rights. She's yours, old chap. Cling to her. Remember your ancestors. You'll get her, and if Jack chooses to make a fool of himself, let him!"

After this expression of opinion, I replaced my last pipe and tumbler, and resumed my seat. Over my head the clouds rolled; through my brain penetrated the gentle influence, bringing tranquillity and peace; bringing also wisdom, and the power of planning and of resolving.

My reflections made me feel that Nora must be mine. She seemed dearer than all the world, and all that. Hadn't I saved her life? I had. Then that life was mine. No one else had such a claim on her as I had. Jack's absurd pretence at a claim was all confounded stuff and nonsense. I considered his attitude on this occasion a piece of the worst kind of selfishness, not to speak of its utter madness. The dog in the manger was nothing to this. I was not the man to let myself be pushed aside in this way. He would not have thought of her if I had not put in my claim. Before that she was no more to him than "Number Three," one of his tormentors from whom he longed to get free, one who annoyed him with letters. All this he had confessed to me. Yet the moment that I told him my story, and informed him of her identity with the Lady of the Ice, at once he changed about, and declared he would never give her up.

All of which reminded me forcibly of the language of a venerable female friend, who used to hold up her hands and exclaim, "Oh, dear! Oh, my! Oh, the corruption of the human heart! Oh, dear! Oh, my!"

On the other hand, I was not so blind but that I could see that Jack's impudent and ridiculous claim to Miss O'Halloran had made her appear in a somewhat different light from that in which I had hitherto viewed her. Until that time I had no well-defined notions. My mind vibrated between her image and that of Marion. But now Miss O'Halloran suddenly became all in all to me. Jack's claim on her made me fully conscious of my superior claim, and this I determined to enforce at all hazards. And thus the one end, aim, and purpose of my life, suddenly and almost instantaneously darted up within me, and referred to making Miss O'Halloran my own.

But, if this was to be done, I saw that it

must be done quickly. Jack's blood was up. He had declared that he would win her, and had departed with this declaration. I knew him well enough to feel sure that his action would be prompt. He was capable of any act of folly or of desperation. If I could hope to contend successfully against him, it would be necessary for me to be as foolish and as desperate. I must go in for a headlong game. It was to be a regular steeple-chase. No dilly-dallying—no shuffling—no coquetting—no wooing — but bold, instant, and immediate action. And why not? Our intercourse on the ice had been less than a day, but those hours were protracted singly to the duration of years, and we had been forced into intimacy by the peril of our path and the horror of our way. We were beaten together by the tempest, rocked by the ice, we sank together in the wave, together we crossed the tottering ice-ridge—together we evaded the fall of avalanches. Again and again, on that one unparalleled journey, she had received her life from me. Was all this to count for nothing? This! Why, this was every thing. What could her recollections of Jack be when compared to her recollections of me? For one who came to her as I had come there need be no delay. Enough to tell her what my feelings were —to urge and implore her for immediate acceptance of my vows.

This was my fixed resolve; but when, where, and how? I could not go to the house again for two days, and, during two days, Jack would have the advantage. No doubt he would at once reply to that last letter of hers. No doubt he would fling away every thought but the one thought of her. No doubt he would write her a letter full of protestations of love, and implore her, for the last time, to fly with him. He had done so before. In his new mood he might do it again. The thought made my blood run cold. The more I dwelt upon it, the more confident I was that Jack would do this.

And what could I do?

One of two ways could be adopted:

First, I might go there on the following day, and call on Miss O'Halloran. Her father would be away.

And, secondly, I might write her a letter.

But neither of these plans seemed satisfactory. In the first place, I did not feel altogether prepared to go and call on her for such a purpose. It came on a fellow too suddenly. In the second place, a letter did not seem to be the proper style of thing. The fact is, when a fellow seeks a lady, he ought to do it face to face, if possible.

The more I thought of it, the more strongly I felt the absolute necessity of waiting for those two days which should intervene before I could go. Then I might go on a regular invitation. Then I might have an additional opportunity of finding out her sentiments toward me. In fact, I concluded to wait.

And so I waited.

The two days passed slowly. Jack, of course, kept aloof, and I saw nothing and heard nothing of him. Where he was, or what he was doing, I could not tell. I could only conjecture. And all my conjectures led to the fixed conviction that Jack in his desperation had written to her, and proposed flight.

This conviction became intensified more and more every hour. I grew more and more impatient. My mood became one of constant and incessant fidgetiness, nervousness, and harrowing suspense.

CHAPTER XXIV.

TREMENDOUS EXCITEMENT. — THE HOUR AP-
PROACHES, AND WITH IT THE MAN.—THE
LADY OF THE ICE.—A TUMULTUOUS MEET-
ING.—OUTPOURING OF TENDER EMOTIONS.—
AGITATION OF THE LADY.—A SUDDEN IN-
TERRUPTION.—AN INJURED MAN, AN AWFUL,
FEARFUL, DIREFUL, AND UTTERLY-CRUSHING
REVELATION.—WHO IS THE LADY OF THE ICE?

AT last the appointed evening came, and I prepared to go to O'Halloran's. By this time I was roused up to a pitch of excitement such as I had never before experienced. For two days and two nights I had been brooding and dreaming over this one subject, imagining all sorts of things, making all sorts of conjectures about Jack's letter and Miss O'Halloran's reception of it. Was it possible that she could share his madness and his desperation? That I could not tell. Women in love, and men in love also, will always act madly and desperately. But was she in love? Could that serene, laughing, merry, happy face belong to one who was capable of a sudden act of desperation—of one who would flit with Jack, and fling her father into sorrow at a moment's warning? How could that be? So by turns my hopes and my fears rose in the ascendant, and the end of it all was that, by the time I reached O'Halloran's door, Jack himself, in his most frantic mood, could not have been more perfectly given up to any headlong piece of rashness, folly, and desperation, than I was.

I knocked at the door.

I was admitted, and shown into the room. O'Halloran, I was told, had just arrived, and was dressing. Would I be kind enough to wait?

I sat down.

In about two minutes I heard a light footstep,

My heart beat fast.

Some one was coming.

Who?

The light footstep and the rustling dress showed that it was a lady.

But who?

Was it the servant?

Or Marion?

Was it Nora?

My heart actually stood still as these possibilities suggested themselves, and I sat glaring at the door.

The figure entered.

My heart gave a wild bound; the blood surged to my face, and boiled in my veins. It was Nora's self! It was—it was—my Nora!

I rose as she entered. She greeted me with her usual beaming and fascinating smile. I took her hand, and did not say a word for a few moments. The hour had come. I was struggling to speak. Here she was. This was the opportunity for which I had longed. But what should I say?

"I've been longing to see you alone," I cried, at last. "Have you forgotten that day on the ice? Have you forgotten the eternal hours of that day? Do you remember how you clung to me as we crossed the ice-ridge, while the waves were surging behind us, and the great ice-heaps came crashing down? Do you remember how I raised you up as you fell lifeless, and carried your senseless form, springing over the open channel, and dashing up the cliff? And I lost you, and now I've found you again!"

I stopped, and looked at her earnestly, to see how she received my words.

And here let me confess that such a

mode of address was not generous or chivalrous, nor was it at all in good taste. True chivalry would have scorned to remind another of an obligation conferred; but then, you see, this was a very peculiar case. In love, my boy, all the ordinary rules of life, and that sort of thing, you know, must give way to the exigencies of the hour. And this was a moment of dire exigency, in which much had to be said in the most energetic manner. Besides, I spoke what I thought, and that's my chief excuse after all.

I stopped and looked at her; but, as I looked, I did not feel reason to be satisfied with my success so far. She retreated a step, and tried to withdraw her hand. She looked at me with a face of perplexity and despair. Seeing this, I let go her hand. She clasped both hands together, and looked at me in silence.

"What!" said I, tragically, yet sincerely—for a great, dark, bitter disappointment rose up within me—"what! Is all this nothing? Has it all been nothing to you? Alas! what else could I expect? I might have known it all. No. You never thought of me. You could not. I was less than the driver to you. If you had thought of me, you never would have run away and left me when I was wandering over the country thinking only of you, with all my heart yearning after you, and seeking only for some help to send you. And yet there was that in our journey which might at least have elicited from you some word of sympathy."

There again, my friend, I was ungenerous, unchivalrous, and all that. Bad enough is it to remind one of favors done; but, on the heels of that, to go deliberately to work and reproach one for want of gratitude, is ten times worse. By Jove! And for this, as for the other, my only excuse is the exigencies of the hour.

Meanwhile she stood with an increasing perplexity and grief in every look and gesture. She cast at me a look of utter despair. She wrung her hands; and at last, as I ended, she exclaimed:

"Oh, what shall I do? what shall I do? Oh, dear! Oh, what a dreadful, dreadful thing! Oh, dear!"

Her evident distress touched me to the heart. Evidently, she was compromised with Jack, and was embarrassed by this.

"Follow your own heart," said I, mournfully. "But say—can you not give me some hope? Can you not give me one kind word?"

"Oh, dear!" she cried; "it's dreadful. I don't know what to do. It's all a mistake. Oh, I *wish* you could only know all! And me!! What in the world *can* I do!"

"Oh, Miss O'Halloran!" said I; "I love you—I adore—you— and—oh, Miss O'Halloran!—I—"

"Miss O'Halloran!" she cried, starting back as I advanced once more, and tried to take her hand.

"*Nora*, then," said I. "Dearest, sweetest! You cannot be indifferent. Oh, Nora!" and I grasped her hand.

But at that moment I was startled by a heavy footstep at the door. I dropped Nora's hand, which she herself snatched away, and turned.

IT WAS O'HALLORAN!!!!!

He stood for a moment looking at us, and then he burst out into a roar of laughter.

"Macrorie!" he cried—"Macrorie! May the divil saize me if I don't beleeve that ye're indulgin' in gallanthries."

Now, at that moment, his laughter sounded harsh and ominous; but I had done no wrong, and so, in conscious innocence, I said:

"Mr. O'Halloran, you are right in your conjecture; but I assure you that it was no mere gallantry; for, sir, I have a strong affection for Miss O'Halloran, and have just asked her for her hand."

"*Miss* O'Halloran!" cried he. "*Miss* O'Halloran! Sure, why didn't ye ask her-silf, thin, like a man?"

"Oh, dear!" cried Nora, taking O'Hallo-ran's arm, and turning her beautiful, plead-ing face up to his—"oh, dear! It's all a dreadful, dreadful mistake. He doesn't know who I am. He thinks that *I* am Miss O'Halloran."

"You!" I cried. "You! Why, are you not? Of course, you are. Who else are you?"

"Oh, tell him, tell him!" cried Nora. "It's so dreadful! Such a horrid, horrid mistake to make!"

A bright light flashed all over O'Hallo-ran's face. He looked at me, and then at Nora; and then there came forth a peal of laughter which would have done honor to any of the gods at the Olympian table. This time the laughter was pure, and fresh, and joyous, and free.

"*Miss* O'Halloran!" he cried—"ha, ha, ha, ha, ha! *Miss* O'Halloran! ha, ha, ha, ha, ha! *Miss* O'Halloran! Oh, be the powers, it's me that'll nivir get over that same! *Miss* O'Halloran! An' givin' wee to sintiment—ha, ha, ha, ha, ha! an' askin' for riciproceetee av' tindir attachmint—ha, ha, ha, ha, ha! What in the woide wurruld ivir injuiced ye to think that me own little Nora was *Miss* O'Halloran?"

"Miss O'Halloran? Why," said I, "what else could I suppose? I recollect now, when you introduced me the other night, you didn't mention her name; and, if she isn't Miss O'Halloran, who is she?

Let me know now, at least. But my senti-ments remain the same," I concluded, "whatever name she has."

"The divull they do!" said O'Halloran, with a grin. "Well, thin, the quicker ye cheenge yer sintimints, the betther. Me own Nora—she's not *Miss* O'Halloran—an' lucky for me—she's somethin' betther—she's—MRS. O'HALLORAN!!!"

Let the curtain fall. There, reader, you have it. We won't attempt to enlarge—will we? We'll omit the exploding thun-der-bolt—won't we? I will quietly put an end to this chapter, so as to give you leisure to meditate over the woes of Macrorie.

CHAPTER XXV.

RECOVERY FROM THE LAST GREAT SHOCK.— GENIALITY OF MINE HOST. — OFF AGAIN AMONG ANTIQUITIES. — THE FENIANS. — A STARTLING REVELATION BY ONE OF THE INNER CIRCLE. — POLITICS, POETRY, AND PATHOS.—FAR-REACHING PLANS AND DEEP-SEATED PURPOSES.

I WAS to dine with O'Halloran, and, though for some time I was overwhelmed, yet I rallied rapidly, and soon recovered. O'Halloran himself was full of fun. The event had apparently only excited his laugh-ter, and appeared to him as affording mate-rial for nothing else than endless chaff and nonsense.

As for Nora, she had been so agitated that she did not come to dinner, nor did Marion make her appearance. This was the only thing that gave me discomfort. O'Halloran seemed to understand how natu-ral my mistake was, and I supposed that he made every allowance, and all that.

We sat at table for a long time. O'Hal-loran discoursed on his usual variety of subjects. Something occurred which suggested the Fenians, whereupon he suddenly stopped; and, looking earnestly at me, he said:

"Ye know I'm a Fenian?"

"Oh, yes."

"I make no saycrit of it," said he. "As a British officer, you're my mortal inimee in my capaceetee as a Fenian; but at this table, and in this house, we're nayther one thing nor the other. You're only Macrorie, and I'm only O'Halloran. Still I don't mind talking of the subject of Fenianism; it's an important one, and will one day take up a great speece in histhory. I don't intind to indulge in any offinsive objurgeetions ageenst the Saxon, nor will I mintion the wrongs of Oireland. I'll only enloighten you as to the purpose, the maining, and the attichood of the Fenian ordher."

With these words he rose from the table, and chatted on general subjects, while the servants brought in the spoons, glasses, tumblers, and several other things. Beneath the genial influence of these, O'Halloran soon grew eloquent, and resumed his remarks on the Fenians.

"The Fenian ordher," he began, "has two eems. One is abroad; the other is at home.

"The first is that which is kipt before the oyes of the mimbers of the outher circles. It manes the libereetion of Oireland, and perpitual inmity to England. This purpose has its maneefesteetion in the attacks which have alriddy been made on the inimy. Two inveesions have been made on Canada. Innumerable and multeefeerious small interproises have been set on fut in Oireland and in England; and these things serve the purpose of keeping before the moinds of the mimbers the prospict of some grand attack on the inimy, and of foirin' their ardhor.

"But there is an innermost circle, saycludhid from the vulgar oi, undher the chootelar prayiminence of min of janius, in whose moinds there is a very different eem. It is the second which I have mintioned. It is diricthid against America.

"Thus—

"In the American raypublic there are foive millions of Oirish vothers. Now, if these foive millions cud only be unoited in one homojaneous congreegeetion, for some one prayiminent objict, they cud aisly rule the counthree, an' dirict its policee intoirely, at home and abroad.

"This, thin, is the thrue and genuoine eem of the shuparior min of the intayrior circles. It is a grand an' comprayhinsive schayme to consoleedeete all the Oirish votes into one overwhilming mass which can conthrol all the ilictions. It is sweed by a few min of praysoiding moinds and shupayrior janius.

"And hince you bayhowld a systim roising within the boosom of the American raypublic, which will soon be greather thin the raypublic itself. At prisint, though, we do not number much over a million. But we are incraysing. We have hoighly-multifeerious raysourcis. All the *hilps* are in our pee. These are our spoys. They infarrum us of all the saycrit doings of the American payple. They bring constint accisions to our numbers. They meek us sure of our future.

"Oirishmin," he continued, "will nivir roise iffikeeciouslee in Oireland. They can only roise in Amirica. Here, in this counthry, is their only chance. And this chance we have sayzed, an', begorra, we'll follow it up till all Amirica is domeeneetid by the Oirish ilimint, and ruled by Oirish votes. This is the only Oirish raypublic for which we care."

"But you've been divided in your counsels," I suggested. "Did'nt this interfere with your prospects?"

"Oh," said he, "that was all our diplomeecee."

"And were you never really divided?"

"Nivir for a momint. These were only thricks intindid to disave and schtoopeefy the Amirican and English governmints."

"So your true aim refers to America?"

"Yis. And we intind to saycure to Amirica a perpetual succession of Oirish prisidints."

"When will you be able to begin? At the next election?"

"No—not so soon. Not for two or three to come. By the third eliction though, all the Oirish populeetion will be riddy to vote, and thin we'll have our oun Oirish Prisidint. And afther that," said O'Halloran, in an oracular tone, and pausing to quaff the transparent draught—"afther that, Amirica will be simplee an Oirish rapublic. Then we'll cast our oys across the say. We'll cast there our arrums. We'll sind there our flates and armies. We'll take vingince out of the Saxon for the wrongs of foive cinturies. We'll adopt Ould Oireland into the fameelee of the Steetes, as the youngest, but the fairist and the broightist of thim all. We'll throw our laygions across the Oirish Channel into the land of the Saxon, and bring that counthry down to its proimayval insignifeecance. That," said O'Halloran, "is the one schtoopindous eem of the Fenian Ordher."

O'Halloran showed deep emotion. Once more he quaffed the restoring draught.

"Yis, me boy," he said, looking tenderly at me. "I'll yit return to the owld land. Perhaps ye'll visit the eeged O'Halloran before he doise. Oi'll teek up me risidince at Dublin. Oi'll show ye Oireland—free—troiumphint, shuprame among the neetions. Oi'll show ye our noble pisintry, the foinist

in the wurruld. Oi'll take ye to the Rotondo. Oi'll show ye the Blarney-stone. Oi'll show ye the ruins of Tara, where me oun ancisthors once reigned."

At this his emotion overcame him, and he was once more obliged to seek a restorative.

After this he volunteered to sing a song, and trolled off the following to a lively, rollicking air:

" ' Ye choonful Noine !
Ye nymphs devoine,
Shuprame in Jove's dominions !
Assist me loyre,
Whoile oi aspoire
To cilibreet the Fenians.

" ' Our ordher bowld
All onconthrowled
Injued with power, be dad, is
To pleece in arrums
The stalwart farrums
Of half a million Paddies.

" ' To Saxon laws
For Oireland's cause
Thim same did break allaygiance,
An' marched away
In war's array
To froighten the Canajians.

" ' We soon intind
Our wee to wind
Across the wolde Atlantic,
Besaige the ports,
Blow up the forts,
An' droive the Saxon frantic.

" ' An' thin in loine,
Our hosts will join
Beneath the Oirish pinnint,
Till Dublin falls,
An' on its walls
We hang the lord-liftinnint.

" ' The Saxon crew
We'll thin purshoo
Judiciously and calmly—
On Windsor's plain
We'll hang the Quane
An' all the royal family.

"'An' thin—begob!
No more they'll rob
Ould Oireland of her taxes,
An' Earth shall rowl
From powl to powl
More aisy on its axis.'"

Now all the time O'Halloran was talk-ing and singing, I had scarcely heard a word that he said. Once I caught the gen-eral run of his remarks, and said a few words to make him think I was attending; but my thoughts soon wandered off, and I was quite unconscious that he was talking rank treason. How do I know so much about it now, it may be asked. To this I reply that after-circumstances gave me full information about was said and sung. And of this the above will give a general idea.

But my thoughts were on far other sub-jects than Fenianism. It was the Lady of the Ice that filled my heart and my mind. Lost and found, and lost again! With me it was nothing but—"O Nora! Nora! Wherefore art thou, Nora?"—and all that sort of thing, you know.

Lost and found! Lost and found! A capital title for a sensation novel, but a bad thing, my boy, to be ringing through a poor devil's brain. Now, through my brain there rang that identical refrain, and nothing else. And all my thoughts and words the melan-choly burden bore of never—never more. How could I enjoy the occasion? What was conviviality to me, or I to convivial-ity? O'Halloran's words were unheeded and unheard. While Nora was near, he used to seem a brilliant being, but Nora was gone!

And why had she gone? Why had she been so cut up? I had said but little, and my mistake had been hushed up by O'Hal-loran's laughter. Why had she retired? And why, when I spoke to her of my love, had she showed such extraordinary agita-tion? Was it—oh, was it that she too loved, not wisely but too well? O Nora! Oh, my Lady of the Ice! Well did you say it was a dreadful mistake! Oh, mistake—irreparable, despairing! And could I never see her sweet face again?

By this, which is a pretty fair specimen of my thoughts, it will be plainly seen that I was in a very agitated frame of mind, and still clung as fondly and as frantically as ever to my one idea of the Lady of the Ice.

One thing came amid my thoughts like a flash of light into darkness, and that was that Jack, at least, was not crossing my path, nor was he a dog in my manger; Miss O'Halloran might be his, but she was noth-ing to me. Who Miss O'Halloran was, I now fully understood. It was Marion—Marion with the sombre, sad face, and the piercing, lustrous eyes.

Well, be she who she might, she was no longer standing between Jack and me. I could regain my lost friend at any rate. I could explain every thing to him. I could easily anticipate the wild shrieks of laugh-ter with which he would greet my mistake, but that mattered not. I was determined to hunt him up. All my late bitter feeling against him vanished, and I began to feel a kind of longing for his great broad brow, his boyish carelessness, his never-ending blunders. So at an early hour I rose, and informed O'Halloran that I had an engage-ment at eleven o'clock, and would have to start.

"It's sorry I am," said he, "but I won't deteen ye."

———•———

CHAPTER XXVI.

A FEW PARTING WORDS WITH O'HALLORAN.—
HIS TOUCHING PARENTAL TENDERNESS, HIGH
CHIVALRIC SENTIMENT, AND LOFTY SENSE
OF HONOR.—PISTOLS FOR TWO.—PLEASANT
AND HARMONIOUS ARRANGEMENT. — " ME
BOY, YE'RE AN HONOR TO YER SEX !"

"It's sorry I am," said O'Halloran, "but
I won't deteen ye, for I always rispict an
engeegemint."

He stopped and looked at me with a benevolent smile. I had risen from my chair,
and was standing before him.

"Sit down a momint," said he. "There's
a subject I wish to mintion, the considheree-
tion of which I've postponed till now."

I resumed my seat in some surprise.

"Me boy," said he, in a tender and paternal voice, "it's now toime for me to speak
to ye about the ayvint of which I was a
casual oi-witniss. I refer to your addhrissis
to me woife. Don't intherrupt me. I comprayhind the whole matter. The leedies
are all fond of ye. So they are of me.
Ye're a divvil of a fellow with them—an'
so am I. We comprayhind one another.
You see we must have a mayting."

"A meeting !"

"Yis—of coorse. A jool. There's nothing else to be done."

"You understand," said I, "of course,
the nature of my awkward mistake, and the
cause of it."

"Don't mintion it. Me ondherstand?
Of coorse. Am I an owl? Be dad, I
nivir laughed so much these tin years.
Ondherstand! Every bit of it. But we
won't have any expleeneetions about that.
What concerns us is the code of honor,
and the jewty of gintlemin. A rigid sinse
of honor, and a shuprame reygard for the

sancteties of loife, requoire that any voio-
leetion, howivir onintintional, be submitted
and subjected to the only tribunal of chivalry—the eencient and maydoayvàl orjil of
the jool."

I confess I was affected, and deeply, by
the lofty attitude which O'Halloran assumed.
He hadn't the slightest hard feeling toward
me. He wasn't in the smallest degree jealous. He was simply a calm adherent to a
lofty and chivalrous code. His honor had
been touched ignorantly, no doubt—yet
still it had been touched, and he saw no
other course to follow than the one laid
down by chivalry.

"My friend," said I, enthusiastically, " I
appreciate your delicacy, and your lofty sentiment. This is true chivalry. You sur-
pass yourself. You are sublime ! "

"I know I am," said O'Halloran, naïvely.

A tear trembled in his eye. He did not
seek to conceal his generous emotion. That
tear rolled over and dropped into his tumbler, and hallowed the draught therein.

"So then," said I, " we are to have a
meeting—but where, and when ? "

"Whinivir it shoots you, and wherivir.
I'm afraid it'll take you out of your wee.
We'll have to go off about twinty moiles.
There's a moighty convaynient place there,
I'm sorry it's not nayrer, but it can't be
helped. I've had three or fower maytings
there mesilf this last year. You'll be de-
loighted with it whin you once get there.
There's good whiskey there too. The best
in the country. We'll go there."

"And when ? "

"Well, well—the seconds may areenge
about that. How'll nixt Monday do ? "

"Delightfully, if it suits you."

"Oh, I'll be shooted at any toime."

"What shall we meet with ? " I asked.

"Sure that's for you to decoide."

"Pistols," I suggested.

O'Halloran nodded.

"I really have no preference. I'll leave it to you if you like," said I.

O'Halloran rose—a benevolent smile illumined his face. He pressed my hand.

"Me boy," said he, with the same paternal tone which he had thus far maintained, "don't mintion it. Aihter will do. We'll say pistols. Me boy, ye're as thrue as steel—" He paused, and then wringing my hand, he said in a voice tremulous with emotion—"Me boy, ye're an honor to yer sex!"

CHAPTER XXVII.

SENSATIONAL !—TERRIFIC !—TREMENDOUS !—I LEAVE THE HOUSE IN A STRANGE WHIRL. —A STORM.—THE DRIVING SLEET.—I WANDER ABOUT.—THE VOICES OF THE STORM, AND OF THE RIVER.—THE CLANGOR OF THE BELLS.—THE SHADOW IN THE DOORWAY.— THE MYSTERIOUS COMPANION.—A TERRIBLE WALK.—FAMILIAR VOICES.—SINKING INTO SENSELESSNESS.—THE LADY OF THE ICE IS REVEALED AT LAST AMID THE STORM !

As I left the house there came a blast of stinging sleet, which showed me that it was a wild night. It was not many days now since that memorable journey on the river; and the storm that was blowing seemed to be the counterpart and continuation of that. It had been overcast when I entered O'Halloran's; when I left it, the storm had gathered up into fury, and the wind howled around, and the furious sleet dashed itself fiercely against me. The street was deserted. None would go out on so wild a night. It was after eleven; half-past, perhaps.

For a moment I turned my back to the sleet, and then drew forth my cloud from my pocket, and bound it about my head.

Thus prepared, and thus armed, I was ready to encounter the fiercest sleet that ever blew. I went down the steps, took the sidewalk, and went off.

As I went on, my mind was filled with many thoughts. A duel was before me; but I gave that no consideration. The storm howled about and shrieked between the houses; but the storm was nothing. There was that in my heart and in my brain which made all these things trivial. It was the image of my Lady of the Ice, and the great longing after her, which, for the past few days, had steadily increased.

I had found her! I had lost her! Lost and found! Found and lost!

The wrath of the storm had only this one effect on me, that it brought before me with greater vividness the events of that memorable day on the river. Through such a storm we had forced our way. From such pitiless peltings of stinging sleet I had sheltered her fainting, drooping head. This was the hurricane that had howled about her as she lay prostrate, upheld in my arms, which hurled its wrathful showers on her white, upturned face. From this I had saved her, and from worse—from the grinding ice, the falling avalanche, the dark, deep, cold, freezing flood. I had brought her back to life through all these perils, and now—and now !—

Now, for that Lady of the Ice, whose image was brought up before me by the tempest and the storm, there arose within me a mighty and irrepressible yearning. She had become identified with Nora, but yet it was not Nora's face and Nora's image that dwelt within my mind. That smiling face, with its sparkling eyes and its witching smile, was another thing, and seemed to belong to another person. It was not Nora herself whom I had loved, but Nora as she stood the representative of my Lady of the Ice. Moreover, I had seen Nora in unfeigned distress; I had seen her wringing her hands and looking at me with piteous entreaty and despair; but even the power of these strong emotions had not given her the face that haunted me. Nora on the ice and Nora at home were so different, that they could not harmonize; nor could the never-to-be-forgotten lineaments of the one be traced in the other. And, could Nora now have been with me in this storm, I doubted whether her face could again assume that marble, statuesque beauty—that immortal sadness and despair, which I had once seen upon it. That face—the true face that I loved—could I ever see it again?

I breasted the storm and walked on I knew not where. At last I found myself on the Esplanade. Beneath lay the river, which could not now be seen through the blackness of the storm and of the night, but which, through that blackness, sent forth a voice from all its waves. And the wind wailed mournfully, mingling its voice with that of the river. So once before had rushing, dashing water joined its uproar to the howl of pitiless winds, when I bore her over the river; only on that occasion there was joined in the horrid chorus the more fearful boom of the breaking ice-fields.

And now the voice of the river only increased and intensified that longing of which I have spoken. I could not go home. I thought of going back again to O'Halloran's house. There was my Lady of the Ice—Nora. I might see her shadow on the window—I might see a light from her room.

Now Nora had not at all come up to my ideal of the Lady of the Ice, and yet there was no other representative. I might be mad in love with an image, a shadow, an idea; but if that image existed anywhere in real life, it could exist only in Nora. And thus Nora gained from my image an attractiveness, which she never could have had in her own right. It was her identity with that haunting image of loveliness that gave her such a charm. The charm was an imaginary one. Had I never found her on the river and idealized her, she might have gained my admiration; but she would never have thrown over me such a spell. But now, whatever she was in herself, she was so merged in that ideal, that in my longing for my love I turned my steps backward and wandered toward O'Halloran's, with the frantic hope of seeing her shadow on the window, or a ray of light from her room. For I could find no other way than this of satisfying those insatiable longings that had sprung up within me.

So back I went through the storm, which seemed still to increase in fury, and through the sleet, which swept in long horizontal lines down the street, and whirled round the corner, and froze fast to the houses. As I went on, the violence of the storm did not at all weaken my purpose. I had my one idea, and that one idea I was bent on carrying out.

Under such circumstances I approached the house of O'Halloran. I don't know what I expected, or whether I expected anything or not. I know what I wanted. I wanted the Lady of the Ice, and in search of her I had thus wandered back to that house in which lived the one with whom she had been identified. A vague idea of seeing her shadow on the window still possessed me, and so I kept along on the opposite sidewalk, and looked up to see if there was any light or any shadow.

There was no light at all.

I stood still and gazed.

Was there a shadow? Or what was it? There was something moving there—a dark, dusky shadow, in a niche of the gateway, by the corner of the house—a dark shadow, dimly revealed in this gloom—the shadowy outline of a woman's form.

I do not know what mad idea possessed me. I looked, while my heart beat fast and painfully. A wild idea of the Lady of the Ice coming to me again, amid the storm, to be again my companion through the storm, flashed like lightning through my brain.

Suddenly, wild and clear and clanging, there came the toll of a bell from a neighboring tower, as it began to strike the hour of midnight. For a moment I paused in a sort of superstitious terror, and then, before the third stroke had rung out, I rushed across the street.

The figure had been watching me.

As I came, she started. She hurried forward, and met me at the curb. With a wild rush of joy and exultation, I caught her in my arms. I felt her frame tremble. At length she disengaged herself and caught my arm with a convulsive clasp, and drew me away. Mechanically, and with no fixed idea of any kind, I walked off.

She walked slowly. In that fierce gale, rapid progress was not possible. She, however, was well protected from the blast. A cloud was wrapped around her head, and kept her face from the storm.

We walked on, and I felt my heart throb to suffocation, while my brain reeled with a thousand new and wild fancies. Amid these, something of my late superstition still lingered.

"Who is she?" I wondered; "Who is she? How did she happen to wait for me here? Is it my Lady of the Ice? Am I a haunted man? Will she always thus come to me in the storm, and leave me when the storm is over? Where am I going? Whither is she leading me? Is she taking me back to the dark river from which I saved her?"

Then I struggled against the superstitious fancy, and rallied and tried to think calmly about it.

"Yes. It's Nora," I thought; "it's herself. She loves me. This was the cause of her distress. And that distress has overmastered her. She has been unable to endure my departure. She has been convinced that I would return, and has waited for me.

"Nora! Yes, Nora! Nora! But, Nora! what is this that I am doing? This Nora can never be mine. She belongs to another. She was mine only through my mistake. How can she hope to be mine, or how can I hope to be hers? And why is it that I can dare thus to take her to ruin? Can I have the heart to?"

I paused involuntarily, as the full horror of this idea burst upon me. For, divested of all sentiment, the bald idea that burst upon my whirling brain was simply this, that I was running away with the wife of another man, and that man the very one who had lately given me his hospitality, and called me his friend. And even so whirling a brain as mine then was, could not avoid being penetrated by an idea that was so shocking to every sentiment of honor, and loyalty, and chivalry, and duty.

But as I paused, my companion forced me on. She had not said a single word. Her head was bent down to meet the storm. She walked like one bent on some desperate purpose, and that purpose was manifestly too strong and too absorbing to be checked by any thing so feeble as my fitful and uncertain irresolution. She walked on like some fate that had gained possession of me. I surrendered to the power that thus held me. I ceased even to think of pausing.

At length we came to where there was a large house with lights streaming from all the windows. It was Colonel Berton's—I knew it well. A ball had been going on, and the guests were departing. Down came the sleighs as they carried off the guests, the jangle of the bells sounding shrilly in the stormy night. Thus far in my wanderings all had been still, and this sudden noise produced a startling effect.

One sleigh was still at the door, and as we approached nearer we could see that none others were there. It was probably waiting for the last guest. At length we reached the house, and were walking immediately under the bright light of the drawing-room windows, when suddenly the door of the house opened, and a familiar voice sounded, speaking in loud, eager, hilarious tones.

At the sound of that voice my companion stopped, and staggered back, and then stood rigid with her head thrust forward.

It was Jack's voice.

"Thanks," he said. "Ha! ha! ha! You're awfully kind, you know. Oh, yes. I'll be here to-morrow night. Good-by. Good-by."

He rushed down the steps. The door closed. He sprang into the sleigh. It started ahead in an opposite direction, and away it went, till the jangle of the bells died out in the distance, amid the storm.

All was still. The street was deserted. The storm had full possession. The lights of the house flashed out upon the snow-drifts, and upon the glittering, frozen sleet.

For a moment my companion stood rooted to the spot. Then snatching her arm from mine, she flung up her hand with a sudden gesture, and tore my cloud down from off my face. The lights from the windows shone upon me, revealing my features to her.

The next instant her arms fell. She staggered back, and with a low moan of heart-broken anguish, she sank down prostrate into the snow.

Now hitherto there had been on my mind a current of superstitious feeling which had animated most of my wild fancies. It had been heightened by the events of my wanderings. The howl of the storm, the voice of the dark river, the clangor of the midnight bell, the shadowy figure at the doorway—all these circumstances had combined to stimulate my imagination and disorder my brain. But now, on my arrival at this house, these feelings had passed away. These signs of commonplace life—the jangling sleigh-bells, the lighted windows, the departing company—had roused me, and brought me to myself. Finally, there came the sound of Jack's voice, hearty, robust, healthy, strong—at the sound of which the dark shadows of my mind were dispelled. And it was at this moment, when all these phantasms had vanished, that my companion fell senseless in the snow at my feet.

I stooped down full of wonder, and full too of pity. I raised her in my arms. I supported her head on my shoulder. The storm beat pitilessly; the stinging sleet pelted my now uncovered face; the lights of the house shone out upon the form of my companion. All the street was deserted. No one in the house saw us. I, for my part, did not think whether I was seen or not. All my thoughts were turned to the one whom I held in my arms.

I took the cloud which was wrapped around her head, and tenderly and delicately drew it down from her face.

Oh, Heavens! what was this that I saw?

The lights flashed out, and revealed it unmistakably. There—then—resting on my shoulder—under my gaze—now fully revealed—there lay the face that had haunted me—the face for which I had longed, and yearned, and craved! There it lay—that never-to-be-forgotten face—with the marble features, the white lips, the closed eyes, the stony calm—there it lay—the face of her whom alone I loved—the Lady of the Ice!

What was this? I felt my old mood returning. Was this real? Was it not a vision? How was it that she came to me again through the storm, again to sink down, and again to rest her senseless form in my arms, and her head upon my breast?

For a few moments I looked at her in utter bewilderment. All the wild fancies which I had just been having now came back. I had wandered through the storm in search of her, and she had come. Here she was—here, in my arms!

Around us the storm raged as once before; and again, as before, the fierce sleet dashed upon that white face; and again, as before, I shielded it from its fury.

As I looked upon her I could now recognize her fully and plainly; and at that recognition the last vestige of my wild, superstitious feeling died out utterly. For she whom I held in my arms was no phantom, nor was she Nora. I had been in some way intentionally deceived, but all the time my own instinct had been true; for, now, when the Lady of the Ice again lay in my arms, I recognized her, and I saw that she was no other than *Marion*.

———◆———

CHAPTER XXVIII.

MY LADY OF THE ICE.—SNOW AND SLEET.—REAWAKENING.—A DESPERATE SITUATION.—SAVED A SECOND TIME.—SNATCHED FROM A WORSE FATE.—BORNE IN MY ARMS ONCE MORE.—THE OPEN DOOR.

So there she lay before me—the Lady of the Ice, discovered at last, and identified with Marion. And she lay there reclining on my arms as once before, and in the snow, with the pitiless blast beating upon her. And the first question that arose was, "What can I do?"

Ay—that was the question. What could I do?

I leave to the reader to try and imagine the unparalleled embarrassment of such a situation. For there was I, in an agony of eagerness to save her—to do something—and yet it was simply impossible to think of any one place to which I could take her.

Could I take her into Colonel Berton's? That was my first impulse. The lights from his windows were flashing brightly out into the gloom close beside us. But how could I take her there? With what story? Or if I trumped up some story—which I easily could do—would she not betray herself by her own incoherencies as she recovered from her faint? No, not Colonel Berton's. Where, then? Could I take her anywhere? To an hotel? No. To any friends? Certainly not. To her own home?—But she had fled, and it was locked against her. Where—where could I take her?

For I had to do something. I could not let her lie here—she would perish. I had to take her somewhere, and yet save her from that ruin and shame to which her rashness and Jack's perfidy had exposed her. Too plain it all seemed now. Jack had urged her to fly—beyond a doubt—she had consented, and he had not come for her.

I raised her up in my arms, and carried her on. Once before I had thus carried her in my arms—thus, as I saved her from death; and now, as I thus bore her, I felt that I was trying to save her from a fate far worse—from scandal, from evil speaking—from a dishonored name—from a father's curse. And could I but save her from this—could I but bear her a second time from this darker fate back to light, and life, and safety; then I felt assured that my Lady of the Ice could not so soon forget this second service.

I raised her up and carried her thus I knew not where. There was not a soul in the streets. The lamps gave but a feeble light in the wild storm. The beating of the sleet and the howling of the tempest increased at every step. My lady was senseless in my arms. I did not know where I was going, nor where I could go; but breasted the storm, and shielded my burden from it as well as I could; and so toiled on, in utter bewilderment and desperation.

Now I beg leave to ask the reader if this situation of mine was not as embarrassing a one as any that he ever heard of. For I thus found forced upon me the safety, the honor, and the life of the very Lady of the Ice for whom I had already risked my life—whose life I had already saved; and about whom I had been raving ever since. But now that she had thus been thrown upon me, with her life, and her honor, it was an utterly impossible thing to see how I could extricate her from this frightful difficulty; though so fervent was my longing to do this, that, if my life could have done it, I would have laid it down for her on the spot.

At last, to my inexpressible relief, I heard from her a low moan. I put her down on the door-step of a house close by, and sat by her side supporting her. A lamp was burning not far away.

She drew a long breath, and then raised herself suddenly, and looked all around. Gradually the truth of her position returned to her. She drew herself away from me, and buried her face in her hands, and sat in silence for a long time. I waited in patience and anxiety for her to speak, and feared that the excitement and the anguish which she had undergone might have affected her mind.

Suddenly she started, and looked at me with staring eyes.

"Did *he* send *you?*" she gasped, in a strange, hoarse, choking voice.

Her face, her tone, and the emphasis of her words, all showed the full nature of the dark suspicion that had flung itself over her mind.

"*He! Me!*" I cried, indignantly. "Never! never! Can you have the heart to suspect *me?* Have I deserved this?"

"It looks like it," said she, coldly.

"Oh, listen!" I cried; "listen! I will explain my coming. It was a mistake, an accident. I swear to you, ever since that day on the ice, I've been haunted by your face—"

She made an impatient gesture.

"Well, not your face, then. I did not know it was yours. I called it the Lady of the Ice."

"I do not care to hear," said she, coldly.

"Oh, listen!" I said. "I want to clear myself from your horrid suspicion. I was at your house this evening. After leaving, I wandered wildly about. I couldn't go home. It was half madness and superstition. I went to the Esplanade, and there seemed voices in the storm. I wandered back again to your house, with a vague and half-crazy idea that the Lady of the Ice was calling me. As I came up to the house, I saw a shadowy figure on the other side. I thought it was the Lady of the Ice, and crossed over, not knowing what I was doing. The figure came and took my arm. I walked on, frozen into a sort of superstitious silence. I swear to you, it happened exactly in this way, and that for a time I really thought it was the Lady of the Ice who had come to meet me in the storm. I held back once or twice, but to no avail. I swear to you that I never had the remotest idea that it was you, till the moment when you fell, and I saw that you yourself were the Lady of the Ice. I did not recognize you before; but, when your face was pale, with suffering and fear upon it, then you became the same one whom I have never forgotten."

"*He* did not send you, then?" said she again.

"He? No. I swear he didn't; but all is just as I have said. Besides, we have quarrelled, and I have neither seen nor heard of him for two days."

She said nothing in reply, but again buried her face in her hands, and sat crouching on the door-step. The storm howled about us with tremendous fury. All the houses in the street were dark, and the street itself showed no living forms but ours. A lamp, not far off, threw a feeble light upon us.

"Come," said I at last; "I have saved you once from death, and, I doubt not, I have been sent by Fate to save you once again. If you stay here any longer, you must perish. You must rouse yourself."

I spoke vehemently and quickly, and in the tone of one who would listen to no refusal. I was roused now, at last, from all irresolution by the very sight of her suffer-ing. I saw that to remain here much longer would be little else than death for her.

"Oh, what shall I do?" she moaned.

"Tell me of some place where I can take you."

"There is no place. How could I dare to go to any of my friends?"

"Why should you not?"

"I cannot—I cannot."

"You can easily make up some story for the occasion. Tell me the name of some one, and I will take you."

"No," said she.

"Then," said I, "you must go home."

"Home! home!" she gasped.

"Yes," said I, firmly, "home. Home you must go, and nowhere else."

"I cannot."

"You must."

"I will not; I will die first."

"You shall not die!" I cried, passionately. "You shall not die while I am near you. I have saved your life before, and I will not let it end in this. No, you shall not die—I swear by all that's holy! I myself will carry you home."

"I cannot," she murmured, feebly.

"You must," said I. "This is not a question of death—it's a question of dishonor. Home is the only haven where you can find escape from that, and to that home I will take you."

"Oh, my God!" she wailed; "how can I meet my father?"

She buried her face in her hands again, and sobbed convulsively.

"Do not be afraid," said I. "I will meet him, and explain all. Or say—answer me this," I added, in fervid, vehement tones—"I can do more than this. I will tell him it was all my doing. I will accept his anger. I'll tell him I was half mad, and repented. I'll tell any thing—any thing you like. I'll shield you so that all his fury shall fall on me, and he will have nothing for you but pity."

"Stop," said she, solemnly, rising to her feet, and looking at me with her white face—"stop! You must not talk so. I owe my life to you already. Do not overwhelm me. You have now deliberately offered to accept dishonor for my sake. It is too much. If my gratitude is worth having, I assure you I am grateful beyond words. But your offer is impossible. Never would I permit it."

"Will you go home, then?" I asked, as she paused.

"Yes," said she, slowly.

I offered my arm, and she took it, leaning heavily upon me. Our progress was slow, for the storm was fierce, and she was very weak.

"I think," said she, "that in my haste I left the back door unlocked. If so, I may get in without being observed."

"I pray Heaven it may be so," said I, "for in that case all trouble will be avoided."

We walked on a little farther. She leaned more and more heavily upon me, and walked more and more slowly. At last she stopped.

I knew what was the matter. She was utterly exhausted, and to go farther was impossible. I did not question her at all. I said nothing. I stooped, and raised her in my arms without a word, and walked vigorously onward. She murmured a few words of complaint, and struggled feebly; but I took no notice whatever of her words or her struggles. But her weakness was too great even for words. She rested on me like a dead weight, and I would have been sure that she had fainted again, had I not felt the convulsive shudders that from time to time passed through her frame, and heard her frequent heavy sighs and sobbings.

7

So I walked on through the roaring storm, beaten by the furious sleet, bearing my burden in my arms, as I had done once before. And it was the same burden, under the same circumstances—my Lady of the Ice, whom I thus again uplifted in my arms amid the storm, and snatched from a cruel fate, and carried back to life and safety and home. And I knew that this salvation which she now received from me was far more precious than that other one; for that was a rescue from death, but this was a rescue from dishonor.

We reached the house at last. The gate which led into the yard was not fastened. I carried her in, and put her down by the back door. I tried it. It opened.

The sight of that open door gave her fresh life and strength. She put one foot on the threshold.

Then she turned.

"Oh, sir," said she, in a low, thrilling voice, "I pray God that it may ever be in my power to do something for you—some day—in return—for all this. God bless you! you have saved me—"

And with these words she entered the house. The door closed between us—she was gone.

I stood and listened for a long time. All was still.

"Thank Heaven!" I murmured, as I turned away. "The family have not been alarmed. She is safe."

I went home, but did not sleep that night. My brain was in a whirl from the excitement of this new adventure. In that adventure every circumstance was one of the most impressive character; and at the same time every thing was contradictory and bewildering to such an extent that I did not know whether to congratulate myself or not, whether to rejoice or lament. I might rejoice at finding the Lady of the Ice; but my joy was modified by the thought that I found her meditating flight with another man. I had saved her; but then I was very well aware that, if I had not come, she might never have left her home, and might never have been in a position to need help. Jack had, no doubt, neglected to meet her. Over some things, however, I found myself exulting—first, that, after all, I *had* saved her, and, secondly, that she had found out Jack.

As for Jack, my feelings to him underwent a rapid and decisive change. My excitement and irritation died away. I saw that we had both been under a mistake. I might perhaps have blamed him for his treachery toward Marion in urging her to a rash and ruinous elopement; but any blame which I threw on him was largely modified by a certain satisfaction which I felt in knowing that his failure to meet her, fortunate as it was for her, and fortunate as it was also for himself, would change her former love for him into scorn and contempt. His influence over her was henceforth at an end, and the only obstacle that I saw in the way of my love was suddenly and effectually removed.

CHAPTER XXIX.

PUZZLING QUESTIONS WHICH CANNOT BE ANSWERED AS YET.—A STEP TOWARD RECONCILIATION.—REUNION OF A BROKEN FRIENDSHIP.—PIECES ALL COLLECTED AND JOINED.—JOY OF JACK.—SOLEMN DEBATES OVER THE GREAT PUZZLE OF THE PERIOD.—FRIENDLY CONFERENCES AND CONFIDENCES.—AN IMPORTANT COMMUNICATION.

THE night passed, and the morning came, and the impression of these recent events grew more and more vivid. The very circumstances under which I found my Lady of the Ice were not such as are generally chosen by the novelist for an encounter between the hero and heroine of his novel. Of that I am well aware; but then I'm not a novelist, and I'm not a hero, and the Lady of the Ice isn't a heroine—so what have you got to say to that? The fact is, I'm talking about myself. I found Marion running away, or trying to run away, with my intimate friend. The elopement, however, did not come off. She was thrown into my way in an amazing manner, and I identified her with my Lady, after whom I longed and pined with a consuming passion. Did the discovery of the Lady of the Ice under such circumstances change my affections? Not at all. They only grew all the stronger. The Lady was the same as ever. I had not loved Nora, but the Lady of the Ice; and now that I found out who she was, I loved Marion. This happens to be the actual state of the case; and, whether it is artistic or not, does not enter into my mind for a single moment.

Having thus explained my feelings concerning Marion, it will easily be seen that any resentment which I might have felt against Jack for causing her grief, was more than counterbalanced by the prospect I now had that she would give him up forever. Besides, our quarrel was on the subject of Nora, and this had to be explained. Then, again, my duel was on the *tapis*, and I wanted Jack for a second. I therefore determined to hunt him up as soon as possible.

But in the course of the various meditations which had filled the hours of the night, one thing puzzled me extremely, and that was the pretension of Nora to be my Lady of the Ice. Why had she done so? Why did Marion let her? Why did O'Halloran announce his own wife to me as the lady whom I had saved? No doubt Nora and Marion had some reason. But what, and why? And what motive had O'Halloran for deceiving me? Clearly none. It was evident that he believed Nora to be the lady. It was also evident that on the first night of the reading of the advertisement, and my story, he did not know that the companion of that adventure of mine was a member of his family. The ladies knew it, but he didn't. It was, therefore, a secret of theirs, which they were keeping from him. But why? And what possible reason had Marion for denying it, and Nora for coming forward and owning up to a false character to O'Halloran?

All these were perplexing and utterly bewildering mysteries, of which I could make nothing.

At length I cut short the whole bother by going off to Jack's.

He was just finishing his breakfast.

The moment he saw me, he started to his feet, and gave a spring toward me. Then he grasped my hand in both of his, while his face grew radiant with delight.

"Macrorie! old boy!" he cried. "What a perfect trump! I'll be hanged if I wasn't going straight over to you! Couldn't stand this sort of thing any longer.—What's the use of all this beastly row? I haven't had a moment's peace since it begun. Yes, Macrorie," he continued, wringing my hand hard, "I'll be hanged if I wouldn't give up every one of the women—I was just thinking that I'd give them all for a sight of your old face again—except, perhaps, poor little Louie—" he added. "But, come, sit down, load up, and fumigate."

And he brought out all his pipes, and drew up all his chairs, and showed such unfeigned delight at seeing me, that all my old feelings of friendship came back, and resumed their places.

"Well, old fellow," said I, "do you know in the first place—our row—you know—"

"Oh, bother the row!"

"Well, it was all a mistake."

"A mistake?"

"Yes. We mistook the women."

"How's that? I'm in the dark."

"Why, there are two ladies at O'Halloran's."

"Two?"

"Yes, and they weren't introduced, and, as they're both young, I thought they were both his daughters."

"Two women! and young? By Jove!" cried Jack—"and who's the other?"

"His wife!"

"His wife? and young?" The idea seemed to overwhelm Jack.

"Yes," said I, "his wife, and young, and beautiful as an angel."

"Young, and beautiful as an angel!" repeated Jack. "Good Lord, Macrorie!"

"Well, you know, I thought his wife was Miss O'Halloran, and the other Miss Marion."

"What's that? his wife? You thought she was Miss O'Halloran?"

"Yes, and the one I saved on the ice, you know—"

"Well, all I can say is, old fellow, I'm confoundedly sorry for your sake that she's a married woman. That rather knocks your little game. At the same time it's a very queer thing that I didn't know any thing about it. Still, I wasn't at the house much, and Mrs. O'Halloran might have been out of town. I didn't know any thing about their family affairs, and never heard them mentioned. I thought there was only a daughter in the family. Never dreamed of there being a wife."

"Well, there is a wife—a Mrs. O'Halloran—so young and beautiful that I took her for the old man's daughter; and Jack, my boy, I'm in a scrape."

"A scrape?"

"Yes—a duel. Will you be my second?"

"A duel!" cried Jack, and gave a long whistle.

"Fact," said I, "and it all arose out of my mistaking a man's wife for his daughter."

"Mistaking her?" cried Jack, with a roar of laughter. "So you did. Oh, Macrorie! how awfully spooney you were about her, you know—ready to fight with your best friend about her, and all that, you know. And how did it go on? What happened? Come, now, don't do the reticent. Out with it, man. Every bit of it. A duel! And about a man's wife! Good Lord! Macrorie, you'll have to leave the regiment. An affair like this will rouse the whole town. These infernal newspapers will give exaggerated accounts of every thing, you know. And then you'll get it. By Jove, Macrorie, I begin to think your scrape is worse than mine."

"By-the-way, Jack, how are you doing?"

"Confound it man, what do you take me for? Do you think I'm a stalk or a stone. No, by Jove, I'm a man, and I'm crazy to hear about your affair. What happened? What did you do? What did you say? Something must have taken place, you know. You must have been awfully sweet on her. By Jove! And did the old fellow see you at it? Did he notice any thing? A duel! Something must have happened. Oh, by Jove! don't I know the old rascal! Not boisterous, not noisy, but keen, sir, as a razor, and every word a dagger. The most savage, cynical, cutting, insulting old scoundrel of an Irishman that I ever met with. By Heaven, Macrorie, I'd like to be principal in the duel instead of second. By Jove, how that old villain did walk into me that last time I called there!"

"Well, you see," I began, "when I went to his house he introduced *me*, and didn't introduce *her*."

"Yes."

"Well, I talked with her several times, but for various reasons, unnecessary to state, I never mentioned her name. I just chatted with her, you know, the way a fellow generally does."

"Was the old fellow by?"

"Oh, yes, but you know yesterday I went there and found her alone."

"Well?"

"Well—you know—you were so determined at the time of our row, that I resolved to be beforehand, so I at once made a rush for the prize, and—and—"

"And, what?"

"Why—did the spooney—you know—told her my feelings—and all that sort of thing, you know."

I then went on and gave Jack a full account of that memorable scene, the embarrassment of Nora, and the arrival of O'Halloran, together with our evening afterward, and the challenge.

To all this Jack listened with intense eagerness, and occasional bursts of uncontrollable laughter.

I concluded my narrative with my departure from the house. Of my return, my wanderings with Marion, my sight of him at Berton's, and all those other circumstances, I did not say a word. Those things were not the sort that I chose to reveal to anybody, much less to Jack.

Suddenly, and in the midst of his laughter and nonsense, Jack's face changed. He grew serious. He thrust his hand in his pocket with something like consternation, and then drew forth—

CHAPTER XXX.

A LETTER!—STRANGE HESITATION.—GLOOMY FOREBODINGS.—JACK DOWN DEEP IN THE DUMPS. — FRESH CONFESSIONS. — WHY HE MISSED THE TRYST.—REMORSE AND REVENGE. —JACK'S VOWS OF VENGEANCE.—A VERY SINGULAR AND UNACCOUNTABLE CHARACTER.—JACK'S GLOOMY MENACES.

"By Jove!" he exclaimed, "I'll be hanged if I haven't forgot all about it. It's been in my pocket ever since yesterday morning."

Saying this, he held up the letter, and looked at it for some time without opening it, and with a strange mixture of embarrassment and ruefulness in his expression.

"What's that?" said I, carelessly. "A letter? Who's it from, Jack?"

Jack did not give any immediate answer. He turned the letter over and over, looking at it on the front and on the back.

"You seem hit hard, old man," said I, "about something. Is it a secret?"

"Oh, no," said Jack, with a sigh.

"Well, what's the matter?"

"Oh, only this," said he, with another sigh.

"What, that letter?"

"Yes."

"It don't look like a dun, old chap—so, why fret?"

"Oh, no," said Jack, with a groan.

"What's the reason you don't open it?"

Jack shook his head.

"I've a pretty good idea of what's in it," said he. "There are some letters you can read without opening them, old boy, and this is one of them. You know the general nature of the contents, and you don't feel altogether inclined to go over all the small details."

"You don't mean to say that you're not going to open it?"

"Oh, I'll open it," said Jack, more dolefully than ever.

"Then, why don't you open it now?"

"Oh, there's no hurry—there's plenty of time."

"It must be something very unimportant. You say you've had it lying in your pocket ever since the day before yesterday. So, what's the use of getting so tragic all of a sudden?"

"Macrorie, old chap," said Jack, in a tone of hollow despair.

"Well?"

"Do you see that letter?" and he held it up in his hand.

"Yes."

"Well, in that I am to read a convincing proof that I am a scoundrel!"

"A what? Scoundrel? Pooh, nonsense! What's up now? Come, now, old boy, no melodrama. Out with it. But, first of all, read the letter."

Jack laid the unopened letter on the table, filled his pipe, lighted it, and then, throwing himself back in his chair, sat staring at the ceiling, and sending forth great clouds of smoke that gathered in dense folds and soon hung overhead in a dark canopy.

I watched him in silence for some time. I suspected what that letter might be, but did not in any way let my suspicion appear.

"Jack," said I, at last, "I've seen you several times in trouble during the last few days, but it is now my solemn conviction, made up from a long observation of your character, your manner, your general style, and your facial expression, that on this present occasion you are hit harder than ever you've been since I had the pleasure of your acquaintance."

"That's a fact," said Jack, earnestly and solemnly.

"It isn't a secret, you said?"

"No, not from you. I'll tell you presently. I need one pipe, at least, to soothe my nerves."

He relapsed into silence, and, as I saw that he intended to tell me of his own accord, I questioned him no further, but sat waiting patiently till he found strength to begin the confession of his woes.

At length he reached forward, and once more raised the letter from the table.

"Macrorie, my boy."

"Well?"

"Do you see this letter?"

"Yes."

"Whom do you think it's from?"

"How do I know?"

"Well," said Jack, "this letter is the sequel to that conversation you and I had, which ended in our row."

"The sequel?"

"Yes. You remember that I left threatening that Number Three should be mine."

"Oh, yes; but don't bother about that now," said I.

"Bother about it? Man alive, that's the very thing that I have to do! The bother, as you call it, has just begun. This letter is from Number Three."

"Number Three? Marion!"

"Yes, Marion, Miss O'Halloran, the one I swore should be mine. Ha, ha!" laughed Jack, wildly; "a precious mess I've made of it! Mine? By Jove! What's the end of it? To her a broken heart—to me dishonor and infamy!"

"My dear boy," said I, "doesn't it strike you that your language partakes, to a slight extent, of the melodramatic? Don't get stagy, dear boy."

"Stagy? Good Lord, Macrorie! Wait till you see that letter."

"That letter! Why, confound it, you haven't seen it yourself yet."

"Oh, I know, I know. No need for me to open it. Look here, Macrorie, will you promise not to throw me over after I tell you about this?"

"Throw you over?"

"Yes. You'll stick by a fellow still—"

"Stick by you? Of course, through thick and thin, my boy."

Jack gave a sigh of relief.

"Well, old chap," said he, "you see, after I left you, I was bent on nothing but Marion. The idea of her slipping out of my hands altogether was intolerable. I was as jealous of you as fury, and all that sort of thing. The widow and Miss Phillips were forgotten. Even little Louie was given up. So I wrote a long letter to Marion."

Jack paused, and looked hard at me.

"Well," said I.

"Well," said he, "you know her last letter to me was full of reproaches about the widow and Miss Phillips. She even alluded to Louie, though how under heaven she had heard about her is more than I can imagine. Well, you know, I determined to write her a letter that would settle all these difficulties, and at the same time gain her for myself, for good and all. You see I had sworn to get her from you, and I could think of nothing but that oath. So I wrote—but, oh, Macrorie, Macrorie, why, in Heaven's name, did you make that mistake about Mrs. O'Halloran, and force that infernal oath out of me? Why did that confounded old blockhead forget to introduce her to you? That's the cause of all my woes. But I won't bore you, old fellow; I'll go on. So, you see, in my determination to get her, I stuck at nothing. First of all, instead of attempting to explain away her reproaches, I turned them all back upon her. I was an infatuated fool, Macrorie, when I wrote that letter, but I was not a villain. I wrote it with an earnest desire that it should be effective. Well, I told her that she should not blame me for my gallantries, but herself for forcing me to them. I reproached her for refusing to elope with me when I offered, and told her she cared far more for her father's ease and comfort than she did for my happiness. I swore that I loved her better than any of them, or all of them put together, and I'll be hanged if I didn't, Macrorie, when I wrote it. Finally, I told her there was yet time to save me, and, if she had a particle of that love which she professed, I implored her now to fly with me. I besought her to name some time convenient to her, and suggested—oh, Macrorie, I suggested—swear at me—curse me—do something or other—Macrorie, I suggested last night—midnight—I did, by Heaven!"

And, saying this, Jack looked at me for some minutes in silence, with a wild expression that I had never before seen on his face.

"Last night, Macrorie!" he repeated —"midnight! Think of that. Why don't you say something?"

"Say?" said I. "Why, hang it, man, what can I say? It's a case beyond words. If you've made such an appointment, and broken it, you've—well, there's nothing to say."

"That's true," said Jack, in a sepulchral tone. "That's true. I made the appointment, and, Macrorie—I was not there."

"Well, of course, I gathered as much from the way you go on about it—but that's what I should like to understand, if it isn't a secret."

"Oh, no. I'll make no secret about any thing connected with this business. Well, then, I put the letter in the post-office, and strolled off to call on Miss Phillips. Will you believe it, she was 'not at home?' At that, I swear I felt so savage that I forgot all about Marion and my proposal. It was a desperate cut. I don't know any thing that has ever made me feel so savage. And I feel savage yet. If she had any thing against me, why couldn't she have seen me, and had it out with me, fair and square? It cut deep. By Jove! Well, then, I could think of nothing else but paying her off. So I organized a sleighing-party, and took out the Bertons and some other girls. I had Louie, you know, and we drove to Montmorency. Fun, no end. Great spirits. Louie teasing all the way. We got back so late that I couldn't call on the widow. That evening I was at Chelmsford's —a ball, you know—I was the only one of ours that went. Yesterday, didn't call on Miss Phillips, but took out Louie. On my way I got this letter from the office, and carelessly stuffed it into my pocket. It's been there ever since. I forgot all about it. Last evening there were a few of us at Berton's, and the time passed like lightning. My head was whirling with a cram of all sorts of things. There was my anger at Miss Phillips, there was a long story Louie had to tell about the widow, and then there was Louie herself, who drove every other thought away. And so, Macrorie, Marion and my letter to her, and the letter in my pocket, and the proposed elopement, never once entered into my head. I swear they had all passed out of my mind as completely as though it had all been some confounded dream."

Jack stopped, and again relapsed into moody silence.

"I'll tell you what it is, old fellow," said he, after a pause. "It's devilish hard to put up with."

"What is?" I asked.

"This 'not-at-home' style of thing. But never mind—I'll pay her up!"

Now here was a specimen of rattle-brainishness—of levity—and of childishness; so desperate, that I began to doubt whether this absurd Jack ought to be regarded as a responsible being. It seemed simply impossible for him to concentrate his impulsive mind on any thing. He flings himself one day furiously into an elopement scheme —the next day, at a slight, he forgets all about the elopement, and, in a towering rage against Miss Phillips, devotes himself desperately to Louie. And now when the elopement scheme has been brought before him, even in the midst of his remorse —remorse, too, which will not allow him to open her letter—the thought of Miss Phillips once more drives away all recollection of Marion, even while he has before him the unopened letter of that wronged and injured girl. Jack's brain was certainly of a harum-scarum order, such as is not often found—he was a creature of whim and impulse—he was a rattle-brain, a scatter-brain —formed to win the love of all—both men and women—formed, too, to fall into endless difficulties—formed also with a native buoyancy of spirit which enabled him to float where others would sink. By those who knew him, he would always be judged lightly—by those who knew him not, he would not fail to be judged harshly. Louie knew him, and laughed at him—Marion knew him not, and so she had received a stroke of anguish. Jack was a boy—no, a child—or, better yet, a great big baby. What in the world could I say to him or do with him? I alone knew the fulness of the agony which he had inflicted, and yet I could not judge him as I would judge another man.

"I'll pay her up!" reiterated Jack, shaking his head fiercely.

"But before paying her up, Jack," said I, "wouldn't it be well to read that letter?"

Jack gave a sigh.

"*You* read it, Macrorie," said he; "I know all about it."

"Well," said I, "that is the most astonishing proposal that I ever heard even from you. To read a letter like that!—Why, such a letter should be sacred."

Jack's face flushed. He seized the letter, tore it open, and read. The flush on his face deepened. As he finished, he crushed it in his hand, and then relapsed into his sombre fit.

"It's just as I said, Macrorie," said he. "She promised to meet me at the time I mentioned. And she was there. And I was not. And now she'll consider me a scoundrel."

In a few moments Jack opened out the crushed note, and read it again.

"After all," said he, "she isn't so awfully affectionate."

"Affectionate!"

"No—she seems afraid, and talks a great deal too much of her father, and of her anguish of soul—yes, that's her expression—her anguish of soul in sacrificing him to me. By Jove!—sacrifice! Think of that! And she says she only comes because I reproach her with being the cause of grief—heavens and earth! and she says that she doesn't expect any happiness, but only remorse. By Jove! See here, Macrorie—did you ever in your life imagine that a woman, who loved a fellow well enough to make a runaway match with him, could write him in such a way? Why, hang it! she might have known that, before our honeymoon was over, that confounded old Irish scoundrel of a father of hers would have been after us, insisting on doing the heavy father of the comedy, and giving us his blessing in the strongest of brogues.

And, what's more, he'd have been borrowing money of me, the beggar! Borrowing money! of me—me—without a penny myself and head over heels in debt. Confound his impudence!"

And Jack, who had begun this with remorse about Marion, ended with this burst of indignation at Marion's father, consequent upon a purely imaginary but very vivid scene, in which the latter was supposed to be extorting money from him. And he looked at me with a face that craved sympathy for such unmerited wrongs, and showed still more plainly the baby that was in him.

I made no answer. His quotations from Marion's letter showed me plainly how she had been moved, and what a struggle of soul this resolve had cost her. Now I could understand the full meaning of that sombre face which I had seen in O'Halloran's parlor, and also could see why it was that she had absented herself on that last evening. Did this letter change my sentiments about her? How could it, after what I already knew? It only elevated her, for it showed that at such a time her soul was racked and torn by the claims of filial duty. Under her hallucination, and under the glamour which Jack had thrown over her, she had done a deep wrong—but I alone knew how fearful was her disenchantment, and how keen was the mental anguish that followed.

"She'll never forgive me," said Jack, after a long silence.

"Who?" said I, with some bitterness, which came forth in spite of my new-found conviction of Jack's utter babyhood.— "Who, Miss Phillips?"

"Oh, no," said Jack—"Marion."

"Forgive you!" I ejaculated.

"Of course not. It's bosh to use the word in such a connection. She'll hate and scorn me till her dying day."

"No, Jack," said I, somewhat solemnly, "I think from what little I know of her, that if she gets over this, she'll feel neither hate nor scorn."

"Yes, she will," said Jack, pettishly.

"No," said I.

"You don't know her, my boy. She's not the one to forget this."

"No, she'll never forget it—but her feelings about you will be different from hate and scorn. She will simply find that she has been under a glamour about you, and will think of you with nothing but perfect indifference—and a feeling of wonder at her own infatuation."

Jack looked vexed.

"To a woman who don't know you, Jack, my boy—you become idealized, and heroic; but to one who does, you are nothing of the kind. So very impressible a fellow as you are, cannot inspire a very deep passion. When a woman finds the fellow she admires falling in love right and left, she soon gets over her fancy. If it were some one other woman that had robbed her of your affection, she would be jealous; but when she knows that all others are equally charming, she will become utterly indifferent."

"See here, old boy, don't get to be so infernally oracular. What the mischief does a fellow like you know about that sort of thing? I consider your remarks as a personal insult, and, if I didn't feel so confoundedly cut up, I'd resent it. But as it is, I only feel bored, and, on the whole, I should wish it to be with Marion as you say it's going to be. If I could think it would be so, I'd be a deuced sight easier in my mind about her. If it weren't for my own abominable conduct, I'd feel glad that this sort of thing had been stopped—only I don't like to think of Marion being disappointed, you know—or hurt—and that sort of thing, you know. The fact is, I have no business to get married just now—no—not even to the angel Gabriel—and this would have been so precious hard on poor little Louie."

"Louie—why," said I, "you speak confidently about her."

"Oh, never fear about her," said Jack.

"She's able to take care of herself. She does nothing but laugh at me—no end."

"Nothing new, then, in that quarter?" I asked, feeling desirous now of turning away from the subject of Marion, which was undergoing the same treatment from Jack which a fine and delicate watch would receive at the hands of a big baby. "No fresh proposals?"

"No," said Jack, dolefully, "nothing but chaff."

"And Miss Phillips?"

"Affairs in that quarter are in *statu quo*," said Jack. "She's chosen to not-at-home me, and how it's going to turn out is more than I can tell. But I'll be even with her yet. I'll pay her off!"

"Perhaps you won't find it so easy as you imagine."

"Won't I?" said Jack, mysteriously; "you'll see."

"Perhaps she's organizing a plan to pay *you* off."

"That's more than she can do."

"By-the-way—what about the widow?"

"Well," said Jack, seriously, "whatever danger is impending over me, may be looked for chiefly in that quarter."

"Have you seen her lately?"

"No—not since the evening I took the chaplain there."

"You must have heard something."

"Yes," said Jack, moodily.

"What?"

"Well, I heard from Louie, who keeps well up in my affairs, you know. She had gathered something about the widow."

"Such as what?"

"Well, you know—she wouldn't tell."

"Wouldn't tell?"

"No—wouldn't tell—chaffed me—no end, but wouldn't go into particulars."

"But could you find out whether it affected you or not?"

"Oh, of course, I took that for granted. That was the point of the whole joke, you know. Louie's chaff consisted altogether of allusions to some mysterious plan of the widow's, by which she would have full, ample, perfect, complete, and entire vengeance on me."

"That's bad."

"It is."

"A widow's a dangerous thing."

"Too true, my boy," said Jack, with a sigh; "nobody knows that better than I do."

"I wonder you don't try to disarm her."

"Disarm her?"

"Yes—why don't you call on her?"

"Well, confound it, I did call only a day or two ago, you know. The last two or three days I've been engaged."

"Yes, but such an engagement will only make the widow more furious."

"But, confound it, man, it's been simply impossible to do any thing else than what I have been doing."

"I'll tell you what it is, Jack," said I, solemnly, "the widow's your chief danger. She'll ruin you. There's only one thing for you to do, and that is what I've already advised you to do, and Louie, too, for that matter. You must fly."

"Oh, bosh!—how can I?"

"Leave of absence—sell out—any thing."

Jack shook his head, and gave a heavy sigh.

CHAPTER XXXI.

A FRIENDLY CALL.—PRELIMINARIES OF THE
DUEL NEATLY ARRANGED.—A DAMP JOUR-
NEY, AND DEPRESSED SPIRITS.—A SECLUDED
SPOT.—DIFFICULTIES WHICH ATTEND A DUEL
IN A CANADIAN SPRING.—A MASTERLY DE-
CISION.—DEBATES ABOUT THE NICETIES OF
THE CODE OF HONOR.—WHO SHALL HAVE
THE FIRST SHOT, STRUGGLE FOR PRECEDENCE.
—A VERY SINGULAR AND VERY OBSTINATE
DISPUTE.—I SAVE O'HALLORAN FROM DEATH
BY RHEUMATISM.

BEFORE the close of the day a gentleman called on me from O'Halloran, whom
I referred to Jack, and these two made
arrangements for the duel. It was to take
place in a certain locality, which I do not
intend to mention, and which was no matter how many miles out of town.

We left at an early hour, and the doctor
accompanied us. Jack had sufficient fore-
sight to fill the sleigh with all the refresh-
ments that might be needed on such an
occasion. We drove to O'Halloran's house,
where we found his sleigh waiting, with
himself and a friend all ready to start.
They led the way, and we followed.

It was a nasty time, the roads were terrible. They were neither one thing nor the
other. There was nothing but a general
mixture of ice heaps, slush, thawing snow-
drifts, bare ground, and soft mud. Over
this our progress was extremely slow.
Added to this, the weather was abominable. It was warm, soft, slimy, and muggy.
The atmosphere had changed into a universal drizzle, and was close and oppressive.
At first O'Halloran's face was often turned
back to hail us with some jovial remark, to
which we responded in a similar manner;
but after a time silence settled on the par-

ty, and the closeness, and the damp, and
the slow progress, reduced us one and all to
a general state of sulkiness.

At length we came to a little settlement
consisting of a half-dozen houses, one of
which bore a sign on which we read the
words *Hôtel de France.* We kept on without stopping, and O'Halloran soon turned
to the right, into a narrow track which
went into the woods. In about half an hour
we reached our destination. The sleighs
drew up, and their occupants prepared for
business.

It was a small cleared space in the middle of the woods. The forest-trees arose
all around, dim, gloomy, and dripping. The
ground was dotted with decayed stumps,
and covered with snow in a state of semi-
liquefaction. Beneath all was wet; around
all was wet; and above all was wet. The
place with its surroundings was certainly
the most dismal that I had ever seen, and
the dank, dark, and dripping trees threw an
additional gloom about it.

We had left Quebec before seven. It
was after twelve when we reached this place.

"Well, me boy," said O'Halloran to me,
with a gentle smile, "it's an onsaisonable
toime of year for a jool, but it can't be
helped—an' it's a moighty uncomfortable
pleece, so it is."

"We might have had it out in the road
in a quiet way," said I, "without the trouble of coming here."

"The road!" exclaimed O'Halloran.
"Be the powers, I'd have been deloighted
to have had it in me own parrulor. But
what can we do? Sure it's the barbarous
legisleetion of this counthry, that throis to
stoifle and raypriss the sintiments of honor,
and the code of chivalry. Sure it's a bad
pleece intoirely. But you ought to see it
in the summer. It's the most sayquisthered
localeetee that ye could wish to see."

Saying this, O'Halloran turned to his friend and then to us.

"Gintlemin," said he, "allow me to inthrojuice to ye me very particular friend, Mr. Murtagh McGinty."

Mr. Murtagh McGinty rose and bowed, while we did the same, and disclosed the form of a tall, elderly, and rather dilapidated Irishman.

All this time we had remained in our sleighs. The surrounding scene had impressed us all very forcibly, and there was a general disinclination to get out. The expanse of snow, in its half-melted condition, was enough to deter any reasonable being. To get out was to plunge into an abyss of freezing slush.

A long discussion followed as to what ought to be done. Jack suggested trying the road; McGinty thought we might drive on farther. The doctor did not say any thing. At last O'Halloran solved the difficulty.

He proposed that we should all remain in the sleighs, and that we should make a circuit so as to bring the backs of the sleighs at the requisite distance from one another.

It was a brilliant suggestion; and no sooner was it made, than it was adopted by all. So the horses were started, and the sleighs were turned in the deep slush until their backs were presented to one another. To settle the exact distance was a matter of some difficulty, and it had to be decided by the seconds. Jack and McGinty soon got into an altercation, in which Jack appealed to the light of reason, and McGinty to a past that was full of experience. He overwhelmed Jack with so many precedents for his view of the case, that at last the latter was compelled to yield. Then we drove forward, and then backward; now we were too far away, again we were too near, and

there didn't appear to be any prospect of a settlement.

At last O'Halloran suggested that we should back the sleighs toward one another till they touched, and then his sleigh would move forward twelve paces.

"But who's to pace them?" asked Jack.

"Why the horse, of course," said O'Halloran. "Sure it's a regular pacer he is, and bred up to it, so he is."

To this Jack had nothing to say.

So the horses backed and the sleighs touched one another.

"Wait a minute McGinty, me boy," said O'Halloran — putting his hand on his friend's arm—"let's all take somethin' warrum. Me system is slowly conjaylin, an' such a steete of things is moighty onwholesome."

This proposition was received with the same unanimity which had greeted O'Halloran's other propositions. Flasks were brought out; and some minutes were passed in a general, a convivial, and a very affectionate interchange of courtesies.

"Me boy," said O'Halloran to me, affectionately, "ye haven't had so much ixpayrieence as I have, so I'll teek the liberty to give ye a small bit of instherruction. Whin ye foire, eem low! Moind that, now—ye'll be sure to hit."

"Thank you," said I.

He wrung my hand heartily; and then motioning to McGinty, his sleigh started off, and advanced a few paces from ours, a little farther than the usual distance on such an occasion. With this he seemed to be satisfied, and, as nobody made any objection, we prepared for the business of the day.

O'Halloran and I stood up in the sleighs, while the seconds kept their seats. Jack and the doctor sat in the front seat of our sleigh. McGinty sat beside O'Halloran as he stood up. I stood in the after-seat of our sleigh.

"Shall I give the word?" said Jack.

"No," said McGinty. "I've had more exparience. I've been sicond at elivin jools—an' hope to assist at as minny more."

"Shure we won't throuble ayther of ye," said O'Halloran. "It's me that's fought more jools than you've been sicond at. Me friend Macrorie and I'll manage it to shoot ourselves—so we will."

"Ye can't give the word yersilves," said McGinty.

"An' what do we want of a word, thin?" said O'Halloran.

"To foire by," said McGinty.

"There's a peculeeareetee," said O'Halloran, loftily, "in the prisint occeesion that obveeates the nicissitee of such prosaydings, and inables us to dispinse with any worrd of command. Macrorie, me boy—frind of me sowl—I addhriss you as the Oirish addhrissed the English at Fontenoy: '*Fire first!*'"

And saying this, O'Halloran bowed and then stood erect, facing me with a grave countenance.

"Fire first?" said I. "Indeed, Mr. O'Halloran, I'll do nothing of the kind."

"Indade and you shall," said he, with a laugh. "I insist upon it!"

"Well, if it comes to that," said I, "what's to prevent me from insisting that you shall fire the first shot?"

"Shure and ye wouldn't dayproive me of the plisure of giving you the prasaydince," said he.

"Then, really," said I, "you will force me to insist upon your having the precedence. You're an older man than I am, and ought to have the first place. So, Mr. O'Halloran—fire first!"

"Thank you," said he, with a bow, "but really, me boy, you must excuse me if I insist upon it."

"Oh, no," said I. "If it were any other occasion, I would cheerfully give you the precedence, and so I give it to you here."

"But, you see," said O'Halloran, "you must considher me in the loight of an intertainer. Ye're my guest to a certain ixtint. I must give up all the honors to you. So foire awee, me boy, and eem low."

"No," said I, "I really couldn't think of it."

This friendly altercation went on for some time, while the others sat listening in amazement.

McGinty was the first to interrupt.

"It's in defoince of all the joolin' code," said he, starting up. "I must inter my protest."

"So say I," cried Jack. "I say let the usual word be given—or else if one must have the first shot, let them draw for it."

O'Halloran looked upon them both with a smile of benevolent pity.

"McGinty," said he.

"Well."

"Ye know me?"

"Sure an' I do."

"And how many jools I've fought?"

"Meself does."

"Am I a choild at it? Will ye be koind enough to mintion any one that has any cleem to considher himself the shupayrior of Phaylim O'Halloran in the noiceties and the dilicacies of the jooling code? Will ye be so good as to infarrum me what there is lift for me to lerrun?"

At this appeal Mr. Murtagh McGinty subsided into silence, and sat down again, shaking his head.

Jack still insisted that the word of command should be given; but O'Halloran silenced him effectually by asking him if he had ever fought a duel.

"No," said Jack.

"Have ye ivir been seccond at one before?"

"No," said Jack, again.

"So this is your first time out?"

"Yes," said Jack, who looked deeply humiliated.

"Will, thin," said O'Halloran, loftily, "allow me to infarrum you, sir, that this is the thirty-seventh toime that I've had the plisure of taking part in a jool, ayther as principal or sicond."

Whereupon Jack was suppressed.

In all this the doctor took no part. He looked cold, wet, uncomfortable, and unhappy.

And now O'Halloran turned to me again.

"Me boy," said he, "if ye'll not grant me this as a feevor, I'll cleem it as a roight."

"A right?" said I.

"Yis," said O'Halloran, solemnly, "a roight!"

"I don't know what you mean," I said, in some perplexity.

"I'll expleen. I'm undher a debt of obleegeetion to you that I nivir can repee. Ye've seevrd the loife of me daughter, me choild, me Marion—that's one debt—then ye've seevrd my loife, me own. But for you, I'd have been tarrun in payces by a howling mob, so I would. Me oun loife is yours. Jewty, and the cleems of gratichood, and the code of honor, all inspoire me with a desoire to meek some rayturrun for what ye've done for me.

"On the other hand," he continued, "ye've made a misteek of an onplisint nature about Mrs. O'H. Ye didn't main any harrum; but the dade's done, and there it is. It necissitates a jool. We must feece one another to satisfy offindid honor. But at the seem toime, while this jool is thus necissiteeted be the code of honor,

jewty and gratichood must be considhered. It's a moighty noice case," he continued, meditatively, "and I don't think such a case ivir came within my ixpayrience; but that ixtinsive ixpayrience which I've had rinders me the best judge of what may be the most shootable course on the prisint occasion. But the ulteemeete tindincy of all me mideeteetions on the subjict is this —that I must allow you to fire the first shot."

"Well," said I, "if you insist on looking at it in that light, and if you persist in feeling obligation, that sense of obligation ought to make you yield to my wishes, and, if I don't want to fire first, you ought not to insist upon it."

"No, me boy," said O'Halloran; "that's all oidle casuisthree an' impty mitaphysics. There's no process of ratiosheeneetion that'll be iver eeble to overturrun the sintimints of jewty and dilicacy that spring spontaneous in the brist. So blaze away."

"Excuse me, but I insist on your firing first."

"Be the powers, thin! and I insist on your taking the lade."

"Pardon me, but you must."

"I'm inkeepeble of such a lack of common cevileetee," said he. "I must still insist."

"And so must I."

This singular and very original altercation went on for some time. At last O'Halloran took the cushions off the seat, and deliberately sat down, facing me, with his legs dangling over the back of the sleigh. Seeing that our argument was to be continued for some time, and that he was thus making himself comfortable, I did the same. We thus sat facing one another.

The seconds here again interposed, but were again baffled by O'Halloran, who explained the whole situation to them in so forcible a manner that they did not know how to answer him. For my part, I was firm in my resolve, and was not going to fire unless we both fired together. True, I might have fired in the air; but I knew O'Halloran so well by this time that I was convinced, if I did such a thing, he would reproach me for it, and insist on my firing again. And in that case it would all have to be commenced afresh.

So there we sat, with our legs dangling over the backs of our respective sleighs, facing one another, pistol in hand, and occasionally renewing the discussion. He was obstinate, I was equally so, and the time began to pass away, and the situation gradually grew more and more tedious to our companions. Still they could not say any thing. It was a punctilio of honor which they could not argue down, and behind all the argument which might be used there arose the very impressive accumulation of O'Halloran's past experience in the field of honor. So all that they could do was to make the best of the situation.

The situation! It was, at best, a dismal one. Overhead was a leaden sky; underneath, the thawing snow, which every hour assumed a more watery appearance; in the distance arose the dreary, gloomy, melancholy forest-trees; while all around was a thin, fine drizzle, which enveloped us, saturating and soaking us with watery vapor. We all became limp and bedraggled, in soul as well as body. The most determined buoyancy of spirit could not withstand the influence of that drizzle, and, one by one, we all sank beneath it.

But not without a struggle. For, at first, as O'Halloran and I thus sat facing one another, we did not forget the ordinary civilities of life, nor were we satisfied with sitting and staring at one another. On the contrary, we sought to beguile the time with an interchange of courtesy on both sides. I took my flask and drank to the health of O'Halloran. O'Halloran responded. Then the seconds followed. Then O'Halloran drank to the health of Jack and the doctor. Then I drank to the health of McGinty. Then Jack and the doctor drank to the health of O'Halloran, and McGinty pledged me.

Two hours passed, and found each of us sitting there in the same position. Jack and the doctor made a doleful attempt at a game of euchre, but soon gave it up. McGinty sat refreshing himself with his flask, defying the weather, laughing, joking, and singing. Then we all smoked. From time to time the seconds would make fresh efforts to shake our resolve. They proposed once more that we should toss up for it, or drive home now, and come out again—in fact, any thing rather than sit here amid this cold, and drizzle, and wet, and dismal gloom, and miserable, rheumatic atmosphere. But all these proposals were declined, and O'Halloran was immovable in his purpose; while I, on the other hand, was equally resolved that I would not fire first.

Thus time passed, and neither of us would yield. At length, the doctor settled himself down into the bottom of the sleigh, and drew the buffalo-robes over him. After a final expostulation, accompanied with a threat to drive off, Jack imitated his example. McGinty, seeing this, proceeded to make himself comfortable in the same way.

The poor horses had the worst time of it. The cold snow was up to their knees; and, as they stood there, they moved uneasily, tramping it down, till a pool of icy water lay beneath, in which they had to stand. I mentioned this to O'Halloran; but he only turned it against me, and made use of it as a fresh argument to shake my decision.

At last I saw that O'Halloran's face and attitude had undergone a change. For my part, I was wet to the skin, and chilled to my very bones; but I was young and strong, and could stand even that. With O'Halloran, however, it was different. A man of sixty cannot sit with impunity, inactive, and exposed to a cold, slimy drizzle, such as this was, without feeling very serious effects, and anticipating worse. This he soon experienced. I saw his figure crouching down, and an expression of pain coming over his face. In the midst of his pain he still maintained his punctilious resolution; but how much did that cost him! It was his own fault, of course. It was all brought on by his impracticability, his whimsicality, his eccentricity, and his punctiliousness. Nevertheless, there was in him that which excited my deepest commiseration. The wretchedness and the pain of his face, and the suffering which was visible in his attitude, all touched me. He sat crouched down, shivering, shuddering, his teeth chattering, and presented a deplorable picture of one who struggled vainly against an overmastering pain.

My resolution was shaken by this. I rose to my feet.

"Mr. O'Halloran," said I, "pardon me. I see that I am subjecting you to very great suffering. If you sit there any longer, exposed to this damp, you'll never get over it. It would be but poor courtesy to subject you to that any longer. And so I don't see what better I can do than allow you to have your own way. I'll have to give up my scruples, I suppose. I can't sit here any longer, and see you suffer. And so— here goes!—I'm willing to fire as you wish."

At this O'Halloran rose to his feet with a cry of joy.

"The first shot!" he exclaimed.

"Yes," said I, "the first. I'll fire, if you insist on it."

"And that's just what I do," said he, shivering.

At this I took aim.

Bang! went the shot. I afterward found that it passed through his hat.

O'Halloran now raised his pistol, and levelled it at me. But the pleasure of his triumph had excited him; and, besides, he was shivering from head to foot, and his teeth were chattering. An accurate aim was impossible. His hand could scarcely hold the pistol, and his benumbed finger could scarcely pull the trigger. He fired, and the bullet passed through the sleeve of my coat, and close to the doctor's head.

"Me boy," he cried, flinging down the pistol, "there's no ind to the obleegeetions you put me under! I owe ye me loife a second toime. Ye've seeved me from death by fraizing."

CHAPTER XXXII.

HOME AGAIN.—THE GROWLS OF A CONFIRMED GROWLER. — HOSPITALITY. — THE WELL-KNOWN ROOM.—VISION OF A LADY.—ALONE WITH MARION.—INTERCHANGE OF THOUGHT AND SENTIMENT.—TWO BEAUTIFUL WOMEN. —AN EVENING TO BE REMEMBERED. — THE CONVIVIALITY OF O'HALLORAN.—THE HUMORS OF O'HALLORAN, AND HIS BACCHIC JOY.

WE all hurried away from the ground as rapidly as possible, and soon reached the *Hôtel de France*. It was small, stuffy, and rather close, but, to people in our half-frozen condition, the big Canadian stove was a blessing beyond words. O'Halloran seemed like an *habitué* of the place, judging by the way he button-holed the landlord, and by the success with which he obtained "somethin' warrum" for the company. But the *Hôtel de France* was not a place where one might linger; and so, after waiting long enough to allow the heat of the Canadian stove to penetrate us, aided by the blended power of "somethin' warrum" —and long enough also to give oats to the horses, which, after all, must have had the worst of it—poor devils!—we started and dragged on to the town.

All this time O'Halloran did not appear to have recognized Jack at all. On the drive out this might have been accounted for, but, in the *Hôtel de France*, O'Halloran had a full and perfect inspection of him. If he did recognize him, it certainly did not appear in his manner. He exchanged words with Jack in a tone of hilarious cordiality, which did not seem as though he considered Jack an enemy; and Jack, who never failed to respond when greeted in such a way, met him more than half-way. It was evident that O'Halloran had not the smallest idea that Jack was that identical British officer whom he had expelled from his house.

Of all the party the doctor seemed to have suffered most; and, on the journey back, he kept up one prolonged growl at me. I was fated, he said, to bring him bad luck, and I would be the death of him. Once before he had ridden all night in the storm for me; and now here was another fool's errand. He seemed inclined to consider it as a personal insult, and actually felt aggrieved because O'Halloran's bullet had not shattered my arm, or penetrated my brain. Thus he alternated between shivering and swearing all the way back.

"I tell you what it is, Macrorie," he growled, "if you ever come to ask my help again on any occasion whatever, I'll take it as a personal insult. I wouldn't have

come this time, but I thought it was to be an affair of honor. An affair of honor! Rot and nonsense! Dragging a fellow over the country all day to see a couple of pistols fired in the air! What sort of a thing do you call that? And here am I—in for it—yes—damn it, man!—I say again—in for it—to any extent—rheumatism, neuralgia, gout, inflammation, and fifty other things! If I thought you'd have any of them, I'd feel satisfied. But no—you're all right, and can afford to sit there grinning at the sufferings of a better man than yourself."

From which it will appear that the doctor was savage, and I was not.

On reaching Quebec, O'Halloran gave us all a comprehensive invitation to dinner.

But the doctor could not accept it. He had taken cold, and would have to go home. Jack could not accept it. He had a very pressing engagement. Mr. McGinty could not accept it, for he had some important business. So O'Halloran pressed me. I alone was disengaged. I had no rheumatism, no pressing engagement, no important business. O'Halloran was urgent in his invitation. Our duel seemed only to have heightened and broadened his cordiality. I was dying to see Marion—or to find out how she was—so what did I do? Why, I leaped at the invitation, as a matter of course.

So once more I was ushered into that comfortable and hospitable back-parlor. Since I had been there last, what events had occurred! O'Halloran left me for a time, and I was alone. I sat down, and thought of that night when I had wandered forth. I thought of all the wild fancies that had filled my brain, as I wandered about amid the storm, listening to the howl of the wind, and the deep, sullen moan

8

of the river. I recalled that strange, weird superstition, which had drawn me back once more to the house—and the deep longing and craving which had filled my heart for one glimpse, however faint, of my Lady of the Ice. I thought of my return—of my earnest gaze around, of the deep toll of the midnight bell, and of the sudden revelation of that dim, shadowy figure of a veiled lady, that stood in faint outline by the house, which advanced to meet me as I hurried over to her.

It was quite dark. There were no lamps lighted, but the coal-fire flickered and threw a ruddy glow about the apartment; at times leaping up into brightness, and again dying down into dimness and obscurity. O'Halloran had gone up-stairs, leaving me thus alone, and I sat in the deep arm-chair with my mind full of these all-absorbing fancies; and, in the midst of these fancies, even while I was thinking of that veiled figure which I had seen under the shadow of the house—even thus—I became aware of a light footfall, and a rustling dress beside me.

I turned my head with a quick movement of surprise.

There was the figure of a lady—graceful, slender, formed in a mould of perfect elegance and loveliness, the dark drapery of her dress descending till it died away among the shadows on the floor. I stared for a moment in surprise. Then the light of the fire, which had subsided for a moment, leaped up, and flashed out upon the exquisite features, and the dark, lustrous, solemn eyes of Marion.

I sprang to my feet, with my heart beating so fast that it seemed impossible to breathe. The surprise was overwhelming. I had thought of her as raving in brain-fever, descending deep down into the abyss of delirium, and now—here she was—here —by my side!—my Lady of the Ice!—Marion!

"I heard that you were here," she said, in a low, tremulous voice, "and I could not help coming down to tell you how I—how I bless you for—for that night."

She stopped—and held out her hand in silence.

I seized it in both of mine. For a few moments I could not speak. At last I burst forth:

"Oh, my God! What bliss it is for me to see you!—I've been thinking about it. ever since—I've been afraid that you were ill—that you would never get over it."

And still holding her hand in mine, I raised it with tremulous eagerness, and pressed it to my lips.

She gently withdrew it, but without any appearance of anger.

"No," said she, "I was not ill. A wakeful night, a very feverish excitement—that was all."

"I listened long after you left," said I, in a low voice; "and all was still."

"Yes," she said, in the same low voice. "No one heard me. I reached my room without any one knowing it. But I had much to sustain me. For oh, sir, I felt deeply, deeply grateful to find myself back again, and to know that my folly had ended so. To be again in my dear home—with my dear papa—after the anguish that I had known!"

She stopped.—It was a subject that she could not speak on without an emotion that was visible in every tone. Her voice was sad, and low, and solemn, and all its intonations thrilled to the very core of my being. And for me—I had nothing to say —I thrilled, my heart bounded at the sight of her face, and at the tones of her voice; while within me there was a great and unspeakable joy. If I had dared to say to her all that I felt at that moment! But how dare I? She had come in the fulness of her warm gratitude to thank me for what I had done. She did not seem to think that, but for me, she would not have left her home at all. She only remembered that I had brought her back. It was thus that her generous nature revealed itself.

Now, while she thus expressed such deep and fervent gratitude, and evinced such joy at being again in her home, and at finding such an ending to her folly, there came to me a great and unequalled exultation. For by this I understood that her folly was cured—that her infatuation was over—that the glamour had been dissipated—that her eyes had been opened—and the once-adored Jack was now an object of indifference.

"Have you told any one about it?" I asked.

"No," said she, "not a soul."

"*He* is my most intimate friend," said I, "but I have kept this secret from him. He knows nothing about it."

"Of course he does not," said she, "how was it possible for you to tell him? This is *our* secret."

I cannot tell the soft, sweet, and soothing consolation which penetrated my inmost soul at these words. Though few, they had a world of meaning. I noticed with delight the cool indifference with which she spoke of *him*. Had she expressed contempt, I should not have been so well pleased. Perfect indifference was what I wanted, and what I found. Then, again, she acknowledged me as the only partner in her secret, thus associating me with herself in one memorable and impressive way. Nor yet did she ask any questions as to whom I meant. Her indifference to him was so great that it did not even excite curiosity as to how I had found out who

he was. She was content to take my own statement without any questions or observations.

And there, as the flickering light of the coal-fire sprang up and died out; as it threw from time to time the ruddy glow of its uprising flames upon her, she stood before me —a vision of perfect loveliness—like a goddess to the devotee, which appears for an instant amid the glow of some mysterious light, only to fade out of sight a moment after. The rare and perfect grace of her slender figure, with its dark drapery, fading into the gloom below—the fair outline of her face—her sad, earnest, and melancholy expression ; the intense and solemn earnestness of her dark, lustrous eyes—all these conspired to form a vision such as impressed itself upon my memory forever. This was the full realization of my eager fancy—this was what I had so longed to see. I had formed my own ideal of my Lady of the Ice—in private life—in the parlor—meeting me in the world of society. And here before me that ideal stood.

Now, it gives a very singular sensation to a fellow to stand face to face with the woman whom he worships and adores, and to whom he dares not make known the feelings that swell within him; and still more singular is this sensation, when this woman, whom he adores, happens to be one whom he has carried in his arms for an indefinite time; and more singular yet is it, when she happens to be one whom he has saved once, and once again, from the most cruel fate; by whose side he has stood in what may have seemed the supreme moment of mortal life; whom he has sustained and cheered and strengthened in a dread conflict with Death himself; singular enough is the sensation that arises under such circumstances as these, my boy—singular, and overwhelming, and intolerable ; a sensation which paralyzes the tongue and makes one mute, yet still brings on a resistless and invincible desire to speak and make all known; and should such a scene be too long continued, the probability is that the desire and the longing thus to speak will eventually burst through all restraint, and pour forth in a volume of fierce, passionate eloquence, that will rush onward, careless of consequences. Now, such was my situation, and such was my sensation, and such, no doubt, would have been the end of it all, had not the scene been brought to an end by the arrival of O'Halloran and his wife, preceded by a servant with lights, who soon put the room in a state of illumination.

Nora, as I must still call her, was somewhat embarrassed at first meeting me—for she could not forget our last interview; but she gradually got over it, and, as the evening wore on, she became her old, lively, laughing, original self. O'Halloran, too, was in his best and most genial mood, and, as I caught at times the solemn glance of the dark eyes of Marion, I found not a cloud upon the sky that overhung our festivities. Marion, too, had more to say than usual. She was no longer so self-absorbed, and so abstracted, as she once was. She was not playful and lively like Nora; but she was, at least, not sad; she showed an interest in all that was going on, and no longer dwelt apart like a star.

It was evident that Nora knew nothing at all about the duel. That was a secret between O'Halloran and me. It was also evident that she knew nothing about Marion's adventure—that was a secret between Marion and me. There was another secret, also, which puzzled me, and of which O'Halloran must, of course, have known as little as I did, and this was that strange act of Nora's in pretending to be the Lady of the Ice. Why had she done it? For what possible reason? Why had Marion allowed her to do it? All this was a mystery. I also wondered much whether she thought that I still believed in that pretence of hers. I thought she did, and attributed to this that embarrassment which she showed when she first greeted me. On this, as on the former occasion, her embarrassment had, no doubt, arisen from the fact that she was playing a part, and the consciousness that such a part was altogether out of her power to maintain. Yet, why had she done it?

That evening I had a better opportunity to compare these two most beautiful women; for beautiful each most certainly was, though in a different way from the other. I had already felt on a former occasion the bewitching effect of Nora's manner, and I had also felt to a peculiar and memorable extent that spell which had been cast upon me by Marion's glance. Now I could understand the difference between them and my own feelings. For in witchery, in liveliness, in musical laughter, in never-failing merriment, Nora far surpassed all with whom I had ever met; and for all these reasons she had in her a rare power of fascination. But Marion was solemn, earnest, intense; and there was that on her face which sent my blood surging back to my heart, as I caught her glance. Nora was a woman to laugh and chat with; Nora was kind and gracious, and gentle too; Nora was amiable as well as witty; charming in manner, piquant in expression, inimitable at an anecdote, with never-failing resources, a first-rate lady-conversationist, if I may use so formidable a word—in fact, a thoroughly fascinating woman; but Marion!—Marion was one, not to laugh with, but to die for; Marion had a face that haunted you; a glance that made your heart leap, and your nerves tingle; a voice whose deep intonations vibrated through all your being with a certain mystic meaning, to follow you after you had left her, and come up again in your thoughts by day, and your dreams by night—Marion! why Nora could be surveyed calmly, and all her fascinating power analyzed; but Marion was a power in herself, who bewildered you and defied analysis.

During that time when Nora had been confounded in my mind with the Lady of the Ice, she had indeed risen to the chief place in my thoughts, though my mind still failed to identify her thoroughly. I had thought that I loved her, but I had not. It was the Lady of the Ice whom I loved; and, when Marion had revealed herself, then all was plain. After that revelation Nora sank into nothingness, and Marion was all in all.

Oh, that evening, in that pleasant parlor! Shall I ever forget it!

Our talk was on all things. Of course, I made no allusion to my journey over the ice, and Nora soon saw that she was free from any such unpleasant and embarrassing remarks. Freed from this fear, she became herself again. Never was she more vivacious, more sparkling, or more charming. O'Halloran joined the conversation in a manner that showed the rarest resources of wit, of fun, and of genial humor. Marion, as I said before, did not hold aloof, but took a part which was subordinate, it is true, yet, to me, far more effective; indeed, incomparably more so than that of the others. Indeed, I remember now nothing else but Marion.

So the evening passed, and at length the ladies retired. Nora bade me adieu with her usual cordiality, and her kindly and bewitching glance; while Marion's eyes threw upon me their lustrous glow, in which there was revealed a certain deep and solemn earnestness, that only intensified, if such a thing were possible, the spell which she had thrown over my soul.

And then it was "somethin' warrum." Under the effects of this, my host passed through several distinct and well-defined moods or phases.

First of all, he was excessively friendly and affectionate. He alluded to our late adventure, and expressed himself delighted with the result.

Then he became confidential, and explained how it was that he, an old man, happened to have a young wife.

Fifteen years ago, he said, Nora had been left under his care by her father. She had lived in England all her life, where she had been educated. Shortly after he had become her guardian he had been compelled to fly to America, on account of his connection with the Young-Ireland party, of which he was a prominent member. He had been one of the most vigorous writers in one of the Dublin papers, which was most hostile to British rule, and was therefore a marked man. As he did not care about imprisonment or a voyage to Botany Bay, he had come to America, bringing with him his ward Nora, and his little daughter Marion, then a child of not more than three or four. By this act he had saved himself and his property, which was amply sufficient for his support. A few years passed away, and he found his feelings toward Nora somewhat different from those of a parent—and he also observed that Nora looked upon him with tenderer feelings than those of gratitude.

"There's a great difference intoirely," said he, "between us now. I've lost my youth, but she's kept hers. But thin, at that toime, me boy, Phaylim O'Halloran was a moightily different man from the one you see before you. I was not much over forty—in me proime—feeling as young as any of thim, an' it wasn't an onnatural thing that I should win the love of ayven a young gyerrul, so it wasn't. An' so she became me woife—my Nora—me darlin'—the loight of me loife. And she's accompanied me iver since on all my wandherin's and phelandherin's, and has made the home of the poor ixoile a paradoise, so she has."

All this was very confidential, and such a confidence would probably never have been given, had it not been for the effects of "somethin' warrum;" but it showed me several things in the plainest manner. The first was, that Nora must be over thirty, at any rate, and was therefore very much older than I had taken her to be. Again, her English accent and style could be accounted for; and finally the equally English accent and style of Marion could be understood and accounted for on the grounds of Nora's influence. For a child always catches the accent of its mother rather than of its father, and Nora must, for nearly fifteen years, have been a sort of mother, more or less, to Marion.

And now, why the mischief did Nora pretend to be my Lady of the Ice, and in the very presence of Marion try to maintain a part which she could not carry out? And why, if she were such a loving and faithful wife, did she deliberately deceive the confiding O'Halloran, and make him believe that she was the one whom I had saved? It was certainly not from any want of love for him. It must have been some scheme of hers which she had formed in connection with Marion. But what in the world could such a scheme have been, and why in the world had she formed it?

This was the puzzling question that arose

afresh, as O'Halloran detailed to me very confidentially the history of this romantic experience in his life.

But this was only one of his moods, and this mood passed away. The romantic and the confidential was succeeded by the literary and the scholastic, with a dash of the humorous.

A trivial remark of mine, in the course of some literary criticisms of his, turned his thoughts to the subject of puns. He at once plunged into the history of puns. He quoted Aristophanes, Plautus, Terence, Cicero. He brought forward illustrations from Shakespeare, Ben Jonson, Milton, Puritan writers, Congreve, Cowper, and others, until he concluded with Hood, who he declared had first unfolded to the human mind the possibility of the pun.

From this he passed off lightly and easily into other things, and finally glided into the subject of mediæval Latin. This, he asserted, was born and nourished under peculiar circumstances, so different from classical Latin as to be almost a new language, yet fully equal to it in all the best characteristics of a language. He defied me to find any thing in classical poetry that would compare with the "Dies Iræ," the "Stabat Mater," or the "Rhythm of Bernard de Morlaix." As I was and am rather rusty in Latin, I did not accept the challenge. Then he asserted that mediæval Latin was so comprehensive in its scope that it was equally good for the convivial and for the solemn, and could speak equally well the sentiments of fun, love, and religion. He proved this by quotations from the immortal Walter Mapes. He overwhelmed me, in fact, with quotations. I caved in. I was suppressed. I became extinct. Finally he offered to show me an original song of his own, which he asserted was "iminintly shooted to the prisint occasion."

As I had no other way of showing my opinion of it, I begged the paper from him, and give here a true copy of it, *verbatim et literatim*, notes and all :

PHELIMII HALLORANII CARMEN.

Omnibus Hibernicis
  Semper est ex more
Vino curas pellere
  Aut montano rore ; *
Is qui nescit bibere,
  Aut est cito satur,
Ille, Pol ! me judice
  Parvus est potator.†

Omnibus Americis
  Semper est in ore
Tuba, frondes habens ex
  Nicotino flore ;
Densis fumi nubibus
  Et vivunt et movent,
Hoc est summum gaudium
  Sic Te Bacche ! fovent.‡

Omnis tunc Hibernicus
  Migret sine mora,
Veniat Americam
  Vivat hac in ora,
Nostram Baccam capiat, §
  Et montanum rorem,
Erit, Pol ! Americus ‖
  In sæcula sæculorum.
          Amen.

---

  * *Montano rore*—cf., id. Hib., *mountain-dew ;* item, id. Scot., Hib., et Amer., *whiskey.*

  † *Parvus potator*—cf., id. Amer., *small potater.*

  ‡ *Te Bacche*—cf., id. Amer., *Tebaccy,* i. e., *tobacco.*

  § *Baccam*—in America vulgo dici solet, *Backy.*

  ‖ *Americus*—cf., id. Amer., *a merry cuss.*

CHAPTER XXXIII.

FROM APRIL TO JUNE.—TEMPORA MUTANTUR, ET NOS MUTAMUR IN ILLIS.—STARTLING CHANGE IN MARION !—AND WHY ?—JACK AND HIS WOES.—THE VENGEANCE OF MISS PHILLIPS.—LADIES WHO REFUSE TO ALLOW THEIR HEARTS TO BE BROKEN.—NOBLE ATTITUDE OF THE WIDOW.—CONSOLATIONS OF LOUIE.

TIME passed on, and week succeeded to week, without any occurrence of a decisive nature. April died out, May passed, and June came. Then all the trees burst into leaf, and the fields arrayed themselves in green, and all Nature gave one grand leap from winter into summer.

During all this time I was a constant and a favored guest at O'Halloran's. I really don't think I ever went anywhere else. I cut off all visits to others—that is, in the evening—and went there only. O'Halloran always received me with the same cordiality, and the ladies always met me with the same smile.

So many evenings in that comfortable parlor, so many chats with the ladies, so many interviews with my host, could not fail to bring us nearer together. Such was, indeed, the case with O'Halloran and Nora ; but with Marion it was different. There was, indeed, between us the consciousness of a common secret, and she could not fail to see in my manner something warmer than common — something more tender than friendship, for instance —something, in fact, which, without being at all spooney, was still expressive of very delicate regard. Yet there came over her something which excited my fears, and filled me with gloomy forebodings. She seemed to lose that cordiality which she evinced on that first evening when I talked with her alone. She never threw at me those deep glances which then had made my nerves tingle. She seemed constrained and reserved. Only in speaking to me, there was always in her voice an indefinable sweetness and gentleness, which made her tones ring in my memory afterward like soft music. That showed me that there was no coldness on her part; and so, too, when I did catch at times the glance of her dark eyes, there was something in them so timid, so soft, and so shy, that I could not think of her as wearying of me. Yet this Marion, timid, tender, and shy; this Marion, holding aloof under evident constraint, keeping apart, giving me no opportunity; this Marion, who had now exchanged the intensity and the solemnity of former days for something so very different —became a puzzle to me.

Why had she changed? Was it her returning regard for Jack? Impossible. His name had several times been mentioned without causing any emotion in her. His approaching marriage with Mrs. Finnimore had once been mentioned by Nora, who spoke of it as an interesting item of news. Marion heard it with indifference. Or was she trying to withdraw from any further intimacy with me? Was she suspicious of my intentions, and desirous of giving me no hope? Was she trying to repel me at the outset? It seemed so. And so a great fear gradually arose in my heart.

So went the time away, and toward the latter part of May and the beginning of June I used to take the ladies out driving, hoping that these new circumstances might elicit some show of cordiality in Marion. But this proved a complete failure; for, the closer we were thrown together, the greater seemed her shy reticence, her timid reserve, and her soft and gentle yet persistent manner of keeping me at a distance.

And so, here was I. I had found my Lady of the Ice; yet no sooner had I found her than she withdrew herself to an inaccessible height, and seemed now as far out of my reach as on that eventful morning when I sought her at the hut at Montmorency, and found that she had fled.

Spending so much time as I did at O'Halloran's, I did not see so much of Jack as before; yet he used to drop in from time to time in the morning, and pour forth the sorrows of his soul.

Marion's name he never mentioned. Either he had forgotten all about her, which was not improbable; or the subject was too painful a one for him to touch upon, which also was not improbable; or, finally, her affair became overshadowed by other and weightier matters, which was in the highest degree natural.

His first great trouble arose from the action of Miss Phillips.

He had gone there a second time to call, and had again been told that she was not at home. He turned away vowing vengeance, but in the following morning found that vengeance was out of the question; for he received a parcel, containing all the letters which he had ever written to Miss Phillips, and all the presents that he had ever given her, with a polite note, requesting the return of her letters. This was a blow that he was not prepared for. It struck home. However, there was no help for it—so he returned her letters, and then came to me with all kinds of vague threats.

Such threats, however, could not be carried out; and as for Miss Phillips, she was quite beyond the reach of them. She accepted the situation wonderfully well. She did more—she triumphed over it. In a short time she had others at her feet, prominent among whom was Colonel Blount—a dashing officer, a Victoria Cross, and a noble fellow in every respect. Thus Miss Phillips revenged herself on Jack. She tossed him aside coolly and contemptuously, and replaced him with a man whom Jack himself felt to be his superior. And all this was gall and wormwood to Jack. And, what was more, he was devoured with jealousy.

The worst thing about it all, however, was the crushing blow which it gave to his self-love. I am inclined to think that he was very much taken down, on one occasion, when I informed him incidentally that Marion was in excellent spirits, and was said to be in better health than she had known for years. Miss Phillips's policy, however, was a severer blow. For it had all along been his firm belief that his tangled love-affairs could not end without a broken heart, or melancholy madness, or life-long sorrow, or even death, to one or more of his victims. To save them from such a fate, he talked of suicide. All this was highly romantic, fearfully melodramatic, and even mysteriously tragic. But, unfortunately for Jack's self-conceit, the event did not coincide with these highly-colored views. The ladies refused to break their hearts. Those organs, however susceptible and tender they may have been, beat bravely on. Number Three viewed him with indifference. Miss Phillips coolly and contemptuously cast him off, and at once found new consolation in the devotion of another. Broken hearts! Melancholy madness! Life-long sorrow! Not they, indeed. They didn't think of him. They didn't confide their wrongs to any avenger. No brother or other male relative sent Jack a challenge. He was simply dropped. He was forgotten. Now any one may see the chagrin which such humiliation must have caused to one of Jack's temper.

And how did the widow treat Jack all this time? The widow! She was sublime; for she showed at once the fostering care of a mother, and the forgiveness of a saint. Forgiveness? That's not the word. I am wrong. She showed nothing of the kind. On the contrary, she evinced no consciousness whatever that any offence had been committed. If Jack had deceived her as to Miss Phillips, she showed no knowledge of such deceit; if he had formed other entanglements of which he had never told her, she never let him know whether she had found out or not; if Jack went every evening to console himself with Louie, any discovery which the widow may have made of so very interesting yet transparent a fact was never alluded to by her. Such was the lofty ground which the widow took in reference to Jack and his affairs, and such was the manner with which she viewed him and them—a manner elevated, serene, calm, untroubled—a manner always the same. For she seemed above all care for such things. Too high-minded, you know. Too lofty in soul, my boy, and all that sort of thing. Like some tall cliff that rears its awful form, swells from the vale, and midway cleaves the storm, and all the rest of it. Such was the demeanor of the widow Finnimore.

She was so kind and cordial that Jack had not a word to say. After a few days of absence, during which he had not dared to call on her, he had ventured back, and was greeted with the gentlest of reproaches for his neglect, and was treated with an elaboration of kindness that was positively crushing. So he had to go, and to keep going. She would not suffer a single cloud to arise between them. An unvarying sweetness diffused itself evermore over her very pretty face, and through all the tones of her very musical voice. And so Jack was held fast, bound by invisible yet infrangible bonds, and his soul was kept in complete subjection by the superior ascendency of the widow.

So he went to see her every day. About six, generally dined there. Always left at eight, or just as dinner was over. Not much time for tenderness, of course. Jack didn't feel particularly inclined for that sort of thing. The widow, on the other hand, did not lay any stress on that, nor did she allow herself to suspect that Jack was altogether too cold for a lover. Not she. Beaming, my boy. All smiles, you know. Always the same. Glad to see him when he came—a pleasant smile of adieu at parting. In fact, altogether a model *fiancée*, such as is not often met with in this vale of tears.

Now always, after leaving this good, kind, smiling, cordial, pretty, clever, fascinating, serene, accomplished, hospitable, and altogether unparalleled widow, Jack would calmly, quietly, and deliberately go over to the Bertons', and stay there as long as he could. What for? Was he not merely heaping up sorrow for himself in continuing so ardently this Platonic attachment? For Louie there was no danger. According to Jack, she still kept up her teasing, quizzing, and laughing mood. Jack's break-up with Miss Phillips was a joke. He had confided to her that he had also broken off with Number Three; and, though she could not find out the cause, this became another joke. Finally, his present attitude with regard to the widow was viewed by her as the best joke of all. She assured him that the widow was to be his fate, and that she had driven the others from the field, so as to have him exclusively to herself.

And thus Jack alternated and vibrated between the widow and Louie, and all his entanglements were now reduced to these two.

Such is a full, frank, fair, free, ample, lucid, and luminous explanation of the progress of affairs, which explanation was necessary in order to make the reader fully understand the full meaning of what follows.

CHAPTER XXXIV.

JACK'S TRIBULATIONS.—THEY RISE UP IN THE VERY FACE OF THE MOST ASTONISHING GOOD FORTUNES.—FOR, WHAT IS LIKE A LEGACY?—AND THIS COMES TO JACK!—SEVEN THOUSAND POUNDS STERLING PER ANNUM!—BUT WHAT'S THE USE OF IT ALL?—JACK COMES TO GRIEF!—WOE! SORROW! DESPAIR! ALL THE WIDOW!—INFATUATION.—A MAD PROPOSAL.—A MADMAN, A LUNATIC, AN IDIOT, A MARCH HARE, AND A HATTER, ALL ROLLED INTO ONE, AND THAT ONE THE LUCKY YET UNFORTUNATE JACK.

JACK had been falling off more and more. I was taken up with the O'Hallorans; he, with those two points between which he oscillated like a pendulum; and our intercourse diminished, until at length days would intervene without a meeting between us.

It was in the middle of June.

I had not seen Jack for more than a week.

Suddenly, I was reminded of him by a startling rumor that reached my ears after every soul in the garrison and in the city had heard it. It referred to Jack. It was nothing about the widow, nothing about Louie, nothing about Marion, nothing about Miss Phillips.

It did not refer to duns.

He had not been nabbed by the sheriff.

He had not put an end to himself.

In short, the news was, that an uncle of his had died, and left him a fortune of unknown proportions. *Omne ignotum pro mirifico*, of course; and so up went Jack's fortune to twenty thousand a year. Jack had told me about that uncle, and I had reason to know that it was at least six or seven thousand; and, let me tell you, six or seven thousand pounds per annum isn't to be laughed at.

So here was Jack—raised up in a moment —far above the dull level of debt, and duns, and despair; raised to an upper and, I trust, a better world, where swarms of duns can never arise, and bailiffs never come; raised, my boy, to a region of serene delight, where, like the gods of Epicurus, he might survey from his cloudless calm the darkness and the gloom of the lower world. A fortune, by Jove! Seven thousand pounds sterling a year! Hard cash! Why, the thing fairly took my breath away. I sat down to grapple with the stupendous thought. Aha! where would the duns be now? What would those miserable devils say now, that had been badgering him with lawyers' letters? Wouldn't they all haul off? Methought they would. Methought! why, meknew they would—mefancied how they would fawn, and cringe, and apologize, and explain, and lick the dust, and offer to polish his noble boots, and present themselves for the honor of being kicked by him. Nothing is more degrading to our common humanity than the attitude of a creditor toward a poor debtor—except the attitude of that same creditor, when he learns that his debtor has suddenly become rich.

Having finally succeeded in mastering this great idea, I hurried off to Jack to congratulate him.

I found him in his room. He was lying down, looking very blue, very dismal, and utterly used up. At first, I did not notice this, but burst forth in a torrent of congra-tulations, shaking his hand most violently. He raised himself slightly from the sofa on which he was reclining, and his languid hand did not return my warm grasp, nor did his face exhibit the slightest interest in what I said. Seeing this, I stopped short suddenly.

"Hallo, old boy!" I cried. "What's the matter? Any thing happened? Isn't it true, then?"

"Oh, yes," said Jack, dolefully, leaning forward, with his elbows on his knees, and looking at the floor.

"Well, you don't seem very jubilant about it. Any thing the matter? Why, man, if you were dying, I should think you'd rise up at the idea of seven thousand a year."

Jack said nothing.

At such a check as this to my enthusiastic sympathy, I sat in silence for a time, and looked at him. His elbows were on his knees, his face was pale, his hair in disorder, and his eyes were fixed on the wall opposite with a vacant and abstracted stare. There was a haggard look about his handsome face, and a careworn expression on his broad brow, which excited within me the deepest sympathy and sadness. Something had happened—something of no common kind. This was a something which was far, very far, more serious than those old troubles which had oppressed him. This was something far different from those old perplexities—the entanglements with three engagements. Amid all those he was nothing but a big, blundering baby; but now he seemed like a sorrow-stricken man. Where was the light of his eyes, the glory of his brow, the music of his voice? Where was that glow that once used to pervade his fresh, open, sunny face? Where! It was Jack—but not the Jack of old. It was Jack—but

"Alas! how changed from him
That life of pleasure, and that soul of whim!"

Or, as another poet has it—

"'Twas Jack—but living Jack no more!"

"Jack," said I, after a long and solemn silence, in which I had tried in vain to conjecture what might possibly be the cause of this—"Jack, dear boy, you and I have had confidences together, a little out of the ordinary line. I came here to congratulate you about your fortune; but I find you utterly cut up about something. Will you let me ask you what it is? I don't ask out of idle curiosity, but out of sympathy. At the same time, if it's any thing of a private nature, I beg pardon for asking you to tell it."

Jack looked up, and a faint flicker of a smile passed over his face.

"Oh, all right, old boy!" he said. "I'm hit hard—all up—and that sort of thing—hit hard—yes, damned hard—serves me right, too, you know, for being such an infernal fool."

He frowned, and drew a long breath.

"Wait a minute, old chap," said he, rising from the sofa; "I'll get something to sustain nature, and then I'll answer your question. I'm glad you've come. I don't know but that it'll do me good to tell it all to somebody. It's hard to stay here in my den, fretting my heart out—damned hard!—but wait a minute, and I'll explain."

Saying this, he walked over to the sideboard.

"Will you take any thing?"

"Thanks, no," said I; "a pipe is all I want." And I proceeded to fill and light one.

Thereupon Jack poured out a tumbler of raw brandy, which he swallowed. Then he came back to the sofa. A flush came to his face, and his eyes looked brighter; but he had still the same haggard aspect.

"I'm in for it, Macrorie," said he at last, gloomily.

"In for it?"

"Yes—an infernal scrape."

"What?"

"The widow—damn her!" and he struck his clinched fist against the head of the sofa.

"In for it? The widow?" I repeated. "What do you mean?"

Jack drew a long breath, and regarded me with a fixed stare.

"I mean," said Jack, fixing his eyes upon me with an awful look, "I mean this—that I have to marry that woman."

"Marry her?"

"Yes," he exclaimed, dashing his fist upon the table savagely, "marry her! There you have it. I'm in for it. No escape. Escape—ha! ha! Nabbed, sir. All up! Married and done for—yes, eternally done for!"

He jerked these words out in a fierce, feverish way; and then, flinging himself back, he clasped his knees with his hands, and sat regarding me with stern eyes and frowning brow.

This mood of Jack's was a singular one. He was evidently undergoing great distress of mind. Under such circumstances as these, no levity could be thought of. Had he not been so desperate, I might have ventured upon a jest about the widow driving the others from the field and coming forth victorious; but, as it was, there was no room for jest. So I simply sat in silence, and returned his gaze.

"Well?" said he at last, impatiently.

"Well?" said I.

"Haven't you got any thing to say about that?"

"I don't know what to say. Your manner of telling this takes me more by surprise than the thing itself. After all, you must have looked forward to this."

"Looked forward? I'll be hanged if I did, except in a very general way. Damn it, man! I thought she'd have a little pity on a fellow, and allow me some liberty. I didn't look forward to being shut up at once."

"At once? You speak as though the event were near."

"Near? I should think it was. What do you say to next week? Is that near or not? Near? I should rather think so."

"Next week? Good Lord! Jack, do you really mean it? Nonsense!"

"Next week—yes—and worse—on Tuesday—not the end, but the beginning, of the week—Tuesday, the 20th of June."

"Tuesday, the 20th of June!" I repeated, in amazement.

"Yes, Tuesday, the 20th of June," said Jack.

"Heavens, man! what have you been up to? How did it happen? Why did you do it? Couldn't you have postponed it? It takes two to make an agreement. What do you mean by lamenting over it now? Why didn't you get up excuses? Haven't you to go home to see about your estates? Why, in Heaven's name, did you let it be all arranged in this way, if you didn't want it to be?"

Jack looked at me for a few moments very earnestly.

"Why didn't I?" said he, at length; "simply because I happen to be an unmitigated, uncontrollable, incorrigible, illimitable, and inconceivable ASS! That's the reason why, if you must know."

Jack's very forcible way of putting this statement afforded me no chance whatever of denying it or combating it. His determination to be an ass was so vehement, that remonstrance was out of the question. I therefore accepted it as a probable truth.

For some time I remained silent, looking at Jack, and puffing solemnly at my pipe. In a situation of this kind, or in fact in any situation where one is expected to say something, but doesn't happen to have any thing in particular to say, there's nothing in the world like a pipe. For the human face, when it is graced by a pipe, and when the pipe is being puffed, assumes, somehow, a rare and wonderful expression of profound and solemn thought. Besides, the presence of the pipe in the mouth is a check to any overhasty remark. Vain and empty words are thus repressed, and thought, divine thought, reigns supreme. And so as I sat in silence before Jack, if I didn't have any profound thoughts in my mind, I at least had the appearance of it, which after all served my purpose quite as well.

"I don't mind telling you all about it, old chap," said Jack, at last, who had by this time passed into a better frame of mind, and looked more like his old self. "You've known all about the row, all along, and you'll have to be in at the death, so I'll tell you now. You'll have to help me through—you'll be my best man, and all that sort of thing, you know—and this is the best time for making a clean breast of it, you know: so here goes."

Upon this Jack drew a long breath, and then began:

"I've told you already," he said, "how abominably kind she was. You know when I called on her after the row with Miss Phillips, how sweet she was, and all that, and how I settled down on the old terms. I hadn't the heart to get up a row with her, and hadn't even the idea of such a thing. When a lady is civil, and kind, and all that, what can a fellow do? So you see

I went there as regular as clock-work, and dined, and then left. Sometimes I went at six, and stayed till eight; sometimes at five, and stayed till nine. But that was very seldom. Sometimes, you know, she'd get me talking, and somehow the time would fly, and it would be ever so late before I could get away. I'm always an ass, and so I felt tickled, no end, at her unfailing kindness to me, and took it all as so much incense, and all that—I was her deity, you know—snuffing up incense—receiving her devotion—feeling half sorry that I couldn't quite reciprocate, and making an infernal fool of myself generally.

"Now you know I'm such a confounded ass that her very reticence about my other affairs, and her quiet way of taking them, rather piqued me; and several times I threw out hints about them, to see what she would say. At such times she would smile in a knowing way, but say nothing. At last there was one evening—it was a little over a week ago—I went there, and found her more cordial than ever, more amusing, more fascinating—kinder, you know, and all that. There was no end to her little attentions. Of course all that sort of thing had on me the effect which it always has, and I rapidly began to make an ass of myself. I began to hint about those other affairs—and at last I told her I didn't believe she'd forgiven me."

Here Jack made an awful pause, and looked at me in deep solemnity.

I said nothing, but puffed away in my usual thoughtful manner.

"The moment that I said that," continued Jack, "she turned and gave me the strangest look. 'Forgiven you,' said she; 'after all that has passed, can *you* say that?'

"'Well,' I said, 'you don't seem altogether what you used to be—'

"'I!' she exclaimed. 'I not what I used to be?—and *you* can look *me* in the face and say that.'

"And now, Macrorie, listen to what an ass can do.

"You see, her language, her tone, and her look, all piqued me. But at the same time I didn't know what to say. I didn't love her—confound her!—and I knew that I didn't—but I wanted to assert myself, or some other damned thing or other—so what did I do but take her hand."

I puffed on.

"She leaned back in her chair.

"'Ah, Jack,' she sighed, 'I don't believe you care any thing for poor me.'"

Jack paused for a while, and sat looking at the floor.

"Which was quite true," he continued, at last. "Only under the circumstances, being thus challenged, you know, by a very pretty widow, and being an ass, and being conceited, and being dazzled by the surroundings, what did I do but begin to swear that I loved her better than ever?

"'And me alone!' she sighed.

"'Yes, you alone!' I cried, and then went on in the usual strain in which impassioned lovers go under such circumstances, but with this very material difference, that I didn't happen to be an impassioned lover, or any other kind of a lover of hers at all, and I knew it all the time, and all the time felt a secret horror at what I was saying.

"But the fact of the business is, Macrorie, that woman is—oh—she is awfully clever, and she managed to lead me on, I don't know how. She pretended not to believe me—she hinted at my indifference, she spoke about my joy at getting away from her so as to go elsewhere, and said a thousand other things, all of which had the effect of making me more of an ass than ever, and so I rushed headlong to destruction."

Here Jack paused, and looked at me despairingly.

"Well?" said I.

"Well?" said he.

"Go on," said I. "Make an end of it. Out with it! What next?"

Jack gave a groan.

"Well—you see—somehow—I went on—and before I knew it there I was offering to marry her on the spot—and—heavens and earth! Macrorie—wasn't it a sort of judgment on me—don't you think?—I'd got used to that sort of thing, you know—offering to marry people off hand, you know, and all that—and so it came natural on this occasion; and I suppose that was how it happened, that before I knew what I was doing I had pumped out a violent and vehement entreaty for her to be mine at once.—Yes, at once—any time—that evening—the next day—the day after—no matter when. I'll be hanged if I can say now whether at that moment I was really sincere or not. I'm such a perfect and finished ass, that I really believe I meant what I said, and at that time I really wanted her to marry me. If that confounded chaplain that goes humbugging about there all the time had happened to be in the room, I'd have asked him to tie the knot on the spot. Yes, I'll be hanged if I wouldn't! His not being there is the only reason, I believe, why the knot wasn't tied. In that case I'd now be Mr. Finnimore—no, by Jove—what rot!—I mean I'd now be her husband, and she'd be Mrs. Randolph—confound her!"

Jack again relapsed into silence. His confession was a difficult task for him, and it came hard. It was given piecemeal, like the confession of a murderer on the day before his execution, when his desire to confess struggles with his unwillingness to recall the particulars of an abhorrent deed, and when after giving one fact he delays and falters, and lapses into long silence before he is willing or able to give another.

"Well, after that," he resumed, at last, "I was fairly in for it—no hope, no going back — no escapes — trapped, my boy — nabbed—gone in forever—head over heels, and all the rest of it. The widow was affected by my vehemence, as a matter of course—she stammered—she hesitated, and of course, being an ass, I was only made more vehement by all that sort of thing, you know. So I urged her, and pressed her, and then, before I knew what I was about, I found her coyly granting my insane request to name the day."

"Oh, Jack! Jack! Jack!" I exclaimed.

"Go on," said he. "Haven't you something more to say? Pitch in. Give it to me hot and heavy. You don't seem to be altogether equal to the occasion, Macrorie. Why don't you hit hard?"

"Can't do it," said I. "I'm knocked down myself. Wait, and I'll come to time. But don't be too hard on a fellow. Be reasonable. I want to take breath."

"Name the day! name the day! name the day!" continued Jack, ringing the changes on the words; "name the day! By Jove! See here, Macrorie—can't you get a doctor's certificate for me and have me quietly put in the lunatic asylum before that day comes?"

"That's not a bad idea," said I. "It might be managed. It's worth thinking about, at any rate."

"Wild!" said Jack, "mad as a March hare, or a hatter, or any other thing of that sort — ungovernable — unmanageable, devoid of all sense and reason—what more do you want? If I am not a lunatic, who is? That's what I want to know."

"There's a great deal of reason in that," said I, gravely.

"No there isn't," said Jack, pettishly. "It's all nonsense. I tell you I'm a madman, a lunatic, an idiot, any thing else. I don't quite need a strait-jacket as yet, but I tell you I do need the seclusion of a comfortable lunatic asylum. I only stipulate for an occasional drop of beer, and a whiff or two at odd times. Don't you think I can manage it?"

"It might be worth trying," said I. "But trot on, old fellow."

Jack, thus recalled to himself, gave another very heavy sigh.

"Where was I?" said he. "Oh, about naming the day. Well, I'll be hanged if she didn't do it. She did name the day. And what day do you think it was that she named? What day! Good Heavens, Macrorie! Only think of it. What do you happen to have to say, now, for instance, to the 20th of June? Hey? What do you say to next Tuesday? Tuesday, the 20th of June! Next Tuesday! Only think of it. Mad! I should rather think so."

I had nothing to say, and so I said nothing.

At this stage of the proceedings Jack filled a pipe, and began smoking savagely, throwing out the puffs of smoke fast and furious. Both of us sat in silence, involved in deep and anxious thought—I for him, he for himself.

At last he spoke.

"That's all very well," said he, putting down the pipe, "but I haven't yet told you the worst."

"The worst?"

"Yes; there's something more to be told—something which has brought me to this. I'm not the fellow I was. It isn't the widow; it's something else. It's—

CHAPTER XXXV.

"LOUIE!"—PLATONIC FRIENDSHIP.—ITS RESULTS.—ADVICE MAY BE GIVEN TOO FREELY, AND CONSOLATION MAY BE SOUGHT FOR TOO EAGERLY.—TWO INFLAMMABLE HEARTS SHOULD NOT BE ALLOWED TO COME TOGETHER.—THE OLD, OLD STORY.—A BREAKDOWN, AND THE RESULTS ALL AROUND.—THE CONDEMNED CRIMINAL.—THE SLOW YET SURE APPROACH OF THE HOUR OF EXECUTION.

"IT's Louie!" said Jack again, after a pause. "That's the 'hinc illæ lachrymæ' of it, as the Latin grammar has it."

"Louie?" I repeated.

"Yes, Louie," said Jack, sadly and solemnly.

I said nothing. I saw that something more was coming, which would afford the true key to Jack's despair. So I waited in silence till it should come.

"As for the widow herself," said Jack, meditatively, "she isn't a bad lot, and, if it hadn't been for Louie, I should have taken all this as an indication of Providence that my life was to be lived out under her guidance; but then the mischief of it is, there happens to be a Louie, and that Louie happens to be the very Louie that I can't manage to live without. You see there's no nonsense about this, old boy. You may remind me of Miss Phillips and Number Three, but I swear to you solemnly they were both nothing compared with Louie. Louie is the only one that ever has fairly taken me out of myself, and fastened herself to all my thoughts, and hopes, and desires. Louie is the only one that has ever chained me to her in such a way that I never wished to leave her for anybody else. Louie! why, ever since I've known her, all the rest of the world and of womankind has been nothing, and, beside her, it all sank into insignificance. There you have it! That's the way I feel about Louie. These other scrapes of mine—what are they? Bosh and nonsense, the absurdities of a silly boy! But Louie! why, Macrorie, I swear to you that she has twined herself around me so that the thought of her has changed me from a calf of a boy into a man. Now I know it all. Now I understand why I followed her up so close. Now, now, and now, when I know it all, it is all too late! By Jove, I tell you what it is, I've talked like a fool about suicide, but I swear I've been so near it this last week that it's not a thing to laugh at."

And Jack looked at me with such a wild face and such fierce eyes that I began to think of the long-talked-of head-stone of Anderson's as a possibility which was not so very remote, after all.

"I'll tell you all about it," said he. "It's a relief. I feel a good deal better already after what I have said.

"You see," said he, after a pause, in which his frown grew darker, and his eyes were fixed on vacancy—"you see, that evening I stayed a little later than usual with the widow. At last I hurried off. The deed was done, and the thought of this made every nerve tingle within me. I hurried off to see Louie. What the mischief did I want of Louie? you may ask. My only answer is: I wanted her because I wanted her. No day was complete without her. I've been living on the sight of her face and the sound of her voice for the past two months and more, and never fairly knew it until this last week, when it has all become plain to me. So I hurried off to Louie, because I had to do so—because

every day had to be completed by the sight of her.

"I reached the house somewhat later than usual. People were there. I must have looked different from usual. I know I was very silent, and I must have acted queer, you know. But they were all talking, and playing, and laughing, and none of them took any particular notice. And so at last I drifted off toward Louie, as usual. She was expecting me. I knew that. She always expects me. But this time I saw she was looking at me with a very queer expression. She saw something unusual in my face. Naturally enough. I felt as though I had committed a murder. And so I had. I had murdered my hope—my love—my darling —my only life and joy. I'm not humbugging, Macrorie—don't chaff, for Heaven's sake!"

I wasn't chaffing, and had no idea of such a thing. I was simply listening, with a very painful sympathy with Jack's evident emotion.

"We were apart from the others," he continued, in a tremulous voice. "She looked at me, and I looked at her. I saw trouble in her face, and she saw trouble in mine. So we sat. We were silent for some time. No nonsense now. No laughter. No more teasing and coaxing. Poor little Louie! How distressed she looked! Where was her sweet smile now? Where was her laughing voice? Where was her bright, animated face—her sparkling eyes — her fun — her merriment — her chaff? Poor little Louie!"

And Jack's voice died away into a moan of grief.

But he rallied again, and went on:

"She asked me what was the matter. I told her—nothing. But she was sure that something had happened, and begged me to tell her. So I told her all. And her face, as I told her, turned as white as marble. She seemed to grow rigid where she sat. And, as I ended, she bent down her head— and she pressed her hand to her forehead —and then she gave me an awful look—a look which will haunt me to my dying day —and then—and then—then—she—she burst into tears—and, oh, Macrorie—oh, how she cried!"

And Jack, having stammered out this, gave way completely, and, burying his face in his hands, he sobbed aloud.

Then followed a long, long silence.

At last Jack roused himself.

"You see, Macrorie," he continued, "I had been acting like the devil to her. All her chaff, and nonsense, and laughter, had been a mask. Oh, Louie! She had grown fond of me—poor miserable devil that I am —and this is the end of it all!

"She got away," said Jack, after another long silence—"she got away somehow; and, after she had gone, I sat for a while, feeling like a man who has died and got into another world. Paralyzed, bewildered —take any word you like, and it will not express what I was. I got off somehow— I don't know how—and here I am. I haven't seen her since.

"I got away," he continued, throwing back his head, and looking vacantly at the ceiling—"I got away, and came here, and the next day I got a letter about my uncle's death and my legacy. I had no sorrow for my poor dear old uncle, and no joy over my fortune. I had no thought for any thing but Louie. Seven thousand a year, or ten thousand, or a hundred thousand, whatever it might be, it amounts to noth- ing. What I have gained is nothing to what I have lost. I'd give it all for Louie. I'd give it all to undo what has been done. I'd give it all, by Heaven, for one more

sight of her! But that sight of her I can never have. I dare not go near the house. I am afraid to hear about her. My legacy! I wish it were at the bottom of the Atlan- tic. What is it all to me, if I have to give up Louie forever? And that's what it is!"

There was no exaggeration in all this. That was evident. Jack's misery was real, and was manifest in his pale face and gen- eral change of manner. This accounted for it all. This was the blow that had struck him down. All his other troubles had been laughable compared with this. But from this he could not rally. Nor, for my part, did I know of any consolation that could be offered. Now, for the first time, I saw the true nature of his senti- ments toward Louie, and learned from him the sentiments of that poor little thing toward him. It was the old story. They had been altogether too much with one an- other. They had been great friends, and all that sort of thing. Louie had teased and given good advice. Jack had sought consolation for all his troubles. And now —lo and behold!—in one moment each had made the awful discovery that their supposed friendship was something far more tender and far-reaching.

"I'll never see her again!" sighed Jack.

"Who?" said I. "The widow?"

"The widow!" exclaimed Jack, contemp- tuously; "no—poor little Louie!"

"But you'll see the widow?"

"Oh, yes," said Jack, dryly. "I'll have to be there."

"Why not kick it all up, and go home on leave of absence?"

Jack shook his head despairingly.

"No chance," he muttered—"not a ghost of a one. My sentence is pro- nounced; I must go to execution. It's my own doing, too. I've given my own word."

"Next Tuesday?"

"Next Tuesday."

"Where?"

"St. Malachi's."

"Oh, it will be at church, then?"

"Yes."

"Who's the parson?"

"Oh, old Fletcher."

"At what time?"

"Twelve; and see here, Macrorie, you'll stand by a fellow—of course—won't you? see me off—you know—adjust the noose, watch the drop fall—and see poor Jack Randolph launched into—matrimony!"

"Oh, of course."

Silence followed, and soon I took my departure, leaving Jack to *his meditations and his despair.*

CHAPTER XXXVI.

A FRIEND'S APOLOGY FOR A FRIEND.—JACK DOWN AT THE BOTTOM OF A DEEP ABYSS OF WOE.—HIS DESPAIR.—THE HOUR AND THE MAN!—WHERE IS THE WOMAN!—A SACRED SPOT.—OLD FLETCHER.—THE TOLL OF THE BELL.—MEDITATIONS ON EACH SUCCESSIVE STROKE.—A WILD SEARCH.—THE PRETTY SERVANT-MAID, AND HER PRETTY STORY.—THROWING GOLD ABOUT.

JACK'S strange revelation excited my deepest sympathy, but I did not see how it was possible for him to get rid of his difficulty. One way was certainly possible. He could easily get leave of absence and go home, for the sake of attending to his estates. Once in England, he could sell out, and retire from the army altogether, or exchange into another regiment. This was certainly possible physically; but to Jack it was morally impossible.

Now, Jack has appeared in this story in very awkward circumstances, engaging himself right and left to every young lady that he fancied, with a fatal thoughtlessness, that cannot be too strongly reprehended. Such very diffusive affection might argue a lack of principle. Yet, after all, Jack was a man with a high sense of honor. The only difficulty was this, that he was too susceptible. All susceptible men can easily understand such a character. I'm an awfully susceptible man myself, as I have already had the honor of announcing, and am, moreover, a man of honor—consequently I feel strongly for Jack, and always did feel strongly for him.

Given, then, a man of very great susceptibility, and a very high sense of honor, and what would he do?

Why, in the first place, as a matter of course, his too susceptible heart would involve him in many tendernesses; and, if he was as reckless and thoughtless as Jack, he would be drawn into inconvenient entanglements; and, perhaps, like Jack, before he knew what he was about, he might find himself engaged to three different ladies, and in love with a fourth.

In the second place, his high sense of honor would make him eager to do his duty by them all. Of course, this would be impossible. Yet Jack had done his best. He had offered immediate marriage to Miss Phillips, and had proposed an elopement to Number Three. This shows that his impulses led him to blind acts which tended in a vague way to do justice to the particular lady who happened for the time being to be in his mind.

And so Jack had gone blundering on until at last he found himself at the mercy of the widow. The others had given him up in scorn. She would not give him up. He was bound fast. He felt the bond. In the midst of this his susceptibility drove him on further, and, instead of trying to get out of his difficulties, he had madly thrust himself further into them.

And there he was—doomed—looking forward to the fateful Tuesday.

He felt the full terror of his doom, but did not think of trying to evade it. He was bound. His word was given. He considered it irrevocable. Flight? He thought no more of that than he thought of committing a murder. He would actually have given all that he had, and more too, for the sake of getting rid of the widow; but he would not be what he considered a sneak, even for that.

There was, therefore, no help for it. He was doomed. Tuesday! June 20th! St. Malachi's! Old Fletcher! Launched into matrimony! Hence his despair.

During the intervening days I did not see him. I did not visit him, and he did not come near me. Much as I sympathized with him in his woes, I knew that I could do nothing and say nothing. Besides, I had my own troubles. Every time I went to O'Halloran's, Marion's shyness, and reserve, and timidity, grew more marked. Every time that I came home, I kept bothering myself as to the possible cause of all this, and tormented myself as to the reason of such a change in her.

One day I called at the Bertons'. I didn't see Louie. I asked after her, and they told me she was not well. I hoped it was nothing serious, and felt relieved at learning that it was nothing but a "slight cold." I understood that. Poor Louie! Poor Jack! Would that "slight cold" grow worse, or would she get over it in time? She did not seem to be of a morbid, moping nature. There was every reason to hope that such a one as she was would surmount it. And yet it was hard to say. It is often these very natures—buoy-ant, robust, healthy, straightforward—which feel the most. They are not impressible. They are not touched by every new emotion. And so it sometimes happens that, when they do feel, the feeling lasts forever.

Tuesday, at last, came—the 20th—the fated day!

At about eleven o'clock I entered Jack's room, prepared to act my part and stand by his side in that supreme moment of fate.

Jack was lying on the sofa, as I came in. He rose and pressed my hand in silence. I said nothing, but took my seat in an easy-chair. Jack was arrayed for the ceremony in all respects, except his coat, instead of which garment he wore a dressing-gown. He was smoking vigorously. His face was very pale, and, from time to time, a heavy sigh escaped him.

I was very forcibly struck by the strong resemblance which there was between Jack, on the present occasion, and a condemned prisoner before his execution. So strong was this, that, somehow, as I sat there in silence, a vague idea came into my head that Jack was actually going to be hanged; and, before I knew where my thoughts were leading me, I began to think, in a misty way, of the propriety of calling in a clergyman to administer ghostly consolation to the poor condemned in his last moments. It was only with an effort that I was able to get rid of this idea, and come back from this foolish, yet not unnatural fancy, to the reality of the present situation. There was every reason, indeed, for such a momentary misconception. The sadness, the silence, the gloom, all suggested some prison cell; and Jack, prostrate, stricken, miserable, mute, and despairing, could not fail to suggest the doomed victim.

After a time Jack rose, and, going to the sideboard, offered me something to drink. I declined. Whereupon he poured out a tumblerful of raw brandy and hastily swallowed it. As he had done that very same thing before, I began to think that he was going a little too far.

"See here, old boy," said I, "arn't you a little reckless? That sort of thing isn't exactly the best kind of preparation for the event—is it?"

"What?—this?" said Jack, holding up the empty tumbler, with a gloomy glance toward me; "oh, its nothing. I've been drenching myself with brandy this last week. It's the only thing I can do. The worst of it is, it don't have much effect now. I have to drink too much of it before I can bring myself into a proper state of calm."

"Calm!" said I, "calm! I tell you what it is, old chap, you'll find it'll be any thing but calm. You'll have delirium tremens before the week's out, at this rate."

"Delirium tremens?" said Jack, with a faint, cynical laugh. "No go, my boy—too late. Not time now. If it had only come yesterday, I might have had a reprieve. But it didn't come. And so I have only a tremendous headache. I've less than an hour, and can't get it up in that time. Let me have my swing, old man. I'd do as much for you."

And, saying this, he drank off a half tumbler more.

"There," said he, going back to the sofa. "That's better. I feel more able to go through with it. It takes a good lot now, though, to get a fellow's courage up."

After this, Jack again relapsed into silence, which I ventured to interrupt with a few questions as to the nature of the coming ceremony. Jack's answers were short, reluctant, and dragged from him piecemeal. It was a thing which he had to face in a very short time, and any other subject was preferable as a theme for conversation.

"Will there be much of a crowd?"

"Oh, no."

"You didn't invite any."

"Me? invite any? Good Lord! I should think not!"

"Perhaps she has?"

"Oh, no; she said she wouldn't."

"Well, I dare say the town, by this time, has got wind of it, and the church'll be full."

"No, I think not," said Jack, with a sigh.

"Oh, I don't know; it's not a common affair."

"Well, she told me she had kept it a secret—and you and Louie are the only ones I've told it to—so, unless you have told about it, no one knows."

"I haven't told a soul."

"Then I don't see how anybody can know, unless old Fletcher has proclaimed it."

"Not he; he wouldn't take the trouble."

"I don't care," said Jack, morosely, "how many are there, or how few. Crowd or no crowd, it makes small difference to me, by Jove!"

"Look here, old fellow," said I, suddenly, after some further conversation, "if you're going, you'd better start. It's a quarter to twelve now."

Jack gave a groan and rose from his sofa. He went into his dressing-room and soon returned, in his festive array, with a face of despair that was singularly at variance with his costume. Before starting, in spite of my remonstrances, he swallowed another draught of brandy. I began to doubt whether he would be able to stand up at the ceremony.

St. Malachi's was not far away, and a few minutes' drive brought us there.

The church was quite empty. A few stragglers, unknown to us, had taken seats in the front pews. Old Fletcher was in the chancel. We walked up and shook hands with him. He greeted Jack with an affectionate earnestness of congratulation, which, I was sorry to see, was not properly responded to.

After a few words, we all sat down in the choir.

It wanted about five minutes of the time. The widow was expected every moment.

Old Fletcher now subsided into dignified silence. I fidgeted about, and looked at my watch every half-minute. As for Jack, he buried his face in his hands and sat motionless.

Thus four minutes passed.

No signs of the widow.

One minute still remained.

The time was very long.

I took out my watch a half-dozen times, to hasten its progress. I shook it impatiently to make it go faster. The great empty church looked cold and lonely. The little group of spectators only added to the loneliness of the scene. An occasional cough resounded harshly amid the universal stillness. The sibilant sounds of whispers struck sharply and unpleasantly upon the ear.

At last the minute passed.

I began to think my watch was wrong; but no—for suddenly, from the great bell above, in the church-tower, there tolled out the first stroke of the hour. And between each stroke there seemed a long, long interval, in which the mind had leisure to turn over and over all the peculiarities of this situation.

ONE! I counted.

[No widow. What's up? Did any one ever hear of a bride missing the hour, or delaying in this way?]

TWO!

[What a humbug of a woman! She has cultivated procrastination all her life, and this is the result.]

THREE!

[Not yet. Perhaps she wants to make a sensation. She anticipates a crowded church, and will make an entrance in state.]

FOUR!

[But no; she did not invite anybody, and had no reason to suppose that any one would be here.]

FIVE!

[No, it could not be vanity; but, if not, what can be the possible cause?]

SIX!

[Can it be timidity, bashfulness, and all that sort of thing? Bosh! The widow Finnimore is not a blushing, timid maiden.]

SEVEN!

[Perhaps her watch is out of the way. But, then, on one's marriage-day, would not one see, first of all, that one's watch was right?]

EIGHT!

[Perhaps something is the matter with her bridal array. The dress might not have arrived in time. She may be waiting for her feathers.]

NINE!

[Not yet! Perhaps she is expecting Jack to go to her house and accompany her here. It is very natural Jack may have agreed to do so, and then forgotten all about it.]

TEN!

[Perhaps there has been some misunderstanding about the hour, and the widow is not expecting to come till two.]

ELEVEN!

[Perhaps she is ill. Sudden attack of vertigo, acute rheumatism, and brain-fever, consequent upon the excitement of the occasion. The widow prostrated! Jack saved!]

TWELVE!!!

The last toll of the bell rolled out slowly and solemnly, and its deep tones came along the lofty church, and died away in long reverberations down the aisles and along the galleries. Twelve! The hour had come, and with the hour the man; but where was the woman?

Thus far Jack had been holding his face in his hands; but, as the last tones of the bell died away, he raised himself and looked around with some wildness in his face.

"By Jove!" said he.

"What?"

"The widow!"

"She's not here," said I.

"By Jove! Only think of it. A widow, and too late! By Jove! I can't grapple with the idea, you know."

After this we relapsed into silence, and waited.

The people in the pews whispered more vigorously, and every little while looked anxiously around to see if the bridal party was approaching. Old Fletcher closed his eyes, folded his arms, and appeared either buried in thought or in sleep—probably a little of both. Jack sat stolidly with his legs crossed, and his hands hugging his knee, looking straight before him at the opposite side of the chancel, and apparently reading most diligently the Ten Commandments, the Creed, and the Lord's Prayer, which were on the wall there. I was in a general state of mild but ever-increasing surprise, and endeavored to find some conceivable reason for such very curious procrastination.

So the time passed, and none of us said any thing, and the little company of spectators grew fidgety, and Jack still stared, and I still wondered.

At last old Fletcher turned to Jack.

"You said twelve, I think, sir," said he, mildly and benevolently.

"Twelve — did I? Well — of course; why not? Twelve, of course."

"The lady is rather behind the time, I think—isn't she?" said the reverend gentleman, with mild suggestiveness.

"Behind the time?" said Jack, fumbling at his watch; "why, so she is; why, it's twenty minutes to one. By Jove!"

"Perhaps you mistook the hour," hinted the clergyman.

"Mistook it? Not a bit of it," cried Jack, who looked puzzled and bewildered. "The hour? I'm as confident it was twelve as I'm confident of my existence. Not a bit of doubt about that."

"Perhaps something's happened," said I; "hadn't I better drive round to the house, Jack?"

"Yes; not a bad idea," said Jack. "I'll go too. I can't stand it any longer. I've read the ten commandments through seventy-nine times, and was trying to work up to a hundred, when you interrupted me. Do you know, old chap—I feel out of sorts; that brandy's got to my head—I'd like a little fresh air. Besides, I can't stand this waiting any longer. If it's got to be—why, the sooner the better. Have it out—and be done with it, I say. A fellow don't want to stand all day on the scaffold waiting for the confounded hangman—does he?"

Jack spoke wildly, cynically, and desperately. Old Fletcher listened to these words with a face so full of astonishment and horror, that it has haunted me ever since. And so we turned away, and we left that stricken old man looking after us in amazement and horror too deep for words.

Jack's spirits had flushed up for a moment into a fitful light; but the next mo ment they sank again into gloom. We walked slowly down the aisle, and, as we passed down, the spectators, seeing us go out, rose from their seats with the evident conviction that the affair was postponed, and the determination to follow. Jack's carriage was at the door, and we drove off.

"Macrorie, my boy," said Jack.

"What?"

"You didn't bring your flask, I suppose," said Jack, gloomily.

"No," said I; "and it's well I didn't, for I think you've done enough of that sort of thing to-day."

"To-day? This is the day of all days when I ought. How else can I keep up? I must stupefy myself, that's all. You don't know, old boy, how near I am to doing something desperate."

"Come, Jack, don't knock under that way. Confound it, I thought you had more spirit."

"Why the deuce does she drive me mad with her delay?" cried Jack, a few minutes after. "Why doesn't she come and be done with it? Am I to spend the whole day waiting for her? By Jove, I've a great mind to go home, and, if she wants me, she may come for me."

"Do," said I, eagerly. "She's missed the appointment; why should you care?"

"Pooh! a fellow can't act in that sort of way. No. Have it out. I've acted badly enough, in a general way, but I won't go deliberately and do a mean thing. I dare say this sort of thing will wear off in the long run. We'll go to England next week. We'll start for New York to-night, and never come back. I intend to try to get into the 178th regiment. It's out in Bombay, I believe. Yes. I've made up my mind to that. It's the only thing to be done. Yes—it's the best thing—far the best for both of us."

"Both of you!"

"Both, yes; of course."

"What, you and the widow?"

"The widow? Confound the widow! Who's talking of her?"

"I thought you were talking of her. You said you were going to take her to England."

"The widow? No," cried Jack, peevishly; "I meant Louie, of course. Who else could I mean? Louie. I said it would be far better for me and Louie if I went to Bombay."

And with these words he flung himself impatiently back in the carriage and scowled at vacancy.

And this was Jack. This was my broad-browed, frank-faced, golden-haired, bright, smiling, incoherent, inconsistent, inconsequential, light-hearted, hilarious Jack—the Jack who was once the joy of every company, rollicking, reckless, and without a care. To this complexion had he come at last. Oh, what a moral ruin was here, my countrymen! Where now were his jests and gibes—his wit, that was wont to set the table in a roar? Alas! poor Yorick! *Amour! amour! quand tu nous tiens*, who can tell what the mischief will become of us! Once it was "not wisely but too many"—now it was "not wisely but too well"—and this was the end of it. O Louie! O Jack! Is there no such thing as true Platonic love on earth?

But there was not much time for Jack to scowl or for me to meditate. The widow did not live very far away, and a quarter of an hour was enough to bring us there.

It was a handsome house. I knew it well. Jack knew it better. But it looked dark now, and rather gloomy. The shutters were closed, and there was no sign of life whatever.

Jack stared at the house for a moment,

and then jumped out. I followed. We hurried up the steps, and Jack gave a fierce pull at the bell, followed by a second and a third.

At the third pull the door opened and disclosed a maid-servant.

"Mrs. Finnimore?" said Jack, as he stepped into the hall—and then stopped.

The servant seemed surprised.

"Mrs. Finnimore?" said she.

"Yes," said Jack. "Is she here?"

"Here?"

"Yes."

"Why, sir—she's gone—"

"Gone!" cried Jack. "Gone! Impossible! Why we drove straight here from St. Malachi's, and didn't meet her. Which street did she go?"

"Which street, sir? St. Malachi's, sir?" repeated the servant, in bewilderment.

"Yes—which way did she go?"

"Why, sir—she went to Montreal," said the servant—"to Montreal, you know, sir," she repeated, in a mincing tone, bridling and blushing at the same time.

"To—where? what?" cried Jack, thunderstruck—"Montreal! Montreal! What the devil is the meaning of all that?" And Jack fairly gasped, and looked at me in utter bewilderment. And I looked back at him with emotions equal to his own. And we both stood, to use an expressive but not by any means classical word—dumfounded.

[Had a thunder-bolt burst—and all that sort of thing, you know, my boy.]

Jack was quite unable to utter another word. So I came to his help.

"I think you said your mistress went to Montreal?" said I, mildly and encouragingly, for the servant began to look frightened.

"Yes, sir."

"Will you be kind enough to tell me what she went there for? I wouldn't ask you, but it's a matter of some importance."

"What for, sir?" said the servant—and a very pretty blush came over her rather pretty face. "What for, sir? Why, sir—you know, sir—she went off, sir—on her—her—wedding-tower, sir."

"Her WHAT!!!" cried Jack, wildly.

"Her wedding-tower, sir," repeated the servant, in a faint voice.

"Her wedding-tour!" cried Jack. "Her wedding-tour! Do you mean what you say? Is this a joke? What *do* you mean?"

At this, which was spoken most vehemently by Jack, who was now in a state of frightful excitement, the servant turned pale and started back in fear—so I interposed.

"Don't be at all alarmed," I said, kindly. "We merely want to know, you know, what you mean by saying it was a wedding-tour. What wedding? We want to know, you know."

"Wedding, sir? Lor', sir! Yes, sir. This morning, sir. She was married, you know, sir."

"MARRIED!" cried Jack, in a strange, wild voice.

"This morning!" I exclaimed.

"Lor', sir! Yes, sir," continued the maid, who was still a little frightened at the presence of such excited visitors. "This morning, sir. Early, sir. Six o'clock, sir. And they took the seven o'clock train, sir—for Montreal, you know, sir—and they talked of New York, sir."

"*They* talked? *They? Who? Married! Who* married her? The widow! Mrs. Finnimore! Married! Nonsense! And gone! What do you mean? Who was it?"

The maid started back in fresh fear at Jack's terrible agitation. Terrible? I should rather think so. Imagine a criminal with the noose about his neck hearing a whisper going about that a pardon had arrived. Agitation? I should say that there was occasion for it. Still, I didn't like to see that pretty servant-maid frightened out of her wits. So I interposed once more.

"We merely want to know," said I, mildly, "who the gentleman was to whom your mistress was married this morning, and with whom she went to Montreal?"

"Who, sir? Why, sir—it was the chaplain, sir—of the Bobtails, sir—the Rev. Mr. Trenaman."

"THE CHAPLAIN!!!" cried Jack, with a strange voice that was somewhere between a shout and a sob. He turned to me. There was ecstasy on his face. His eyes were all aglow, and yet I could see in them the moisture of tears. He caught my hand in both of his.

"Oh, Macrorie!" he faltered, "see here, old boy—it's too much—Louie—all right—at last—too much, you know."

And the long and the short of it is, he nearly wrung my hand off.

Then he turned to the servant-maid, and fumbling in his pockets drew out a handful of sovereigns—

"See here!" he said, "you glorious little thing! you princess of servant-maids! here's something for a new bonnet, you know, or any thing else you fancy."

And he forced the sovereigns into her hand.

Then he wrung my hand again.

Then he rushed wildly out.

He flung some more sovereigns at the astonished coachman.

Then he sprang into the carriage, and I followed.

"Where shall I drive to, sir?" said the coachman.

"To Colonel Berton's!" roared Jack.

"Nonsense, Jack!" said I; "it's too early."

"Early—the devil! No it isn't.—Drive on."

And away went the carriage.

I prevailed on Jack to drop me at the corner of one of the streets, and, getting out, I went to my den, meditating on the astonishing events of the day.

The conclusions which I then came to about Mrs. Finnimore, now Mrs. Trenaman, were verified fully by discoveries made afterward.

She had been quick-sighted enough to see that Jack did not care for her, and had given him up. The chaplain was far more to her taste. As Jack came again to her, she could not resist the desire to pay him up. This was the reason why she led him on to an offer of matrimony, and named the day and place. Miss Phillips had paid him up in one way; the widow chose another method, which was more in accordance with her own genius. All this time she had come to a full understanding with the chaplain, and the day which she had named to Jack was the very one on which her real marriage was to come off. I never could find out whether the chaplain knew about it or not. I rather think he did not. If he had known, he would have dropped a hint to Jack. He was such a confoundedly good-hearted sort of a fellow, that he would have interposed to prevent the success of the plan. As it was, it was carried out perfectly.

After all, she wasn't a bad little thing. She knew about Jack's devotion to Louie, and thought that her little plot, while it gratified her own feelings, would not in any way interfere with Jack's happiness. And it didn't. For, ever since then, Jack has never ceased to declare that the widow, as he still called her, was—a brick—a trump—a glorious lot—and every other name that has ever been invented to express whatever is noble, excellent, or admirable in human nature.

The next morning Jack came bursting into my room. One look at him was enough. Jack was himself again. He poured forth a long, a vehement, and a very incoherent account of his proceedings. I can only give the general facts.

He had driven at once to Colonel Berton's. He had dashed into the house and asked for Louie. After a while Louie came down. He didn't say a word to her, but caught her in his arms. She didn't resist. Perhaps she had seen in his face, at one glance, that he was free. It was a long time before the absurd fellow could tell her what had happened. At length he managed to get it all out. He must have acted like a madman, but, as all lovers are more or less mad, his behavior may not have seemed very unnatural to Louie. The poor little girl had been moping ever since her last interview with Jack; every day had made it worse for her; and Jack assured me that, if he hadn't turned up at that particular hour on that particular day, she would have taken to her bed, and never risen from it again. But as it was Jack's inveterate habit to doom to death all the ladies who had cherished a tender passion in his behalf, the assertion may not be absolutely true. Louie might possibly have rallied from the blow, and regained the joy and buoyancy of her old life; yet, however that may be, it was certainly best for her that things should have turned out just as they did.

But I must now leave Jack, and get on to—

CHAPTER XXXVII.

MY OWN AFFAIRS.—A DRIVE AND HOW IT CAME OFF. — VARYING MOODS. — THE EXCITED, THE GLOOMY, AND THE GENTLEMANLY. —STRAYING ABOUT MONTMORENCY.—REVISITING A MEMORABLE SCENE.—EFFECT OF SAID SCENE.—A MUTE APPEAL AND AN APPEAL IN WORDS.—RESULT OF THE APPEALS. —" WILL YOU TURN AWAY ? "—GRAND RESULT.—CLIMAX.—FINALE.—A GENERAL UNDERSTANDING ALL ROUND, AND A UNIVERSAL EXPLANATION OF NUMEROUS PUZZLES.

ALL this was very well. Of course. To a generous nature like mine, the happiness of a friend could not fail to extend itself. For I'm awfully sympathetic, you know. I don't remember whether I've made that remark before or not, but in either case the fact remains. Yet, sympathetic or not, every fellow has his own affairs, you know, and, as a matter of course, these engage his chief attention. Now all my affairs circled around one centre, and that centre was—Marion !

I had seen her on the previous evening. I had made an engagement with her and Nora to go out with me for a drive on the following day, and we had arranged all about it. We were to drive to Montmorency Falls, a place which is the chief attraction among the environs of Quebec. I had not been there since that memorable day when I rode there with the doctor to find my bird flown.

Accordingly on the next day, at the appointed hour, I drew up in front of O'Halloran's and went in. The ladies were there, but Nora was half-reclining on a couch, and seemed rather miserable. She complained of a severe attack of neuralgia, and lamented that she could not go. Up on this I expressed my deepest regrets, and hoped that Miss O'Halloran would come. But Marion demurred, and said she wouldn't leave Nora. Whereupon Nora urged her to go, and finally, after evident reluctance, Marion allowed herself to be persuaded.

It was with an inexpressible feeling of exultation that I drove off with her. At last we were alone together, and would be so for hours. The frigidity which had grown up within her during the last two months might possibly be relaxed now under the influence of this closer association. My heart beat fast. I talked rapidly about every thing. In my excitement I also drove rapidly at first, but finally I had sufficient sense to see that there was no need to shorten so precious an interview by hurrying it through, and so I slackened our speed.

As for Marion, she seemed as calm as I was agitated. Her demeanor was a singular one. She was not exactly frigid or repellent. She was rather shy and reserved. It was rather the constraint of timidity than of dislike. Dislike? No. Not a bit of it. Whatever her feelings might be, she had no reason for dislike. Still she was cold—and her coldness began gradually to affect me in spite of my exultation, and to change my joy to a feeling of depression.

After a few miles this depression had increased sufficiently to sober me down completely. I no longer rattled. I became grave. A feeling of despondency came over me. My spirits sank. There seemed no sympathy between us—no reciprocity of feeling. She had no cordiality of manner —no word, or look, or gesture, to give encouragement.

After a time my mood changed so under the influence of Marion's depressing manner, that I fell into long fits of very ungallant silence—silence, too, which she never attempted to break. Amid these fits of silence I tried to conjecture the cause of her very great coolness, and finally came to the very decision which I had often reached before. "Yes," I thought, "she has discovered how I love her, and she does not care for me. She has gratitude, but she cannot feel love. So she wishes to repel me. She didn't want to come with me, and only came because Nora urged her. She did not like to refuse, for fear of seeming unkind to me. At the same time, now that she is with me, she is trying to act in such a way as will effectually quell any unpleasant demonstrations of mine." Thoughts like these reduced me to such a state of gloom that I found myself indulging in fits of silence that grew longer and longer.

At last I roused myself. This sort of thing would never do. If nothing else could influence me, I felt that I ought to obey the ordinary instincts of a gentleman. I had invited her for a drive, and, because she was constrained, that was no reason why I should be rude. So I rallied my failing faculties, and endeavored now not to secure enjoyment for myself, but rather to make the drive agreeable to my companion.

This better mood lasted all the rest of the way, and the few miles of feverish excitement, which were followed by the few miles of sullenness, were finally succeeded by the ordinary cheerfulness of a travelling companion. The change was very much for the better. My feverish excitement had served to increase the constraint of Marion; and now, since it had passed away, she seemed more inclined to be agreeable. There were many things to attract and interest those who travelled merely for the pleasure of the thing, without any ulterior motives. The long French villages, the huge chapels, the frequent crosses by the way-side, the smooth, level road, the cultivated fields, the overshadowing trees, the rich luxuriance of the vegetation, the radiant beauty of the scene all around, which was now clothed in the richest verdure of June, the *habitants* along the road—all these and a thousand other things sufficed to excite attention and elicit remarks. While I was impassioned, or eager, or vehement, Marion had held aloof; but now, while I was merely commonplace and conventional, she showed herself sufficiently companionable. And so our drive went on, and at last we reached our destination.

If I were inclined to bore the reader, I might go into raptures over this scene—where the river, winding on amid wooded banks, and over rocky ledges, finally tumbles over a lofty precipice, and flings itself in foam into the St. Lawrence; where the dark cliffs rise, where the eddies twirl and twist, where the spray floats upward through the span of its rainbow arch. But at that moment this scene, glorious though it was, sank into insignificance in my estimation in comparison with Marion. I will take it for granted that the reader, like me, finds more interest in Marion than in Montmorency, and therefore will not inflict upon him any description of the scene. I refer him to Byron's lines about Velino. They apply with equal force to Montmorency.

Well. To resume.

We wandered about Montmorency for an hour or more. We walked over the broad, flat ledges. We descended deep slopes. We climbed lofty rocks. I helped her over every impediment. I helped her down. I helped her up. She had to take my hand a hundred times in the course of that scramble.

There was an informal and an uncon-ventional character about such proceedings as these which did much toward thawing the crust of Marion's reserve. She evidently enjoyed the situation—she enjoyed the falls—she enjoyed the rocky ledges—she enjoyed the scramble—she even went so far on one occasion as to show something like enthusiasm. Nor did I, in the delight of that time, which I experienced to the most vivid degree, ever so far forget myself as to do the impassioned in any shape or way. Whatever was to be the final result, I had determined that this day should be a happy one, and, since Marion objected so strongly to the intense style, she should see nothing but what was simply friendly and companionable.

But it was a hard struggle. To see her beautiful, animated face—her light, agile form—to feel her little hand—to hear the musical cadence of her unequalled voice, and yet to repress all undue emotion. By Jove! I tell you what it is, it isn't every fellow who could have held out as long as I did.

At last we had exhausted the falls, and we went back to the little inn where the horses were left. We had still over an hour, and I proposed a walk to the river-bank. To this Marion assented.

We set out, and I led the way toward that very cottage where I had taken her on that memorable occasion when I first met her. I had no purpose in this, more than an irresistible desire to stand on that bank by her side, and, in company with her, to look over that river, and have the eyes of both of us simultaneously looking over the track of our perilous journey. And still, even with such a purpose as this, I resolved to discard all sentiment, and maintain only the friendly attitude.

The cottage was not far away, and, in a short time, we entered the gate of the farm, and found ourselves approaching it.

As we went on, a sudden change came over Marion.

Up to the time of our entering the gate she had still maintained the geniality of manner and the lightness of tone which had sprung up during our wanderings about the falls. But here, as we came within sight of the cottage, I saw her give a sudden start. Then she stopped and looked all around. Then she gave a sudden look at me—a deep, solemn, earnest look, in which her dark, lustrous eyes fastened themselves on mine for a moment, as though they would read my very soul.

And at that look every particle of my commonplace tone, and every particle of my resolution, vanished and passed away utterly.

The next instant her eyes fell. We had both stopped, and now stood facing one another.

"Pardon me," said I, in deep agitation. "I thought it might interest you. But, if you wish it, we may go back. Shall we go back, or shall we go on?"

"As you please," said she, in a low voice.

We went on.

We did not stop at the cottage. We passed by it, walking in silence onward toward the river-bank. We reached it at last, and stood there side by side, looking out upon the river.

We were at the top of a bank which descended steeply for a great distance. It was almost a cliff, only it was not rock, but sandy soil, dotted here and there with patches of grass and clumps of trees. Far below us was the river, whose broad bosom lay spread out for miles, dotted with the white sails of passing vessels. The place where we stood was a slight promontory,

and commanded a larger and more extended view than common. On the left and below us was the Ile d'Orleans, while far away up the river Cape Diamond jutted forth, crowned by its citadel, and, clustering around it, we saw the glistening tin roofs and tapering spires of Quebec. But at that moment it was neither the beauty nor the grandeur of this wonderful scene that attracted my gaze, but rather the river itself. My eyes fastened themselves on that broad expanse of deep and dark-blue water, and wandering from the beach beneath, up the river, to the shore opposite Quebec—many a mile away—in that moment all the events of our memorable journey came back before me, distinctly and vividly. I stood silent. Marion, too, was silent, as though she also had the same thoughts as those which filled me. Thus we both stood in silence, and for a long time our eyes rested upon the mighty river which now rolled its vast flood beneath us, no longer ice-bound, but full and free, the pathway for mighty navies, and the thoroughfare of nations.

Now I was able to grasp the full and complete reality of our fearful adventure. We had wandered from the opposite shore far up near Point Levi, toiling over treacherous ice, which, even as we walked, had moved onward toward the sea, and had thus borne us down for miles till we attained the shore at this place. Looking at the river, I could trace the pathway which we had taken, and could fix the locality of every one of those events which had marked that terrible journey—where the horse ran—where the sleigh floated—where I had drawn it to the ice—where the ice-ridge rose—where we had clambered over—where Marion fell—till finally beside this shore I could see the place where that open channel ran, near which she had fallen for the last time, when I had raised her in my arms and borne her back to life. And there, too, below us, was the steep bank up which I had borne her—how I knew not, but in some way or other most certainly— till I found refuge for her in the hospitable cottage. At this last I looked with the strongest emotion. What strength must have been mine! what a frenzied, frantic effort I must have put forth! what a madness of resolve must have nerved my limbs to have carried her up such a place as that! In comparison with this last supreme effort all the rest of that journey seemed weak and commonplace.

Rousing myself at last from the profound abstraction into which I had fallen, I turned and looked at my companion.

She was standing close beside me; her hands hung in front of her, closed over one another; her head was slightly bent forward; her eyes were opened wide, and fixed steadfastly upon the river at the line which we might have traversed; and there was in her face such rapt attention, such deep and all-absorbed meditation, that I saw her interest in this scene was equal to mine. But there was more than interest. There was that in her face which showed that the incidents of that journey were now passing before her mind; her face even now assumed that old expression which it had borne when first I saw her—it was white, horror-stricken, and full of fear—the face that had fixed itself on my memory after that day of days —the face of my Lady of the Ice.

She did not know that I was looking at her, and devouring her with my gaze. Her eyes wandered over the water and toward the shore. I heard her quick breathing, and saw a sudden shudder pass through her, and her hands clutch one another more tightly in a nervous clasp, as she came to that place where she had fallen

last. She looked at that spot on the dark water for a long time, and in visible agitation. What had taken place after she had fallen she well knew, for I had told it all on my first visit to her house, but it was only from my account that she knew it. Yet here were the visible illustrations of my story—the dark river, the high, precipitous bank. In all these, as in all around, she could see what I had done for her.

Suddenly, with a start, she raised her head, and, turning, looked full upon me. It was a wild, eager, wistful, questioning look—her large, lustrous eyes thrilled me through with their old power; I saw in her face something that set my heart throbbing with feverish madness. It was a mute appeal—a face turned toward me as though to find out by that one eager, piercing, penetrating glance, something that she longed to know. At the same time there was visible in her face the sign of another feeling contending with this—that same constraint, and shy apprehension, and timidity, which had so long marked her manner toward me.

And now, in that moment, as her face thus revealed itself, and as this glance thrilled through me, there flashed upon my mind in a moment the meaning of it all. There was but an instant in which she thus looked at me—the next instant a flush passed over her face, and her eyes fell, but that very instant I snatched her hand in both of mine and held it.

She did not withdraw it. She raised her eyes again, and again their strange questioning thrilled through me.

"Marion," said I, and I drew her toward me. Her head fell forward. I felt her hand tremble in mine.

"Marion," said I—lingering fondly on the name by which I now called her for the first time—"if I ask you to be mine—will you turn away?"

She did not turn away.

She raised her face again for a moment, and again for a moment the thrilling glance flashed from her deep, dark eyes, and a faint smile of heavenly sweetness beamed across the glory of her solemn face.

There!

I let the curtain drop.

I'm not good at describing love-scenes, and all that sort of thing, you know.

What's more, I don't want to be either good or great at that.

For, if a fellow feels like a fool, you know, when he's talking spooney, how much more like a fool must he feel when he sits down and deliberately writes spooney! You musn't expect that sort of thing from me at any rate—not from Macrorie. I can feel as much as any fellow, but that's no reason why I should write it all out.

Another point.

I'm very well aware that, in the story of my love, I've gone full and fair against the practice of the novelist. For instance, now, no novelist would take a hero and make him fall in love with a girl, no matter how deucedly pretty she might be, who had been in love with another fellow, and tried to run off with him. Of course not. Very well. Now, you see, my dear fellow, all I've got to say is this, that I'm not a novelist. I'm an historian, an autobiographer, or any thing else you choose. I've no imagination whatever. I rely on facts. I can't distort them. And, what's more, if I could do so, I wouldn't, no matter what the taste or fashion of the day might be.

There's a lot of miserable, carping sneaks about, whose business it is to find fault with every thing, and it just occurs to me that some of this lot may take it into their heads—notwithstanding the *facts*, mind you—may take it into their heads, I say, to make the objection that it is unnatural, when a girl has already been so madly in love, for another fellow to win her affections in so short a time. Such fellows are beneath notice, of course; but, for the benefit of the world at large, and humanity in general, I beg leave to suggest a few important points which serve to account for the above-mentioned change of affection, and all that sort of thing:

I. The mutability of humanity.

II. The crushing effects of outrage and neglect on the strongest love.

III. My own overwhelming claims.

IV. The daily spectacle of my love and devotion.

V. My personal beauty.

VI. The uniform of the Bobtails.

The above, I think, will suffice.

The drive back was very different from the drive down. On the way I heard from Marion's own lips a full explanation of many of those things which had been puzzling me for the last two months. She explained all about the crossing of the river, though not without some hesitation, for it was connected with her infatuation about Jack. Still, she had got over that utterly, and, as I knew all about it, and as she had nothing but indifference toward him, I was able to get an explanation from her without much difficulty.

It seems, then, that O'Halloran had forbidden Marion to see Jack, but she was infatuated about him, and anxious to see him. She had met him several times at the house of a friend at Point Levi, and a few days before that eventful journey O'Halloran had gone to Montreal. At the same time Jack had written her, telling her that he would be over there. So she took advantage of her father's absence to go over on a visit, hoping also to meet with Jack. But Jack was not there. She stayed as long as she dared, and finally had to return so as to be home before her father got back. This was the day of the storm. She had much difficulty in finding a driver, but at length succeeded by means of a heavy bribe. Then followed her momentous meeting with me. Her departure from the cottage so abruptly was owing to her intense desire to get home before her father should arrive. This she succeeded in doing. She felt deeply grateful to me, but did not dare to take any steps to show gratitude, for fear her father would hear of her journey to Point Levi. Nora knew about it, and kept her secret from O'Halloran most faithfully. Then came my arrival upon the scene. She recognized me at once, and as soon as I told my story Nora recognized me, too, as Marion's mysterious deliverer.

They held counsel together after leaving the room, and, seeing O'Halloran's fancy for me, they thought I might often come again. They saw, too, that I had noticed their agitation, but had not recognized Marion. They judged that I would suspect them, and so Nora volunteered to personate the lady so as to save Marion from that outburst of indignation which was sure to fall on her if her father knew of her disobedience. This, then, was the cause of Nora's assumption of a false part. She had told some plausible story to O'Halloran which satisfied him and saved Marion; but her peculiar frank and open nature made her incapable of maintaining her part, and also led to my absurd proposal to her, and its consequences.

Meanwhile Marion had her troubles. She had not seen Jack, but on her return got his frantic letter, proposing an elopement, and threatening to blow his brains out.

She answered this as we have seen. After this, she heard all about Jack's love-affairs, and wrote to him on the subject. He answered by another proposal to elope, and reproached her with being the cause of his ruin. This reproach stung her, and filled her with remorse. It was not so much love as the desperation of self-reproach which had led to her foolish consent. So at the appointed time she was at the place; but instead of Jack—there was quite another person.

Of course, I did not get all the above from her at that time. Some of it she told; but the rest came out long afterward. Long afterward I learned from her own dear lips how her feelings changed toward me, especially on that night when I saved her and brought her home. Jack became first an object of contempt, then of indifference. Then she feared that I would despise her, and tried to hold aloof. Despise her!——!!!!

All this, and a thousand other things, came out afterward, in the days of our closer association, when all was explained, and Marion had no more secrets to keep from me, and I had none from her.

CHAPTER XXXVIII.

GRAND CONCLUSION. — WEDDING-RINGS AND BALL-RINGS.—ST. MALACHI'S.—OLD FLETCHER IN HIS GLORY.—NO HUMBUG THIS TIME. —MESSAGES SENT EVERYWHERE.—ALL THE TOWN AGOG.—QUEBEC ON THE RAMPAGE. —ST. MALACHI'S CRAMMED. — GALLERIES CROWDED.—WHITE FAVORS EVERYWHERE.— THE WIDOW HAPPY WITH THE CHAPLAIN.— THE DOUBLE WEDDING. — FIRST COUPLE— JACK AND LOUIE!—SECOND DITTO— MACRORIE AND MARION!—COLONEL BERTON AND O'HALLORAN GIVING AWAY THE

BRIDES. — STRANGE ASSOCIATION OF THE BRITISH OFFICER AND THE FENIAN.—JACK AND MACRORIE, LOUIE AND MARION.—BRIDES AND BRIDEGROOMS.—EPITHALAMIUM.—WEDDING IN HIGH LIFE.—SIX OFFICIATING CLERGYMEN.—ALL THE ELITE OF QUEBEC TAKE PART.—ALL THE CLERGY, ALL THE MILITARY, AND EVERYBODY WHO AMOUNTS TO ANY THING.—THE BAND OF THE BOBTAILS DIS- COURSING SWEET MUSIC, AND ALL THAT SORT OF THING, YOU KNOW.

ON reading over the above heading, I find it so very comprehensive that it leaves nothing more for me to say. I will therefore make my bow, and retire from the scene, with my warmest congratulations to the reader at reaching

THE END.

POPULAR WORKS OF FICTION

PUBLISHED BY

D. APPLETON & CO.,

90, 92 & 94 Grand St., New York.

APPLETONS' ILLUSTRATED LIBRARY OF ROMANCE.

In uniform octavo volumes,

Handsomely illustrated, and bound either in paper covers, or in muslin.

Price, in Paper, $1.00; in Cloth, $1.50.

*** In this series of Romances are included the famous novels of LOUISA MUHLBACH. Since the time when Sir Walter Scott produced so profound a sensation in the reading-world, no historical novels have achieved a success so great as those from the pen of Miss MUHLBACH.

1. TOO STRANGE NOT TO BE TRUE. A Novel. By Lady Georgiana Fullerton.
2. THE CLEVER WOMAN OF THE FAMILY. By Miss Yonge, author of "The Heir of Redclyffe," "Heartsease," etc.
3. JOSEPH II. AND HIS COURT. By Louisa Muhlbach.
4. FREDERICK THE GREAT AND HIS COURT. By Louisa Muhlbach.
5. BERLIN AND SANS-SOUCI; or, FREDERICK THE GREAT AND HIS FRIENDS. By Louisa Muhlbach.
6. THE MERCHANT OF BERLIN. By Louisa Muhlbach.
7. FREDERICK THE GREAT AND HIS FAMILY. By Louisa Muhlbach.
8. HENRY VIII. AND CATHARINE PARR. By Louisa Muhlbach.
9. LOUISA OF PRUSSIA AND HER TIMES. By Louisa Muhlbach.
10. MARIE ANTOINETTE AND HER SON. By Louisa Muhlbach.
11. THE DAUGHTER OF AN EMPRESS. By Louisa Muhlbach.
12. NAPOLEON AND THE QUEEN OF PRUSSIA. By Louisa Muhlbach.
13. THE EMPRESS JOSEPHINE. By Louisa Muhlbach.
14. NAPOLEON AND BLUCHER. An Historical Romance. By Louisa Muhlbach.
15. COUNT MIRABEAU. An Historical Novel. By Theodor Mundt.
16. A STORMY LIFE. A Novel. By Lady Georgiana Fullerton, author of "Too Strange not to be True."
17. OLD FRITZ AND THE NEW ERA. By Louisa Muhlbach.
18. ANDREAS HOFER. By Louisa Muhlbach.
19. DORA. By Julia Kavanagh.
20. JOHN MILTON AND HIS TIMES. By Max Ring.
21. BEAUMARCHAIS. An Historical Tale. By A. E. Brachvogel.
22. GOETHE AND SCHILLER. By Louisa Muhlbach.
23. A CHAPLET OF PEARLS. By Miss Yonge.

Grace Aguilar.

HOME INFLUENCE. 12mo. Cloth. $1.00.

MOTHER'S RECOMPENSE. 12mo. Cloth. $1.00.

DAYS OF BRUCE. 2 vols., 12mo. Cloth. $2.00.

HOME SCENES AND HEART STUDIES. 12mo. Cloth. $1.00.

WOMAN'S FRIENDSHIP. 12mo. Cloth. $1.00.

WOMEN OF ISRAEL. 2 vols., 12mo. Cloth. $2.00.

VALE OF CEDARS. 12mo. Cloth. $1.00.

" Grace Aguilar's works possess attractions which will always place them among the standard writings which no library can be without. 'Mother's Recompense' and 'Woman's Friendship' should be read by both young and old."

W. Arthur.

THE SUCCESSFUL MERCHANT. 1 vol., 12mo. Cloth. $1.

J. B. Bouton.

ROUND THE BLOCK. A new American Novel. Illustrated. 1 vol., 12mo. Cloth. $1.25.

" Unlike most novels that now appear, it has no 'mission,' the author being neither a politician nor a reformer, but a story-teller, according to the old pattern; and a capital story he has produced, written in the happiest style."

F. Caballero.

ELIA; or, Spain Fifty Years Ago. A Novel. 1 vol., 12mo. Cloth. $1.

Mary Cowden Clarke.

THE IRON COUSIN. A Tale. 1 vol., 12mo. Cloth. $1.50.

" The story is too deeply interesting to allow the reader to lay it down till he has read it to the end."

Charles Dickens.

The Cheap Popular Edition of the Works of Charles Dickens.

Clear type, handsomely printed, and of convenient size. 18 vols., 8vo. Paper.

	Pages.	Cts.		Pages.	Cts.
OLIVER TWIST	172	25	BLEAK HOUSE	340	35
AMERICAN NOTES	104	15	LITTLE DORRIT	330	35
DOMBEY & SON	356	35	PICKWICK PAPERS	326	35
MARTIN CHUZZLEWIT	342	35	DAVID COPPERFIELD	351	35
OUR MUTUAL FRIEND	330	35	BARNABY RUDGE	257	30
CHRISTMAS STORIES	162	25	OLD CURIOSITY SHOP	221	30
TALE OF TWO CITIES	144	20	SKETCHES	196	25
HARD TIMES, and ADDITIONAL CHRISTMAS STORIES	200	25	GREAT EXPECTATIONS	184	25
NICHOLAS NICKLEBY	340	35	UNCOMMERCIAL TRAVELLER, PICTURES FROM ITALY, Etc.	300	35

THE COMPLETE POPULAR LIBRARY EDITION. Handsomely printed in good, clear type. Illustrated with 32 Engravings, and a Steel-plate Portrait of the Author. 6 vols., small 8vo. Cloth, extra. $10.50.

OUR MUTUAL FRIEND. With Illustrations by Marcus Stone. London edition. 2 vols., 12mo. Scarlet Cloth, $5.00; Half Calf, $9.00.